YOU WERE MADE FOR THIS

YOU WERE MADE FOR THIS

A NOVEL

MICHELLE SACKS

Little, Brown and Company
New York Boston Toronto

The characters and events in this book are fictitious. Any similarity to real persons, living or dead, is coincidental and not intended by the author.

Little, Brown and Company
Hachette Book Group
1290 Avenue of the Americas, New York, NY 10104
littlebrown.com

First Edition: June 2018

Little, Brown and Company is a division of Hachette Book Group, Inc. The Little, Brown and Company name and logo are trademarks of Hachette Book Group, Inc.

The publisher is not responsible for websites (or their content) that are not owned by the publisher.

The Hachette Speakers Bureau provides a wide range of authors for speaking events. To find out more, go to hachettespeakersbureau.com or call (866) 376-6591.

ISBN 978-0-316-47540-2 (Hardcover) / 978-0-316-44941-0 (Canadian edition)
LCCN 2017946995

10 9 8 7 6 5 4 3 2 1

LSC-C

Printed in the United States of America

For my mother, Avril

You must always go carefully into the dark Swedish woods, for within the forests there live many dark, dark creatures. Witches and werewolves and wicked, wicked trolls. Beware the trolls! For they are in the habit of stealing away human children to keep for their own. Oh, you must beware the trolls, for you will not see them coming. They are terribly clever with their disguises.

—Åsa Lindqvist, *Det hämndlystna trollet.*

YOU WERE MADE FOR THIS

Merry

If you saw us you'd probably hate us. We look like the cast of an insurance commercial: shiny, happy us. The perfect little family, living the perfect little life.

Wasn't that another perfect day? is what we always say at the end of days like these. A confirmation. A promise. A warding-off of any days that might be anything less. But most are perfect here in Sweden, many more than I can count.

It's so beautiful, especially now in the middle of the summer, all dappled, dancing light and gentle sun. The little red wooden house we live in is out of a children's picture book—nestled in the forest, snug as a bug, with the trees all around and the garden lush and blooming, an abundance of life—vegetable patches thick with leaves, bushes heavy with sun-ripened summer berries, the smell of blooms everywhere, heady and sweet, drawing in the bees with their charms. The summer evenings are endless and still, the sky bright well past ten, and the vast lake pale and calm like the very faintest shade of blue on a color wheel. And stillness—everywhere just the sound of the birds and the rustling of the leaves on the branches.

★ ★ ★

Our lives here involve no traffic, no pollution, no upstairs neighbors blaring music or downstairs neighbors screeching out their misery; no litter on the sidewalk or rotting Manhattan trash or sweaty L-train commutes to work, no crowds, no tourists; no daily encounters with rats or roaches or perverts or street preachers. No. Nothing but this, an impossible life of lightness and dreams. Sam and the baby and me, on our island of three.

Like most mornings after I put the baby down for his nap, I went into the kitchen to bake. Today, a pie from the blueberries we'd picked in the forest this past weekend. I made the dough myself and rolled it out, pricked it with a fork, baked it blind to crisp it. The sun was already streaming in through the big open windows, rays of light casting themselves across the floors of our bright little house. The ripened berries I cooked low and slow, excising out the juices over the heat with maple syrup and a stick of cinnamon, careful not to let it all burn and spoil. Sam in his studio smelled the butter and the sugar and the sweetness of the fruit; he came out to the kitchen to see what I'd made. He looked at me and grinned, just as pleased as punch.

See, he said, don't I always tell you. You were made for this.

The pie was good; we ate it still warm with mugs of coffee as we sat out in the garden under the early-afternoon sun. The baby tasted a spoonful of the innards and dribbled it all out again, like a miniature office worker who'd just chewed his blue pen. Sam laughed and scooped it back up into the spoon.

Isn't this kid the best? he said. He lifted him and jiggled

him about, so the baby laughed and squealed and spit up some more. I observed them together. The boys. My boys. Father and son. I smiled, and felt the warmth of the sun against my skin.

Down the dirt road that connects the houses on the reserve, one of the neighbors has a paddock full of prizewinning horses nursing their young. The spring foals wobble about on spindly, unsteady legs; the mares nudge them up with their muzzles, coaxing their offspring gently into the world. They are good at mothering. Patient and instinctive. Fierce with love for their young, as nature demands.

Sam and I walked the baby over to watch them in the field. Horse, Sam said, and he pointed and neighed, and the baby was in hysterics. I reached out a hand to a chestnut-brown mare who had approached the fence, felt the quiver of life and taut muscle under my fingers. She was beautiful. Strong and certain. Her black eyes were fierce.

Careful, Sam warned. New mothers can be dangerous.

We left the horses and made our way slowly back to the house. Our home for a little under a year. It's around forty-five minutes outside of Stockholm, on a nature reserve bordering Sigtuna, the oldest town in Sweden. The reserve covers a fairly large stretch of land, mostly fields and forest nestled around the lake, with the odd house dotted in between the pines. Many of the homes have been in a single family for generations, the same red wooden cabin extended or repaired over the years as necessary; the walls within witness to the constant comings and goings of the newly born and the newly departed.

* * *

Sam inherited the house from his grandfather's second wife, Ida, who was born and raised here. She had no children of her own, but always had a soft spot for Sam, who knew even as a child how to charm her, how to compliment her on her rose garden or her spiced cookies or the gentle Swedish accent that made all her words sound like songs. When she died some years ago, Sam discovered she'd left him the house, with the stipulation that it could never be sold, only passed down.

We'd never visited before last year, never even thought much about the house or the country. Actually, our sole point of reference for all of Sweden was one of those little red Dala horses Ida brought back for us after one of her visits. It sat atop the spice rack in our Brooklyn apartment, next to the pepper grinder and the unopened jar of saffron strands I'd bargained for at a night market in Marrakech.

Of course, moving here was Sam's idea.

All the good ones are, he likes to joke.

He said it would be like a fairy tale. That we'd be happier than we've ever been.

He was right. He always is. Pointing us in the right direction; the compass that leads me away from the storms. How lucky I am to have him.

Later in the afternoon, the three of us took a long walk through the forest, the baby in the backpack carrier, hitched snugly to Sam. As we walked, we named the trees and birds we've learned to identify this past year—a spruce, a nest of finches, *Fraxinus excelsior,* a common ash. These are our new-found pleasures and hobbies, the things we busy ourselves with over here. We laugh at ourselves sometimes, imagining the people we once were.

In the little town of Sigtuna, we stopped for thick rye-crumbed herrings and potato salad at the café by the pier; listened to the sounds of the seagulls and the lapping water as they blended hypnotically with the low chatter of the well-turned-out Swedes. The waitress tickled the baby's cheek and took our order in flawless English. *Tack,* we said. *Tack.*

Back home, I gave the baby his bath and rocked him gently to sleep in my arms. I breathed into his neck and traced a hand gently over his downy golden hair, which was slowly beginning to thicken. I touched a hand to his chest, felt the thud of his beating heart, steady and miraculous every time; *doof doof,* the echo of life. Sam and I, tired out from the walk and the fresh air, climbed in between the crisp sheets before it had turned dark outside. I curled into my husband's arms, gazed at his handsome face, the dark eyes, the sharp jaw, that chest of his that feels plated in armor. A solid man, a man who can carry the weight of you, and does.

I let out a contented sigh. Wasn't that another perfect day? I said.

Sam kissed my forehead and closed his eyes. I moved my arm to turn over onto my front.

No, he said, stay.

Yes, it's just as Sam said. A fairy-tale life in the woods.

Sam

Today is our one-year anniversary of moving to Sweden. Hard to believe. A full year, a new country, a new home, a new child. A whole new life. A better one, that's for sure. To celebrate, I returned home from my meeting in Stockholm with a bunch of fresh spring flowers, a bottle of wine, and a knitted Viking hat for Conor that I picked up in one of the tourist stores in the old town.

Merry was in the kitchen, her long dark hair bundled on top of her head, her apron tied around her waist. She smiled when she saw me. I kissed her and she went to fetch a vase for the flowers.

Beautiful, she said.

As is my wife, I replied. I know she likes it when I call her that.

She put her arms around me and I breathed in her smell; perfume and something recently fried. Happy Swede-iversary, she said. Look, I made Swedish meatballs to celebrate.

Where's my boy? I asked, and went to find Conor. He was on the activity mat in the living room, lying on his back, trying to get at the frog that hangs suspended from the green plastic bar. This child. I can't get enough of him. Eight months and counting. He's growing by the day, a little evolution at the speed of light; always changing, always in motion.

How's my champ today, I said, lying down beside him. He smiled at me, the smile that turns my heart on its head: gummy and pink and pure love. I nuzzled my face into his belly, inhaled the smell of talcum powder and diaper cream.

I put the hat on his little head and lifted him up to show Merry. Two blond Viking braids hung down from the hat. Conor grabbed one and put it in his mouth.

Great, Merry laughed, now he's ready to lead an invasion.

She's so happy here. Light and happy. Unburdened. I love to see her like this. It's all I've ever wanted for her. For us.

I handed her the baby so I could go and wash up for dinner. She cradled him close, and I paused a minute to frame the scene.

Beautiful, I said again.

We sat down together around Ida's old oak table, Con in the high chair I built for him, Merry and I across from one another. She'd unpinned her hair, parted it to the side just as I like best. She was wearing a blue blouse that made her gray eyes appear almost translucent, as though they were portals to some other world, or altogether empty behind.

I poured the wine, Merry dished up the food and wiped the rim of the plates where the sauce had spilled. She'd lit candles even though it would still be light out for hours, and set the flowers on the far end of the table.

To Sweden, I toasted.

Merry held up her wine and we clinked our glasses together.

So good, I said, eating a mouthful.

Remember when we met, I laughed, you could hardly make a slice of toast.

It can be hard sometimes to remember that Merry. So much has changed since then.

Another lifetime, Merry said.

Yeah, I agreed. And this one's a far better fit.

She was radiant, the evening light from outside streaming in, painting her edges in a soft golden glow.

She was trying to feed Conor, but he kept turning his head away.

What have you got for him?

Broccoli, carrot, and chicken, she said.

Lucky guy. I smiled. Let me.

I took the blue plastic spoon from her.

Vrooom, vroooom. He opened his mouth wide and was done in no time.

See? I winked. He just wants you to work a little harder for it.

Later, after Con was asleep in his crib, Merry and I lay out on the lawn and finished the bottle of wine. I pulled her to me and kissed her deeply.

The stars above us blanketed the sky in light. The lavender in the garden floated its scent in the air, a little too overpowering. I could make out Merry's eyes, watching me, and within them, the edges of my reflection. I lifted her blouse and moved her down beneath me.

Sam, she protested.

Shhh, I said, we're in the middle of nowhere.

She relaxed under me and shuddered slightly as I pried her open and apart.

Besides, I reminded her, we're supposed to be trying for another baby.

Yes.

This is the life.

This is exactly how it's meant to be.

Merry

Today my project was jam and baby food. There's a surplus of produce from the garden and the refrigerator is almost empty of the little pots of food I make for the baby's meals. Sam and I agreed that he should eat as much organic and homemade food as possible, so we grow most of the vegetables ourselves, and I cook it up and turn it all into puree to bottle and store. It's not that much more work, really. I suppose nothing is when it comes to your children.

When we arrived last year, everything was wild and overgrown, fifteen years of neglect, of unweeded lawn and trees beset with rot. We pulled down the rotted spruces, heaved out the gnarl-rooted bushes and the lawn overrun with chickweed and black grass. We bought books on horticulture and planted rows and rows of seedlings from the nursery. Sam custom-built bricked-in vegetable patches and cold frames for the winter to guard against the frost. There were plagues of snails and fungus, seedlings that refused to sprout, mis-planted produce that we tried and failed to grow in the wrong seasons. Slowly, eventually, we worked out the rhythms of planting and picking, the time it takes to nurture a cabbage, the optimal alkalinity of the soil. We are quite expert now, or at least I am. Like the kitchen, the garden is my domain.

★ ★ ★

There is no shortage of produce these days. Every morning, I am outside sowing the seeds, removing the weeds, harvesting the vegetables from out of the soil. The smell of earth sits heavy in the air; the smell of something wholesome and good. Back to basics, Sam says. He likes to pretend he can taste the difference; he'll take a bite of salad and rule it home-grown or market-bought. I usually lie if he guesses wrong. I hate for him to feel silly.

For the baby's food, I boil the vegetables in pots on the stove, one for carrots, one for broccoli, one for zucchini. I write labels for the jars, as though the baby might be able to read them and choose his own dinner. Sam likes to open the refrigerator and see them all lined up in a row, a little army of food soldiers ready to serve.

Who's been a busy little wife? he'll say.

Oh, that would be me, I'll reply, with a wink. Coy and cute.

I sure am a busy little wife. It is the role I was born for, according to Sam. He cannot get enough of me like this, wifely and domestic and maternal. Perhaps he is right, and I was built for it. I certainly seem to excel at it. A natural, you might say, if you didn't know how hard I work to pull it all off.

Never mind; it's worth it, isn't it? What more could I hope for. What more do I need? The love of a husband, the gift of a child. It is enough—it is everything.

Sometimes this new life makes me feel as though I am living as a quaint eighteenth-century settler wife. Growing things, baking bread, going to the weekly farmer's market to choose my box of greens: zucchini, kale, celery, whatever I can't grow in my own garden. Sam marvels at the offerings—the freshness of wild Norwegian salmon, the taste of real farm butter or eggs plucked right out from under a hen.

How did we ever survive in the States? he says.

You'd wonder, I reply.

We do this frequently, compare life before and after; new world and old. Sweden always wins. There is seldom much need for debate. Sweden is Sam's gift to me, to us. It is the answer to everything, it has been the cure for all that ailed us before. Paradise, he calls it, and waits for me to agree.

I always do. How could I not.

As well as jam and baby food, it was a bathroom and kitchen day, so after finishing with the food, I made my homemade cleaning paste of vinegar and baking soda—the recipe courtesy of a blog Sam found for me. It's full of household tips, like how to make scented candles and the best ways to remove stubborn mold from the grouting. He subscribed me to the newsletter so I need never miss a single tip.

He's good like that. Proactive. I admire that quality in a person, the ability to decide and do, to set plans in motion. It has never been something I'm particularly good at. I often wonder what my life might look like if I was.

On my knees in the bathroom, I started with the bath. Scrubbing and shining the taps till I could see myself reflected back, distorted and inverted, pulling our week of collective shed hair out of the drain in a single swampy ball. The toilet next, finicky work, head in the bowl. What would my mother say if she could see me now? In the mirror, I looked at myself. Unkempt, that's what my mother would say. Or, more likely, hideous. Unwashed, no makeup, skin slicked in oil. A thin trickle of sweat pooling down my T-shirt. I sniffed under my armpits.

Then I smiled into the mirror, dazzling and wide. I opened my arms in a gesture of gracious welcome.

Welcome to our home, I said aloud. Welcome to our lives.

The woman in the mirror looked happy. Convincing.

There was a phone call earlier this morning from Frank. She woke the baby.

I'm coming to Sweden, she said.

What?

I'm coming to visit!

I've said it to her again and again in the year we've been here, at the end of every email and phone call. You must visit, it's wonderful; we'd love to have you.

And now she is coming. She will be here in a few weeks.

Your best friend, Sam said when I told him. That's great news.

Yes, isn't it, I said, smiling.

I'd emailed her just a few days ago. Another missive about my wonderful Swedish life, with photographs as proof. Something home-baked, a smiling child, a shirtless husband. She replied almost immediately, informing me of her new promotion, a sparkling new penthouse in Battersea. She attached a photograph of herself from a recent break to the Maldives. Frank in a pineapple-print bikini, sun-kissed and oiled, the lapping Indian Ocean in the background, a coconut cocktail in her hand.

I wonder what she'll make of all this. The picture of my life, when she sees it in the flesh.

I wiped the mirror and opened the windows to air the room of the stench of vinegar. In the kitchen, I moved the dishwasher and cleaned the dirt gathered against the wall. I scoured the oven of fat and grease, climbed up on the ladder to clean the top of the refrigerator. Sometimes I like to carve out messages in the dust. *HELP,* I wrote this morning, for no particular reason.

The baby woke up and began to cry just as I was halfway through bottling the last of the excess vegetables in brine. Pickling is another of my newfound skills. It's very rewarding. I went into the baby's room and stared at him in his crib.

Boiling over, face red with rage at his neglect. Spit foaming out of his mouth as he cried. He saw me and frowned, held out his arms, rocked on his haunches to try to propel himself up and out.

I watched him. With all my heart, I tried to summon it. Please, I thought, please.

Instincts, they call them, but for me they are the very furthest thing. Buried somewhere deep inside under too many layers, or altogether missing.

Please, I urged again, I coaxed, I begged. But inside, like always, there was only emptiness. Cold and hollow. The great void within.

I could do nothing but stand and watch.

The baby's cries grew more urgent, his face twisted with hot and vicious need. Almost purple. I stood helpless, rooted to the spot. I turned my head away so he would stop appealing to my eyes, imploring me to alleviate his rage. Unable to comprehend that I could not do it.

I looked around his room, filled with books and stuffed toys. A map of the world on the wall, along with stenciled illustrations of Arctic mammals. Polar bear. Moose. Fox. Wolf. I'd done it myself, the last month of pregnancy, balancing a paint box on the mound of my belly. The whole world, just for him. And still it is not enough. I am not enough.

And he is too much.

In the noise, I tried to find my breath, to feel the beating of my heart. It was pounding today, loud with upsets of its own; an angry fist in a cage.

I edged closer to the crib and peered down at the hysterical child. My child. I shook my head.

I'm sorry, I said at last. Mommy is not in the mood.

I left the room and closed the door behind me.

Sam

Karl and I sat outside while the women finished up the salads in the kitchen. He and his wife, Elsa, are our neighbors from across the field, good solid Swedes, wholesome and hardworking. She's in adult education; he runs a start-up that converts heating systems into more energy-efficient models. They invited us to their midsummer party last year right after we moved in, and this is how long it's taken us to have them over.

New baby, I apologized, and Karl shrugged. Of course.

Their daughter, Freja, was sitting on the lawn playing with Conor. Karl and I were talking, and I was trying not to stare at him too intently. It's hard to look away. His startling blue eyes, the height and spread of him. A full-blooded Viking. He'd brought over a gift of vacuum-sealed elk meat.

You'll have to join me for a hunt one day, he said. All the Swedes do it.

So, remind me, Karl said, what is it you do.

I shifted. I'm trying to get into film, I said. Documentary film.

You were doing that before?

No, I said. Before, I was an academic. Associate professor of anthropology. Columbia University.

He raised his eyebrows. Interesting. What was your area of study?

I smiled. The transformative masks of ritual and ceremony in West Africa, particularly the Ivory Coast. How's that for useless information?

It's very interesting, I'm sure.

It was, actually. The masks are fascinating, I said. The way they enable such fluidity of identity and power in these tribes, the way they depend on masking and performance for their—

I stopped myself from continuing. From remembering what I missed.

Onward, onward and up.

Anyway, it was time for a change, I said.

I finished the last of the beer in my glass, thought back to the final meeting with that brittle spinster Nicole from Human Resources. Sign here, initial this. A swift and unceremonious dismissal that took almost two decades of work—all the successes and accolades and titles—and vanished it into the ether.

But they haven't even heard my side, I said.

They know more than enough already, she replied coolly.

So you moved here for a new job, Karl said.

Not exactly, I said. I'm starting out. It's going to take some time. At the moment, it's pretty much just meetings and pitches, trying to show my reel to the right people.

I cracked my knuckles, the reassuring click of bones fitting into place. Karl wasn't letting up.

But why pick Sweden? he asked.

I shrugged. We had the house. We wanted a different kind of life. Americans live so superficially—it's all distraction and noise. I—well, we—we wanted something more real.

America is not real? Karl smiled. He'd already finished his second beer. I reached into the cooler and handed him a third.

America is a country built on myths, I said. Manifest destiny, American exceptionalism. The idea that we're better than we really are.

Karl nodded. So what is the verdict? It's better over here?

Of course, I said. Sweden feels like the best place in the world to be.

Karl laughed. Maybe you're not looking closely enough. He raised his beer and gave a mock toast. Anyway, he said, let's hope you're right.

I looked at Conor on the lawn, bright-eyed and thriving.

Of course this was the place.

Freja came over to show Karl a cut on her finger. He said something to her in Swedish and she nodded and went back to Conor.

So you don't miss home, Karl said. Being around your own people.

There's not a damn thing I miss about the USA, I said.

Elsa came out balancing a bowl of coleslaw and a green salad. Merry followed with a pile of plates and cutlery. She looked tired. She'd been up since early, preparing for the guests. Next to Elsa, she seemed vaguely off-putting, her hair unwashed and pulled back into a messy bun.

No time, she'd said earlier when I asked.

There's always time, I said, just not always good time management.

What about you, Merry, Karl asked. Do you miss being in the States?

Merry glanced over at me and shrugged. What's there to miss?

We sat to eat, passed around bowls of food and saltshakers. Merry had overdressed the salad, but I said nothing.

It's very good, Elsa said.

I noticed she hardly ate a thing.

Merry brought out a bowl with Conor's baby food, and Freja asked if she might feed him. She took a spoon and made an airplane, flying mush into his mouth.

Look at that. I smiled. She's a real natural.

Yes, Karl said, she can't wait for a baby brother or sister to play with.

Elsa put down her knife and fork. Karl took a sip of his beer and gave me a knowing smile. In the meantime, he said, we have bought her a cat.

Elsa looked over at Conor and patted his arm. He is a wonderful baby, she said. Very sweet.

Sure is, I said, wondering how it was possible Karl didn't crack her in half every time he lay on top of her.

Merry stood up to clear the dishes, scraping and stacking, refusing Elsa's offer to help. When she came back out, she carried a cake for dessert; summer berries piled in the middle and drizzled in cream.

My domestic goddess, I said. What have we got here?

Merry passed around glass plates and silver cake forks. I recognized them from her mother's silverware set.

Merry, Karl said, you haven't told us what you do.

I pointed to the cake. She does this, I said, and we all laughed.

I used to work as a set designer, Merry said, almost inaudibly.

For movies? Karl asked.

Movies, TV shows, often just TV commercials.

Yes, I said, she was always constructing these little made-up worlds. Kitchens and living rooms, those generic sets you see on all the crappy ads. Disinfectant hand soap or mattresses.

Well, there were some more interesting projects, Merry said.

I had a sudden memory of her coming home one night with a green armchair she'd spent all day tracking down. She'd asked me to help her haul it up to our apartment. I remember how I resented that chair, and her for interrupting me for help with something so silly while I was grading papers. The job was beneath her. Beneath us.

I looked at her now. She had that look she gets from time to time. Pensive. Melancholic. Like she is slipping away. Forgetting herself.

I took another mouthful of cake. God, this is good, isn't it?

Yes, Karl agreed. It's a very good cake.

Merry blinked and smiled.

Do you plan to find something similar over here? Elsa asked. There are a lot of shows shot locally, in Stockholm or

Gothenburg. It would be very convenient, very close by for you.

I caught Merry's eye, and she shook her head. No, she said. It's good to just focus on motherhood for now. That's really the most important thing.

Before they left, I took Karl inside to show him my collection of African masks. Six carved wooden faces: three from the Ivory Coast, one from Benin, two Igbo fertility masks from my semester in Nigeria.

How exotic, he said.

They are terrifying. Elsa shuddered.

I laughed. Merry feels the same way. She's been begging me to put them away in a box for years.

Elsa smiled. And still they are on the wall, she said.

After we said our goodbyes, I closed the door and pulled Merry to me.

That was fun, I said.

Yes, she said.

Aren't they like wax models, those two?

Yes, she said. Elsa is flawless.

I made a mental note to take Karl up on his offer to go hunting, while Merry went to finish the last of the cleaning up, packing dishes into the dishwasher, wiping down the countertops, gathering the crumbs into her hand.

I lifted Conor off the rug and into my arms. He smelled of Elsa's perfume. And shit.

I handed him over to Merry. Looks like it's time for a diaper change, I said.

Merry

I watch the baby through the bars of his crib. A little prison, to keep him safely inside. He watches me. He does not smile. I do not bring him joy.

Well. The feeling is mutual.

I look at his face. I watch closely for signs of change. They tell you that they transform all the time. They are supposed to resemble their father first, then their mother, then back again. But he is only me. All me. Too much of me.

His eyes stare, a constant reproach. Accusatory. Remember, they say, remember what you have done. I'm sorry, I whisper, and look away.

My bars are not bars. They are glass and trees. The glass cage that is our house, the huge glass windows all around that Ida's father installed to maximize light and space. The ancient tall pines that block off the light. My island exile, all escapes closed off, all outside life shut out. Just us.

Sam and me and the baby.

All we need, Sam says.

Is it? I say. Doesn't it feel like we're the last three survivors of a plane crash?

Oh... He laughs at my silliness.

★ ★ ★

He was off in Stockholm or Uppsala today—I forget which—playing his show reel for ad executives and producers. He is trying hard to make this work. He really is doing his best. He always does. Family, he says: nothing matters more. This is why we moved here, a new start, the very best place to raise a family. How he loves the baby. How he adores every part of him and every little thing he does. Once, he looked at me like this, as though I were a wonder of nature, a rare being to worship and adore.

Ba-ba. Ma-ma. Pa-pa.

Everything we say is broken into two syllables.

Bird-ee.

Hors-ee.

Hous-ie.

The baby eats some of the time but not always. Often I make him food and eat it myself, letting him watch as I spoon it into my mouth.

See? No mess.

I offer him the spoon and he shakes his head.

The baby cries a lot but forms no words. He rocks on his belly but does not yet know how to crawl. There are milestones that I am surely supposed to be checking and am not. The copy Sam bought me of *The Ultimate Guide to Baby's First Year* lies unopened next to the bed, under a tube of organic rose hand cream that sends five percent of its profits to the preservation of the rain forest.

You read it, right?

Of course, I lie. It was terrifically informative.

The baby. My baby. He has a name, but somehow I can't bring myself to say it out loud. Conor Jacob Hurley. Naturally, Sam named him. Conor Jacob, he said, Jacob after his best friend from high school who was lost at sea on a round-the-world sailing trip. Conor in deference to Sam's vaguely Irish roots. Conor Jacob. Conor Jacob Hurley. It was decided, written down on the tag on his tiny wrist. I read it. I mouthed the words of my son's name. Conor Jacob Hurley.

The balloons next to the hospital bed were baby blue. One had already burst, its deflated remains drifting forlornly among the rest.

Would you like to hold your son? the nurse offered.

If Sam was out of the room, I would shake my head.

He believes I am a good mother, the very best kind. Devoted and all-nurturing and selfless. Without a self. Perhaps he is right about the last part. Sometimes I wonder myself: Where am I? Or: Was there anyone there to begin with?

The days Sam isn't home always feel like a vacation. The baby and I have no audience to impress. Usually, I don't shower. I don't change out of my nightgown. I sit on the couch watching reality TV, my dirty little habit (one of many, I should add). I cannot get enough. Plastic women devouring each other, housewives and teen mothers. How they play at being real, when really it's all for the cameras. Still, everyone pretends not to know. The conspiracy is a success.

Most days, I eat wedges of butter to stave off my sugar cravings and keep my weight down, but when Sam's away, I unpack my hidden stash from the barrel of the washing machine and indulge in whole bags of crisps and cookies, which I smuggle home from the grocery store under packs of diapers and organic detergent. I am vile. Terrifically unladylike. I pick at my toenails and squeeze out the ingrown hairs from my legs. Sam would shudder if ever he saw me like this. Sometimes I shudder myself, at this version of me. Well, she will need to be banished once Frank arrives. There will be no such escapes for a while.

Some days, I think it would be nice to go out, to leave our little island territory, but of course Sam has the car. It's an hour on foot to get anywhere from here, and forty minutes' walk to the nearest bus station. Sam bought himself a mountain bike for the trails, but it's been ruled out for me. Too dangerous, he said, with a baby.

That leaves us stuck. Just us. Mother and child, with nothing to do but revel in domestic duties. I suspect Sam likes it. No, I know he does. My lack of distraction. My utter focus. Actually, it surprises me how encouraging he's being about Frank's visit. In New York, I was always hearing complaints about any outside interests or distractions. The parts of me that weren't entirely consumed with Sam. Sam's favorite music, Sam's current reading list, Sam's teaching materials, his new eating habits, or his latest workout. Sam's everything. And now Sam's baby.

The baby. The baby we made. The baby we let into the world. I remember how I felt that day, standing in the pokey beige bathroom of our apartment which always smelled of the deep fryer from the Indian restaurant downstairs, looking at the two lines faint on the stick, the lines of life, imminent and incontrovertible. It was the second test. Whoopsie daisy. A whoopsie baby.

The door burst open, Sam home early and unexpectedly.

Is that? he asked, looking at me, caught red-handed. I did not miss a beat. Yes, Sam, I cried. Isn't it the very best news.

The origin of the word *suffer* is "to bear." You are not supposed to overcome it. You are only supposed to endure. I am free to leave, this is what anyone would say to me, but the question is how, and with what, and to where. These have never been questions I could answer. They have never seemed like my decisions to make. In this world, I have no one but Sam. He knows this. It is surely part of the allure. That and how I am no good on my own. I would not know where to begin.

There are sleepless nights and nights that don't end. I wake sometimes and find the baby in my arms, yet I have no recollection of fetching him. He screams himself awake and I go to his crib, watching him turn red and fuming, tears streaming down his face, cries catching violently in his throat. Feral, raging changeling from the wild. I am reluctant to pick him up, loath to offer him comfort, even though this is all he wants from me, all he asks. I cannot give it. I can only stand and watch, silent and unmoving, until he is all cried out and too exhausted for more.

Sleep training, I'll explain to Sam, if he complains about the crying. I'll quote a reputable pediatric authority, because I like to show him how seriously I take our child's development. Still, he'll find things to point out that I am doing wrong. He'll offer wisdom and advice—minor improvements, he calls them, and there's always room for these. Yes. He does love to educate me. He is very good at it. Filling in the blanks. I think perhaps he considers me to be one of the blanks, too, and slowly he is filling me in. Do this, wear that. Now you should quit your job. Now we should marry. Now we should breed.

Over the years he has shown me what to appreciate and what to disavow. Italian opera, classical Russian pianists. Experimental jazz. Korean food. French wine.

Is it Dvořák? I ask him, as though I don't know. As though I wasn't the one raised in the oceanfront house in Santa Monica, lavished with education and private lessons beyond anything I wanted or deserved.

Husband. *Hūsbonda.* Master of the house.

I suppose he only tells me things I don't know myself. What I need. What I want. Who I am. And in return for this, I give it my all. I give Sam the exact woman he wants me to be. A faultless performance. Nothing else would do.

The men before Sam wanted to rescue me, kiss away the boo-boos. Sam wanted to make me over from scratch. And I hate to disappoint him, because disappointing Sam is the worst feeling in the world. It is the end of the world, actually, and the return of the hopeless, relentless, gnawing vacancy inside.

You'll be a terrific mother, Merry, he told me all through the pregnancy, through the nausea and the discomfort and that feeling of hostile, unstoppable invasion. He couldn't take his eyes off me, or his hands off my swollen belly. He was mesmerized with what he imagined was his singular achievement.

Look at this, he marveled. We made this life; we made this living being inside of you.

The miracle of it, he said.

It felt like the very farthest thing. But Sam had already carried us away on a dream and a plan: Sweden. A brand-new life. Shed the old skin and slip into another. There was something enticing about the idea of it, of leaving New York with its many secrets and shames. Some of them Sam's, the biggest one belonging to me.

The baby, the baby. Sam loves him with such ferocity, it can sometimes make it hard for me to breathe. And now there will be Frank to think of. Frank in my house. Frank in my life. So close. Perhaps too close. We are childhood friends, that most dangerous kind. Bonded over memories and sleepovers and secrets; over betrayals and jealousies and cruelties big and small. She has always been in my life somehow, a lingering presence. Even when we are far apart, separated by cities or continents, it is Frank I think of most. It is Frank I crave. I imagine her reacting to what I do and say, to how I live, to whom I love. I imagine Frank taking it all in. I imagine what it feels like for her, to see my life and hold it up against her own. We need each other like this. We always have.

I remember when she first moved to New York—snapped up after her MBA by one of the top consulting firms. Suddenly she was a different Frank. Jet-setting between cities, dating hedge-fund managers, living in a penthouse apartment with a Russian art dealer for a roommate. Well, I packed my things and moved there myself a few months later. My father paid my rent.

But what are you doing here? Frank asked when I arrived on her doorstep one Saturday morning with two cream cheese bagels.

I've always planned to live here, I said, I told you.

Yes. We need each other. Without the other, how would either of us exist?

It was nine o'clock when Sam returned home, much earlier than he'd said. The baby was in his crib, newly asleep with the help of a teaspoon or two of cough syrup. I do this occasionally, on the more difficult days. It's meant to be harmless. Mother's little helper, is all.

Other things I do too. Like put pillows too close to the baby's head. Or set him down to nap just a touch too near the edge of the bed. I don't know why. I don't know what it is that compels me. I only know I cannot stop it. Often I weep. Other times, all is numb, whole parts of me dead and blackened like a gangrenous limb. Immune to life.

I was on the sofa when I heard Sam's car on the gravel. I startled. I'd been watching a show about women who compete with their best friends to see who can throw the better wedding. I hadn't yet cleaned myself up. I quickly snapped shut the laptop and opened a book on early childhood development.

Hello, wife, Sam said, kissing me on the mouth.

His breath was stale, the smell of rotting meat. My stomach turned.

How did it go today? I asked.

He ignored the question, sat down next to me, and cupped my swollen breasts, weighed them like a medieval merchant.

Our Merry's in musk, it seems, he said, laughing. I know what you'll be wanting, he said, a finger burrowing inside my jeans. I was unwashed; I could smell myself on his fingers.

Have you been using the thermometer? he asked. You have to do it every day so we get the dates right.

A few weeks ago, he bought me a basal thermometer. I am supposed to take my temperature every morning and track the stages of my ovulation. Follicular phase, luteal phase, cycle length, everything recorded and set to a graph that displays on an app on my phone. Conception made science. When I am at my most fertile, the phone beeps frantically and a red circle appears on the screen. It's a red day, it declares. A reminder. A warning.

I'm using it, I said. But it takes a while to work out your cycle.

He is impatient with me. He wants me pregnant again. Insisted we start trying when the baby was barely two months old.

It's too soon, I begged. Everything hurts.

Nonsense, he said. The doctor said six weeks.

I would bleed afterward, shocked pink blood on the sheets and in my underwear the next day. Several pairs I deposited straight into the trash, the blood stiff and dried brown, smelling strongly of rust and decay.

Come, Sam said. He led me to the bedroom, set me down gently, with purpose.

I lay there and pretended to enthuse. Oh, yes. More. Please. He likes it when I beg. When I say thank you afterward, like he has given me a gift.

Some days it is harder than others to remember gratitude. To acknowledge my awful good luck. Sam went slow, stopping to look into my eyes. He repulses me sometimes. A physical reaction to his smell and his touch; the way he breathes through his mouth with his tongue lifted up, the way the hairs on his shoulders sprout in odd patches of wiry black strands.

Something inside me heaves and shudders to have him close.

I suppose that's normal.

I love you, Merry, he said, and then I did feel it. Grateful. Loved. Or at least I think it's what I felt. Sometimes it's hard to know for sure.

Sam on top, inside, he clutched at me with both hands and breathed into my ear.

Let's make a baby, he said, right before he came.

Sam

I was up early this morning, shaved, dressed, half out the door. Merry was setting Conor down in his high chair.

Where are you going?

Uppsala again, I said. I told you a few days ago.

You didn't, she said.

It's okay, I said, giving them each a quick kiss. You probably just forgot. You know how bad your memory can be.

You're going again?

It's a callback, I said. A meeting with the executive creative director this time.

She nodded. Good luck.

In the car, I checked the time, then my phone.

10 a.m., I wrote.

I pulled out of the drive and headed slowly past the neighboring houses. Mr. Nilssen was out with the horses. I raised my hand in greeting. He's supposedly a billionaire. Sells his horses to the Saudis but still drives a Honda. God, I love the Swedes. Gives me a thrill every morning, driving out, seeing where we live and how. The sheer good fortune of it all. Sometimes you get lucky, I guess.

⋆ ⋆ ⋆

The day was going to be a good one. Sunny and clear. The traffic was smooth.

In forty minutes, I was outside her apartment door, ringing the doorbell.

You're early, she said when she opened up. She was wearing a dress, ivory satin, tied tightly against her so it looked like she'd been submerged in thick cream. Her hair was loose, long, and blond and softly curled at the shoulders.

Hello, Malin. I smiled.

Come inside, she said.

Later, around the boardroom table, I looked at six young Swedes as they watched my reel. It's a mix of old footage from the field and some new material I've been working on in the studio I've set up for myself at home. It's good work. I know my way around a scene. I've been told that I have an excellent eye for framing. That I'm a natural at this.

I sipped an espresso from a mint green cup.

This is great, the creative director commented, very dynamic.

I reckon I have a fresh perspective, I said. With my background.

It wasn't so difficult, all this self-promotion. Fake it till you make it and all.

It says here you taught at Columbia?

Yes, I said.

Why the career change?

I gave a wry smile. Well, after enough years teaching young people, you realize you've got it in reverse. They know it all and you're just a dinosaur with a piece of chalk.

Oh, and I was fired. I guess I could have added that.

They laughed. A good answer. Endearing, not too cocky. I've got it down to an art.

So you did a lot of filmmaking as an anthropologist?

Some, yes. Mostly in the early days of my career, the time I spent doing fieldwork in Africa. But film was always what I really wanted to do. That's why I've returned to documentary now.

They looked at me and I smiled. Not one of them a day over thirty, and all of them so effortlessly self-possessed you'd think they were Fortune 500 CEOs.

Snow tires. The shoot is for a company that makes snow tires.

Great, I said. Sounds interesting.

A mobile phone rang and the producer got up to take the call. Before he left the room, he slipped a business card onto the table in front of me.

Sorry, the creative director said, we're busy with a big project at the moment; everyone's a little distracted.

It was my cue to leave. I shut my laptop and stood up, knocking the chair back as I did.

He shook my hand. We'll let you know.

How was your meeting? Merry asked when I got back home.

It was good, I said, really good.

She beamed. Wonderful.

She had Conor in her arms, freshly bathed and ready for bed. His eyes were red, like he'd been crying.

Did you two have a good day? I asked.

Oh, for sure, she said. The best.

Merry

Domestic chores aren't usually Sam's department, but last night he volunteered to bathe the baby. He emerged from the bathroom afterward holding him in a towel.

Hey, he said, what's this over here?

He lifted the towel and showed me the child's thighs. My face flushed. I had not noticed the marks, four little blue bruises against his skin.

That is strange, I said. I swallowed.

I wonder, Sam said, could his clothes be too tight? Could that be it?

Yes, I said, more than likely. I should have bought him the next size up by now.

Sam nodded. Well, you should take care of that in the morning.

Absolutely, I said, first thing.

And so, in the name of new baby clothes, I was permitted the car for today. Sam took the baby and I headed into Stockholm, music blaring, windows open to the warm midsummer air. Exhilarating, the heady feeling of freedom, of leaving the island behind. I had dressed up, a light floral summer skirt, a sleeveless blouse.

In Stockholm, I parked the car and checked my face in the mirror. I loosened my hair and shook it out. I painted on mascara and lined my lips with color. Transformed. I walked a short way to a café in Södermalm I'd read about.

Sometimes I do this, page through travel magazines and imagine all the alternative lives I might be living. Drinks at the newest gin bar in Barcelona, a night in Rome's best boutique hotel.

I picked up an English newspaper from the counter and sat at a table by the window, pretending to read. I love to people-watch in the city. Everyone is so beautiful. Clear skin and bright eyes, hair shining, bodies taut and well proportioned. There is no excess. Nothing bulging out or hanging over or straining at the seams. Even their clothes seem immune to crumpling. It isn't just Karl and Elsa next door: it's a whole country of them.

Immaculate Elsa. I should probably invite her over for *fika,* try to make friends. We could discuss pie recipes and child-rearing; I might ask her about her skincare routine. Only I've never been very good at it. Female friendships. Well, apart from Frank, I suppose.

Sam keeps asking if I'm excited for her visit. I try to be enthusiastic. I do look forward to it, I think. Showing off our lives, showing her everything I have accomplished. Showing her who is ahead.

But there is another part of me that feels deep unease. Something about the way Frank always sees more than she should. She likes to think she knows me better than anyone—maybe even myself. She considers this a triumph. So she pokes at my life like a child with a stick, prodding at a dead seal washed up on the shore. Waiting to see what crawls out. Peekaboo, I see you!

She is always digging, digging, trying to go beyond the surface. The real you, she says, I know the real Merry. Whatever that means.

At the table across from me, I watched a young woman. She must have been in her early twenties, blond and slim and well dressed. She was eating a cinnamon bun, forking small bites of pastry into her mouth. She kept brushing a finger gently to her lips. She talked with an older man, perhaps in his forties, dressed in a gray cashmere sweater and dark jeans. Like me, he watched her movements closely, followed her fork with his eyes into her mouth; followed her fingers as they danced on those red lips. At one point she touched his arm, casual and friendly and innocent of all desire, but for him I could see it was electrifying.

She was showing him something on a laptop screen, pointing with her long fingers. She wore no wedding band, just a thin gold ring on her index finger, set with a small topaz stone in the center. He nodded intently as she spoke; she wrote something down in a notebook that lay open next to her cup. He watched her take a sip, the way she licked her lips to make sure that no foam lingered. Love or infatuation, who could ever tell.

An older woman walked in alone, ordered a coffee and a sandwich from the barista, and sat down at a table near the window. She was flawless. White trousers, neat leather pumps, pearl earrings. She must have been sixty or more, glowing and beautiful, without anything surgically pulled or plumped. It is a mystery here, how their women are permitted to age with such grace.

I thought of my own mother, her freakish final face and all the ones in between. So many years she spent obsessively trying to ward off the inevitabilities of aging. Every few months, something new. Eyes ironed out at the corners, extra skin pulled back and sewn high into the temples. Fatty deposits sucked out and reassigned, either to cheeks or lips. Breasts lifted, stomach fat suctioned through a pump.

As a child, I loved to watch her getting herself ready to go out. My father was always coming home with invitations to galas and balls; charity dinners or openings of new wings at the hospital. It was an elaborate performance, painting on a face, torturing her hair into some elegant updo, squeezing into a dress two sizes too small and two decades too young.

You're so pretty, I'd say.

I'm not pretty enough, she always replied.

Or sometimes: I used to be, before you came along.

There were many things for which I was accused and held accountable. The loss of her figure. The thinning of her hair. The sagging of her skin. The absence of my father's attention.

He never told her to stop the surgeries. Perhaps this was how he punished her.

Sam likes me natural, he says. This means slim. Groomed. Depilated. Scrubbed and lotioned, smooth like a piece of ripe fruit.

He shaved me once, early on in our relationship; made me

stand over him in the bath while he took a razor between my legs and slowly carved away. There, he said, that's how I want you.

I had looked down at my new self with delight. Beloved, I thought, this is what it feels like to be beloved.

Six years in and still, in the early hours of the morning, while Sam lies and dreams, I clean my teeth and shine my face and comb my hair. I shape my eyebrows and tint my lashes and pluck away the stray hairs that plant themselves on my upper lip; I trim my cuticles and buff the dead skin from my heels, I paint my nails to match the seasons. I shave and moisturize and soften my skin, I spray perfume and roll deodorant and use special intimate wipes to make me smell like flowers instead of a woman. All this I do so that when he wakes, I am transformed, when he wants me, I am ready. All yours, I say. I am all yours.

It is a lie; a small part I keep for myself.

It must have been around noon when I realized I was hungry. I left the café and strolled around the cobbled back streets in the glare of the sun. It's a pleasant city, I suppose. Charming, contained in a way that New York is not, and never can be. Here there is none of that current in the air, the pulse of lust and need and ruthlessness. Of longing and secrets.

Around Götgatan I spied a café with a neat little row of quiches sitting in the window. I went inside and ordered at the counter, sat down at a small table in the corner. The waitress brought over my food and laid down cutlery and a napkin. *Tack,* I said, and she smiled sweetly. The quiche was delicate, not too heavy. It felt strange and delicious to eat alone; a forbidden delight from another life.

I ordered a coffee after I finished, not wanting it to end just yet. The café was filling up with people; I saw the waitress glance over at me. She came up to the table.

Would you mind? she said. This man would like to eat something.

It was the same man from earlier.

May I? He indicated the free chair opposite me.

I smiled. Of course.

You are American, he said, as he sat.

Yes, I said. Sorry about that.

He laughed. I tried to recall the movements of the woman from earlier, the way she touched her lips, delicate and deliberate. I brushed my fingers against my mouth. I watched him watch me.

What are you doing here, he said, business or pleasure?

Oh. I smiled. Always pleasure.

Again my fingers went to my lips.

You remind me of someone, he said.

Yes, I said, I hear that all the time.

You're on vacation? he asked.

I hesitated. There was something I had to take care of here, I said.

I wanted to sound enigmatic and mysterious. The kind of woman a man like him aches for. I took a sip of coffee, I touched my lips. I smiled sadly and looked suddenly toward the street, into the middle distance, as though recalling some dark secret or heartache within.

Yes, I had it. I watched him watch me and shift in his seat.

* * *

In New York, there were countless days like this. It's easy in a city that size. You never see the same person twice. Never have to be the same person. Sitting in the park, strolling through the Met, whiling away a few hours in the public library. I was the woman in the red dress, or the blue coat, or the scarf with red lips printed all across it. I was a lawyer, a grad student, a midwife, an anthropologist, a gallerist; I was Dominique or Anna or Lena or Francesca. I was all of these women. Everyone but Merry. It was always a rush, a moment belonging only to me; a spectacle for my own entertainment. My own secret pleasure. Only occasionally did it go too far.

Even as a child, I loved nothing better than to perform in front of the bathroom mirror. Sometimes I'd steal one of my mother's lipsticks or some of her jewelry. I'd pretend to be a model or an actress, sometimes a lovesick girlfriend or a wife betrayed. I liked to watch myself, the transformation into someone else. I'd try out different voices and accents, different expressions on my face. I could play out scenes for hours on end. It never grew dull. It still doesn't. Perhaps this is my gift. The ability to slip in and out of selves, as though they were dresses hanging in a wardrobe, waiting to be tried on and twirled about.

I'm Lars, by the way, the man said.

He extended his hand and I let it linger in mine. While he ate his lunch, I entertained him with stories from my recent trip to the Maldives.

Can you imagine, I laughed, two weeks on a tropical island with only the winter wardrobe of Mr. Oleg Karpalov in my possession!

Which island? he asked.

I tried to recall Frank's email and couldn't. I glanced at my watch.

I have to go, I said.

He grabbed my wrist.

Wait, he said. Give me your number.

He took his phone from his pocket and wrote down the digits I offered.

I smiled.

I had won.

It was late and I had to hurry to Drottninggatan to find a department store. I needed to be Merry again. In the baby section, I threw piles of clothes over my arm. T-shirts, miniature chinos, cargo shorts with dinosaurs on the pockets, little track pants and pajama bottoms.

The phone rang and my heart sank.

Where are you? Sam asked. I thought you'd be back by now. He sounded irritated.

I apologized profusely. I had a hard time finding what I was looking for, I explained. You know I always get lost here, in the city.

Well, come back soon, he said.

Yes, Sam, I said, apologizing once more before I hung up the phone.

I paid for the baby clothes and slipped into the restroom. In front of the mirror, I wet a wad of paper and wiped off the remnants of my makeup under the bright white light. Inside one of the stalls, a woman was retching. Probably an eating disorder, I thought, though it could have been anything.

★ ★ ★

I made my way back to the car and did find myself lost—the cobbled lanes, the tasteful storefronts, the quaint boutiques and antiques shops—all of them blend into the same tepid view: spotless streets, polite pedestrians, the too-orderly flow of people and traffic. The heady freedom of earlier was already in retreat. My chest was constricting, the streets narrowing in parallel, closing me in, squeezing it all back down to size. I hate to upset Sam. It fills me with terror, any time he has a reason to find me lacking.

At last I found the parking lot. An old Roma woman sat begging at the entrance. She looked at me, sucked her teeth, and wagged a finger. A witch casting a curse.

I drove home too fast. When I got back, Sam handed me the baby.

He hasn't eaten yet, he said. And he needs his bath.

He did not kiss me.

Already there was a message waiting from Lars. I deleted it quickly from my phone and went to attend to my child.

Sam

Email this morning from the guys in Uppsala. They're going with another director for the snow tires. Assholes. Top of the class, I was, graduated cum fucking laude. Fellowships, scholarships. Tenure. Now this.

It's all right. I'll get there. Just got to stick it out. Keep at it.

From the studio I could hear Conor whining. He's been out of sorts for a couple of days.

Teething, Merry says. She tells me it's normal. She read it in the parenting book I bought her.

Let's take a long walk, I said. I want to encourage Merry to exercise. Tone up. Lose the baby weight that's still sticking to her. Discipline, I say, all it takes.

I lifted Con into the backpack and hoisted it onto my shoulders. Merry put sunscreen and a hat on him, and dabbed the back of my neck so I wouldn't burn.

We closed the door behind us and made for the forest trails that surround the reserve. The day was warm but not too hot, a low hum of insects and birds. We walked in silence.

A sweat will do us good, I said, heading for one of the more difficult routes.

Merry walked behind us. I could hear her breathing.

Beautiful, I said. The summers here are incredible.

Merry was quiet.

Hon?

Sam, I say it all the time, don't I. It's beautiful. It's perfect. It's amazing.

Jesus, I said. Guess you're not pregnant this month after all.

What?

Take it easy, I said. I'm joking. Clearly this is some heavy-duty PMS, right? Your foul mood. Hormones in a spin.

I laughed. You women, always so sensitive. And you think you want to run the world.

I walked on, leaving her to stew. I won't indulge these moods; she knows better than to think that I will.

Tuesday morning and I'm taking a hike with a baby strapped to my back. Guess this is life in Sweden for you. Transculturation. In anthropological terms, it's what happens when you move to a new society and adopt the culture.

Professor. I always liked being called that. Guess it doesn't work so well out here. Hey, Professor Hurley, can you zoom in on the snow tires?

Conor started to whine and I stopped to check on him.

He'd pulled off the hat and was damp with sweat. Merry caught up to us.

He feels really warm, I said.

He's fine, Merry replied. Just needs some water. She gave him a bottle and he pushed it away. She poured some water onto a cloth and nestled it against his neck to keep him cool.

Wonder-mom, I said. You know all the tricks.

Sorry about earlier, she said. You're probably right. It must be PMS.

We looped back along the trail and made our way down toward the lake.

I bent to feel the temperature. Icy, I said. Give it a couple of weeks, it'll be just right.

Merry stood staring into the endless blue of the water, transfixed.

Thinking about going in? I teased.

Something like that, she said vaguely, and stayed a moment longer, lost in her head.

Back at home, Merry prepared a light lunch, cheese and fresh bread, a salad. She seemed to be distracted still. She forgot the lemon in my soda, the oil for the salad.

You're not yourself today, I said, and she appeared to shrink.

I'm sorry, Sam, I don't know what it is.

Has Frank confirmed dates yet? I asked, trying to brighten her mood.

No, she said, shaking her head. Something about wrapping up work. Apparently she's taking a sabbatical.

Bread's good, I said, and she smiled.

It's a new recipe I tried.

That's my wife, I said. Always outdoing herself.

Merry beamed. She needs this kind of reassurance, I guess. Or she loses sight of herself, starts to fade.

Hey, I said. I got that job.

Oh, Sam, she said, I knew you would.

After lunch, she laid Conor down for a nap and emerged back outside with a couple of blankets, which she spread out on the lawn.

There, now we can take a little nap too. She smiled, squinting her eyes against the light, looking at me the way she does.

Merry, I said, it's Tuesday afternoon. I've got work to do.

I left her alone on the empty lawn and went inside. In the darkened studio, I sat and watched other people's videos on the thirty-inch monitor I bought in anticipation of my new career. I read my emails. There was one from Columbia, an invitation to apply for an upcoming grant. Must be an old mailing list.

After an hour or so, I pulled back the blinds to peer outside. Merry was still sitting on the blanket, cross-legged and facing the house. No sign of any particular pleasure. No sign of anything much at all.

How I love this woman, I thought.

Merry

I lay in the bath, submerged in water that had turned too cool. The body under water, the way it is floating and weightless and expanded all at once. Corpses they pull from the water are always unrecognizable, aren't they, bloated inflated creatures, blimplike parodies of their once-human form. I shuddered, and then stilled myself below the surface. So pale. So slight. There is so little of me. I take up almost no space.

In front of the mirror, my mother's first eyes stared back at me, the ones that were exiled for growing old and sad. Or maybe it was not sadness, but rage that she was trying to disguise. Rage at my father for filling his days with work and his nights with other women.

You marry your father, this is what they tell us. This is what you pray will be untrue. I sometimes think of Sam on all his business trips, so much time to squander while the baby and I are marooned here alone, left to our own devices and wicked ways. He has a history, to put it mildly, a habit of straying. But I dare not mention it. I dare not reveal any concern that he is not what he says—a different man over here, a better man. What do I care, anyway? And what right do I have to judge him. I am no innocent myself.

I am no innocent in anything.

★ ★ ★

I stood and watched my bare chest heave and shake, the breasts undulating, pendulous. Lower than before, bigger and rounder. Sam strokes them with adoration.

Mother's breasts now, he says, as though their divine purpose has been revealed at last.

I breastfed the baby for six full months, tortured milk from my cracked, engorged nipples. Sometimes the pain was so great I had to scream. The baby did not notice.

In the hospital right after he was born, the nurses wanted me to hold him, to bond him to me, flesh against flesh. Latching. Suckling. Feeding. Everything primal and exposed. You are an animal like you've always been.

Cow, sow, bitch; bloody and ruined.

In my arms, the baby kept rooting for my nipples, pink and downy like a truffle pig.

The milk would not come. The body would not comply. The nurses brought different pumps and a lactation consultant called Eve. She gave me little white pills to swallow. She told me to keep holding the baby close, to keep his skin on my skin, to keep his toothless mouth in proximity to my milkless breasts.

How am I here? Still I don't quite know. I feel something leaking out of me daily, slow wafts of weightlessness and life. A little here, a little there. Sometimes it's in response to something benign, like Sam's ceaseless enthusiasm for these shiny new lives, or his tireless adulation of the baby and his latest smile or almost-comprehensible word. Other times it's a moment, a glimpse of my life reflected back at me through a window or a mirror. This is you. This is your life. This is your allowance for happiness and joy. There's nothing wrong with the picture except everything.

If I close my eyes, I see nothing.

No. I see Frank.

So clear, so sure of herself in so many ways. Sharp about the edges. A woman defined. And me, just a blur. A frame that will not hold.

And yet. It is Frank who has always given me shape. A way to see myself clear. Because from where she is standing, the view is spectacular. Something to covet. Something to yearn for, with that deep, guttural longing that knows it can never be properly filled. Best friend. Yes, she really must be.

In the living room, I sat and wrote out a list of everything I'll need to do for her visit. New bed linens, soft-touch pillows and throws. Some woven baskets and succulents in stone pots to warm up the room. Maybe a framed print or two, something graphic and abstract, or an ink drawing from one of the designer homeware stores around Söder.

From the wall, I felt six extra pairs of eyes on me, Sam's masks, hollow and terrifying. I checked them once, for hidden cameras. Those nanny cams that people use to spy on their babysitters. I'd had a sudden flash of an idea, that Sam might be watching. Might be making even more certain to miss nothing of my parenting skills. He does like to be in control. I took them off the wall and examined them closely, the faint whiff of decay coming from the wood. There weren't any cameras behind the masks, but still, they never fail to unsettle me. To remind me that I am always under scrutiny. And now another set of eyes will be on me.

It was time for the baby's lunch. In his room, he held his arms up to me, fraught with expectation. I looked at him, as I do. Waiting. Hoping to feel something.

I wonder if it isn't somehow inherited. Maternal instincts, or the lack thereof. I cannot remember Maureen ever holding me. At six months old, she left me with a nurse so she could go off on a monthlong weight-loss program in Switzerland. As a child, any time I cried, she'd roll her eyes and say, It gets worse, Merry, trust me.

It was Frank's mother, Carol, who showed me what it meant to be loved. To be mothered. How I adored her. The smell of her kitchen, the sturdiness of her body, its ability to hold you firm and rock away any number of sorrows. My mother would deposit me at Frank's house as though it were a day-care center, waving to Carol from the car because she didn't want to endure stepping inside their shabby Brentwood living room. They'd met through the husbands. My father, surgeon in chief at Cedars, and Frank's father, Ian, a gynecologist.

I'd barely be out of the car with my little overnight bag and my mother would be reversing away, hurrying off to lunch with the girls or some act of maintenance. Hairdresser or nail salon or day spa; sometimes it was for a stretch of a few days while she recuperated from a procedure or detoxed at one of her retreats. You're just the best, Carol, my mother would sing, but any time they bumped into one another at a social event, she'd pretend not to know her.

I longed for her never to return, so that I could stay always with Carol, wrapped in her arms, comforted by the sound of her soft southern drawl, safe and warm in the only place that ever felt like a home. My mother always came back for me, and always we regarded each other with that first brief look of disappointment: You again.

In his crib, the baby had turned his attention to Bear. The two of them appeared to be deep in conversation.

I watched. I imagined Frank, seeing my son for the first time, the soft curls starting to collect behind his ears, the gummy smile punctuated with sharp points of new teeth; those sparkling eyes, the fat belly he loves to have tickled. Those pudgy hands that grab and pull at everything in sight. The smell of him newly bathed or sound asleep, the milky sighs and wet open kisses, the tiny arms that reach around your neck to hold you in warm, exquisite embrace.

My child. My son.

I lifted him up into my arms and showered him with all the love I had.

Sam

Oh, Samson, you can't honestly tell me that you're happy over there.

My mother on the phone, calling from the States.

Samson, I know you.

I've told you, Mother, it's wonderful here. I wish you'd come over and see for yourself.

She won't, thankfully.

It's a long flight, she said.

You've never even met your grandson.

Even this is not enough to persuade her. She cannot get over the fact that I left. She wants to punish me for it. Or maybe this is the extent to which she loathes Merry. She doesn't even want to meet our son.

She sighed. That goddamn Ida, she said.

She left me a house, I said. She was a nice woman.

Please, she hissed. It's thanks to her I'm alone and you're a million miles away.

You're being mean-spirited, I said.

Ida was a manipulative bitch, I always said so. Only married my father so she could stay in the country. And then she does this, leaves my son a house so he'll move to the other side of the world.

Anyway, she said, they're all the same.

Who? I said.

Women.

The line was quiet.

Samson, she said slowly. I played bridge with Myra last week.

I sucked in my breath.

You remember her daughter. Josie Rushton, from Columbia.

She paused.

It's just gossip, I said, knowing what was coming.

But she said you were—

Gossip, I said.

That's not why you left, she said. That's not what you're doing there, son, is it? Running away from your problems. I know it wouldn't be the first one. I know you like your—

I'm going now, Mother, I said, and put down the phone.

I went outside. The calls with my mother usually end like this. Me in a rage. I opened the door to the barn at the edge of the garden. Ida's boxes still piled up inside. A lawnmower, a canoe that needs to be stripped and painted. The list of things to do is endless. At least the house is livable now, the garden in check.

God, if I think of the day we arrived and saw what a state it was all in. A boarded-up house half falling apart, a garden overgrown, a tangle of thorns and rotting trees and sharp edges waiting to cut you to pieces. Merry pregnant, me circling the property in a daze as though waiting for it all to come into focus. It's a wonder we didn't run away.

The house was virtually uninhabitable—the few remaining pieces of Ida's furniture covered in sheets brown with dust, the windows cracked, the roof tiles falling down. We covered our mouths with scarves and pulled off the sheets one by one, shoved open the windows and the doors and tried to let the fresh Swedish air do its work. I quickly realized how little I'd thought about logistics like beds and towels and kettles. Water, power, blankets for the cold. We had nothing and nowhere to sleep. No food, nowhere to curl up after more than twenty-four hours of airports and flights.

What are we doing here, Sam? Merry said, her eyes shining with tears and fright. I think it was the first time she ever looked at me that way. Like I didn't have all the answers.

We drove the rental car into town and stopped at three guesthouses before we found somewhere with a vacancy. We left the luggage in the car, found a little café on the main street, and ordered burgers and milk shakes. By two in the afternoon we were back in the room, fast asleep and not to wake until the next evening, even though the jetlag ought to have kept us up through the night.

On the third day, we got up early and drove to the big supermarket on the outskirts of town. We loaded up the car with cleaning products and groceries and candles and a couple of cheap beach towels. We had the water and power set up later that day, and then we went to work with the mops and the window cleaner and the polish, every corner and crevice of the house we scrubbed and shined, every inch of dust we caught and dispensed with, every sign of neglect we reversed and restored. We fitted new light bulbs and tested the old fridge and stove; we ran the taps to clear out the pipes and washed the huge glass windows with soap and water. Together we wrote endless lists of the things we needed to buy for each room, the repairs that needed to be made; every time you looked there was something else.

We bought a car from a dealership in Uppsala and drove to the nearest Ikea, made frequent trips to the hardware store and the garden center. I built the baby's crib and painted the walls of his room. I moved in one of Ida's old armchairs, we bought a woven blanket and cushions to make it comfortable. In Stockholm we shopped for strollers and car seats, bath chairs and diaper bags and thermometers and educational rattles. The prices in krona made your eyes water but we loaded up the cart and handed over the card to swipe.

I bought a wheelbarrow and a toolbox, a power drill and a ladder to fix the roof. The sweat dripped off me; I tied a bandanna around my forehead and removed my shirt. I was pure alpha, man on a mission. It was exhilarating.

Outside, I pulled weeds and hacked down waist-high bushes. I measured frames and bricked in vegetable patches and rebuilt fallen walls.

Fixing, making, shaping. Building our new lives one drop of sweat at a time.

You can't honestly tell me you're happy over there.

My mother refuses to believe any American can be happy anywhere but America. She sends over care packages from the States, all the things she thinks we're missing. Boxed macaroni and cheese dinners, triple-chocolate-chip cookies, hot sauce.

In the last package, she included an American flag, just in case we needed reminding.

You were all I had, son, and now you're gone. With that woman.

The women, the women. Always it's the women.

If I think about the part that's really addictive, the part that's the sweetest, it's the way they look when you've hurt them. The way they crack and break. Even the strongest woman is just a little girl in disguise, desperate for you to notice something about her. So hungry for it, she'll do anything you ask. Low things.

You're a cruel man, Sam.

I have heard this more than once. It always feels good, though I can't say why.

In Ida's shed, I looked for the box marked *Train Set* and removed the bottle I keep stashed away inside. I took a long sip, then another. I examined the wooden trains; they must have belonged to Ida's brother. There was a story about him I can't quite recall. Drowned in the lake or stung by a bee. His trains carefully carved and painted, each carriage a different shape and shade. A labor of love.

Probably his father's. This is what fathers do. I tested out the train on a little stretch of wooden track. Chug-a-chug-a-choo. Conor will love it. I took another sip. It dawned on me suddenly that Ida's dead brother is the only reason I've been left the house. One man's misery is another man's fortune, and all.

* * *

I'll need to call my mother back. Make up a vague apology. Get her to wire over more money. Weave in some guilt about her not bothering to know her grandson. That'll do it.

Our cash is running out, not that Merry knows. Not her department, I always say. Funny, I always thought she'd inherit a decent amount from her mother. But turns out old Gerald wasn't as astute an investor as he was a surgeon. Bad decisions, big losses. After he died, Maureen lived outside her means; in the end there was nothing left but a load of back taxes and a series of unpaid aesthetician bills.

I took out my phone. *Tomorrow?* I wrote.

Yes, came Malin's reply.

She asked me once, Do you love your wife?

Yes, I said, of course.

She nodded sadly but said nothing more.

I downed a final drink in the barn and went inside.

Merry

An email arrived this morning from Frank. Her flight details confirmed. See you soon, she wrote. I felt a wave of unexpected dread, a sort of preemptive exhaustion. Frank in need, always hungry for approval. Always watching to see if there are any slips. Continuity errors. She loves to catch me out.

No, I must focus on the good. Her face when she sees the house. When she holds the baby. When she's confronted with all the parts of her that are lacking.

Just like that, she will be sure of nothing.

And I will have it all.

I wrote down the details and deleted her email. I clicked on the website I visit most days. I came upon it by accident. An anonymous forum. Mothers, all of us, but not the ones who share recipes for birthday cake and ideas for Halloween craft projects.

I don't write anything but I read it all.

Val in Connecticut who drops buttons on the carpet in the hopes her baby daughter might choke on one, dropping a single button each day so that it will be down to fate in the end. Anonymous in Leeds who calls and then hangs up on social services every morning, trying to work up the courage to hand over the twins she cannot bear.

Pretend women, playing at being mothers.

Sam emerged from the studio and I quickly exited the page. He came up behind me and pressed his hands into my shoulders, kissing the top of my head.

Who's Christopher? he said, as an email popped onto the screen.

Just an old client, I said. He probably doesn't know I've left the States.

Better tell him, Sam said, and walked off.

I read the email and then deleted it. I had an overwhelming need suddenly to get out of the house. I pulled on running gear and went to find Sam. I'm going for a hike, I announced.

He was taken aback, but thrilled. Fantastic, he said. Should I watch Con?

Oh no, I said, I really want to have some mommy-son time.

Strange, how the words come so easily, how the untruths roll off the tongue while the rest stays locked away.

You're such a great mom, Sam said.

I nodded. I'm doing my best.

And I am, I am! I must be, because why else would it all feel this torturous—as though I were day and night on stage, under the harsh lights, face melting, body corseted into an ill-fitting borrowed costume. The same show, again and again, enter stage left, deliver the lines you have rehearsed. And into the crowd, looking out at a sea of faces, searching, hoping—desperately needing to hear the sounds of applause. Or even just a single clap. *I see you. You exist.*

★ ★ ★

I settled the baby in his stroller and pulled the door shut behind me. We walked down the path in the direction of the lake, then veered left onto the dirt road that leads to the forest trails. It was a fair climb up the first hill, to the flattish clearing of forest with views of the south side of the lake.

In the last months of my pregnancy, I would wake some nights and find myself here, having wandered through the house in the half darkness, out the door and through the garden and down to the gate, a trance that took me inexplicably all the way to the start of the hiking trails, and out to this clearing. I'd cut my feet on gravel and stones and the pain would make me wince and cramp and cry out. I was weighted down with the life inside, an awkward shape, clunky and dense in the darkened forest, knocking into trees and branches as I lumbered along. There were noises and movements in the night but none of them scared me as much as what was inside. Sometimes in the mornings, Sam would find a thin trail of blood leading from the front door to my side of the bed; nocturnal Odette turned back into the cursed swan. How did I get here, how did I get here? I could not understand it.

It was good to be outside in the cool and the quiet, just the trees and the soft calls of insects at work. I looked around. There was not another soul about. A cabin nearby was boarded up, the windows shut, wooden beams nailed across them. A gingerbread house, I thought, and perhaps inside, a cannibal witch.

I looked into the stroller. The baby had fallen asleep. In the soft dappled sunlight, he looked almost painterly, the golden-haloed child of devotional art. I touched a finger to his nose. He stirred but did not wake. I considered the stroller. I remembered the salesman in Stockholm describing state-of-the-art suspension, a fixed front wheel, pneumatic tires. *Mountain Jogger,* it says on the handlebar. Built for this terrain.

I breathed in the morning air, fresh and warm; held out my arms as though awaiting some divine benediction. Then I began to run. Harder, faster, farther and farther into the trees. Around me, the pines loomed tall and ancient and indifferent; the ground underfoot crunched with fallen leaves and weeds and thick-growing lichen, everything alive and wild, a world unto its own.

I did not look back. I ran and ran, as though running for my life. I ran and ran, until everything ached and stung—heart and lungs and head. I wondered briefly if the baby would be all right, out here in the woods, exposed to all the elements. But surely it could only do us good. Hearty exertion, fresh forest air. I pushed on. The sweat poured off me in sheets. I pushed, I pushed; I ran. I thought: *I may never stop.* I imagined how easy it would be to keep going, to keep running, pushing farther and farther north, to Uppsala, then Gävle, then Sundsvall. And farther still. All the way to the far north, to Kiruna and across into Finland, to Kilpisjärvi. From there you keep going, Alta, then Nordkapp; I've looked on the map, nothing but space and sky, the water and the ice. Svalbard. Greenland. Land so barren you would surely feel like the first person to set foot on earth. Or the last.

All those voyages north, the polar expeditions into nothingness and white. Searching for the unknown, for places to name and land to call one's own. Or maybe it was just blankness they were after, a world made new.

I ran and ran, stumbling occasionally over uneven ground and unfamiliar terrain; rocks and roots and the stumps of felled trees. I ran until I could no longer breathe, until my legs could no longer move me forward or support my weight. I collapsed to the ground. I gasped air into my shocked lungs; I gulped at it like it was water. More, more, pounding heart, ready to burst right out of its fragile cage of bone. I held my hand over it. It would not quieten. It was the feeling of death. Or maybe of being alive.

I lay in the soil, leaves at my back, millions upon millions of subterranean creatures busy belowground with secret endeavors. A discarded husk of snail shell I held and then crushed, the sharp points digging into my fingers. My breath was steadying slowly.

And still, my heart raced. The feeling of being free. Here where I am no one and everyone, a mass of cells and atoms like everything else that lives and breathes and is of this earth. It all came flooding in, the noise of the silence and the stillness and the smell of life uninterrupted. I tried to inhale it, to steal some for myself.

I don't know how long I lay on the ground.

Before the baby and I made our way back home, I paused to take a photograph on my phone. Something about the light and the colors compelled me. Perhaps I would send it to Frank. A taste of what's in store.

Wasn't that fun, I said to the baby, who had woken. Wasn't that a fun adventure for us.

He gifted me with a smile, and I was reassured. His cheeks were a little flush, his hair matted to his skull from all the movement. I made a note to double-check the safety of the forest, to rule out any encounters with wild animals. But I shouldn't think there's anything sinister in these parts.

Did you have a nice bonding session? Sam asked as we walked through the door.

I smiled. I felt genuinely happy. It was just what we needed, I said.

Merry

We had a visitor today. Sam was in Oslo; he took a flight late last night. Before he left, he paused a moment at the door, his new blazer buttoned up, his new sneakers blinding white on his feet. I suppose he is trying to fit in.

I'm sorry, he said. I know it's a lot of travel. I know you're alone a lot—too much, probably.

It's unlike him, to apologize for something. I was caught off-guard. I didn't know what to say.

It's all right, I replied eventually. It's just until you've established yourself, isn't it. You're doing it all for us.

He looked like he might say more, but instead he kissed my cheek, chaste and strange.

I slept soundly, all alone in the big bed. I spread out, I rolled over onto Sam's side, smelled him in the sheets. There was a stain, the dried markings of our reproductive quest. Well, his. I'm not sure how much longer I can hold the wolf from the door, how much more time he'll allow to pass before he sends me off to the doctor to be examined and explored for faults and flaws.

It seemed to happen so quickly before, he said.

It's different every time, I assured him.

★ ★ ★

I dreamed of Frank, a dream or a memory, I don't quite know. The two of us were in my childhood home, that tower of marble and glass. In my bedroom, I had a cabinet with a collection of porcelain dolls inside, beautiful, delicate, fragile things, so inviting for little girls to hold and touch, and yet they stayed always locked away, unmoving behind the glass.

They're not for playing, my mother said. They're special dolls just for looking. If you play with them, they will break.

Trust her to have filled my bedroom with immovable faces. I could never understand the point.

Frank in the dream had the cabinet unlocked, and a doll in her lap—my favorite one—the dark-haired little girl with red painted lips and a blue organza dress. She wore a pearl bracelet and shoes that could be removed from her toeless porcelain feet. Why do you have her, Frank? I shouted. I pulled. The doll was mine. I was crying in the dream; it was too unfair.

Carol came running into the room and took the doll away from us both. There, learn to share or no one plays, she said. Her dress was full of blood. She was trailing her insides all over the white carpet, the womanly parts that killed her in the end.

Carol, Carol. I think I was crying in my sleep.

In the morning, I went into the baby's room. He was lying on his back, eyes open, watching me. Big eyes unblinking. What do they see, I wonder. What secrets will they one day spill?

I dressed in my running clothes and sat him in the stroller.

We go every day now. I salivate for it. I cannot do without my little escape into the woods.

When we returned, I lifted him up. He needed changing, his diaper full and sodden. I lay him on the bed and closed the door behind me; settled onto the sofa to watch my shows. It was supposed to be a laundry and linens day, but I wanted to enjoy the empty house while I still could. I must have spent four hours in front of the screen, following my plastic housewife counterparts in Miami.

At some point, I looked up. Elsa was at the window, waving frantically to get my attention.

I went to the door. I set my face into a smile.

Elsa, what a wonderful surprise, I said.

She looked worried; she was frowning.

Sorry to come over without an invitation, she said. It's just, I wanted to check if everything is all right over here.

It was then that I heard the crying, wailing, actually, deep and pained.

I must have blushed. Oh, I—I am so sorry if he was disturbing you, Elsa.

No, no, she said, looking confused. It is not why I came. It's just . . . a lot of crying. He's been crying a long time.

She looked briefly down at the headphones in my hand.

Sorry, she said quickly, it is of course none of my business.

Oh, Elsa, I said. Thank you so much for coming over. You are very kind. It's just, well, we're trying something. I am trying something new with the baby. Sleep training, I said. To see if it's better. To see if the baby takes to it.

She looked at me and gave a small smile. Yes, she said. Of course.

Would you like to stay for coffee? I said. I can make a fresh pot. I have cookies, too; I baked them just yesterday. Raisin and oatmeal. No added sugar.

The baby was still crying, screeching. Elsa seemed to wince at the sound.

I'll bet Freja didn't cry so much as a baby, I said. She must have been an angel.

She shook her head. I don't know, she said. I am not her mother.

Sorry, I said. I thought.

Freja is Karl's daughter from his first marriage.

I didn't know.

We have been trying for many years to have our own child, she said. Nine times I have miscarried our babies.

Oh, I said. I'm sure it will come eventually.

She shook her head. Karl thinks there is something wrong with me.

The baby was still crying.

You should go to him, she said. I will let myself out.

I nodded. Thank you, I said, as she made her way back across the garden to her own house. From the living room wall, the eyeless masks watched in silent reproach.

In the bedroom, the baby was no longer on the bed where I had left him. He was on the floor.

Oh, baby, I said, lifting him and kissing him and rocking him in my arms. Mommy's sorry. Mommy didn't mean it.

I held him and stroked him and he screeched louder. He was

holding his arm at a strange angle. I touched it and he bellowed and my heart raced with panic. Broken, maybe. I gave him a spoonful of medicine to calm him and kept him gently in my arms.

Mommy's here, I said, Mommy's got you.

My hands were shaking. I wanted to weep. Or vanish, or turn to dust.

At dinnertime, I fed the baby patiently, with many airplanes to amuse him. He did not laugh. Afterward, I held him tenderly on my lap and read him a story.

Who's that hiding in the barn?

Who's that under the blanket?

Who's that in the nest?

He half-heartedly lifted the flaps on each of the pages. He found the horse and the kitten and the bluebird, without much enthusiasm. His eyes were still red from crying. I hugged him to me and kissed his warm head.

I tested his arm, handing him Bear and Biscuit to hold. He winced a little but did not scream. My insides turned over themselves.

When it was time for bed, I let him fall asleep in my arms, held gently to my breast. I could feel his heart beat; I could hear the soft breath coming from his lips, in and out, in and out.

I wanted to hold him in my arms for eternity.

Sam

I was opposite Malin, watching her careful movements, spying those heavy breasts and long, smooth legs. She is older than Merry, but stunning. In her youth, she must have been a tremendous beauty. The girl every man longed to fuck. She still has this quality.

I cannot take my eyes off her.

She was asking about Columbia. Life as an anthropology professor.

You must miss it, she said.

No.

But you spent so long working your way up, all that research, those papers and conferences—the years and years of study.

I folded my arms.

No.

You don't mind that it's gone.

Look, I said, irritated now. It happened. It was bad luck on my part—that some little bitch decided she wanted to ruin me. The rest of the faculty, they couldn't wait to send me down for something—anything. I was too good, too much of a threat to their own pathetic careers.

You know how cutthroat academia is, I said.

But she was your student. It was inappropriate.

Christ, Malin, I said, everyone does it. I just got caught out. They used me as an example. That's all. They made me the fall guy.

She sipped her water. She shook out her hair with her long, slim fingers. The smell of her sat in the air of her apartment, everything touched by those hands, everything brushed by that skin.

There was a photograph of her with a gray-haired man, the two of them set against a flaming pink sky. This your husband? I asked once.

She did not reply.

She looked at me and bowed her head. Forgive me, Sam, she said. I don't mean to pry.

I leaned forward. Then let's change the subject, I said, giving her a wink.

She smiled. Whatever you say.

On my way home, my mother called me.

I've transferred the money, son.

Good, I replied.

You could thank me, she said.

No, Mother, I said. I have nothing to thank you for in this lifetime.

Merry

There are only a few days left before Frank arrives.

In the spare room, I set a vase of lilacs on top of the chest of drawers and hung a dozen hangers in the wardrobe. I pulled the bed straight and puffed up the pillows.

Still I can't work out if this feeling is anxiety or excitement, delight or dread. I don't know if I feel anything at all.

With so much left to arrange, I borrowed the car and drove into Stockholm for a spending spree. Sam was at home preparing for a pitch meeting.

You'll have to take Con along with you, he said. I have too much work to do.

Before I set off, I stood outside and looked toward the house, imagining how it will be for Frank to see it for the first time. You cannot fail to be impressed. You cannot be underwhelmed. Yes. It is beautiful. A sign of achievement. A great big checkmark. And mine. I smiled. The baby was in my arms. I kissed him and took his little hand in mine, feeling the small bones of his fingers against my palm.

That's right, I said, Mommy loves you.

⋆ ⋆ ⋆

In Stockholm, we went winding around the almost-familiar streets, popping into stores to check things off my list. A new brass reading lamp from a Finnish design store, an industrial bench as a side table. New Egyptian cotton sheets in a soft shade of fern, a bright handwoven traditional Norwegian throw for some color. In my head I could see how it would all work together. The ultimate guest room for the ultimate guest. I should be good at this, I suppose, even though my set-building days in New York seem so far away.

Looking back, it surely embarrassed Sam, that job. Well, he got his way, didn't he. In those first whirlwind months he told me he could see me as the mother of his children. I'd laughed. But he knew what he wanted. And how to get it.

Before set design, I tried many things. Failed at most. It was sheer chance, really, that I dated a man who worked on sets, who one day needed an extra pair of hands. You've got a great eye, the director said. He hired me for his next project and from there it grew. Making imaginary worlds, constructing them piece by piece. It was a thrill every time. Creating something out of nothing. The way I could close my eyes and imagine a new world, then open them and make it so. It was hardly empire-building, but to me there was power in it all the same.

In New York, I attended meetings with producers and creative directors. I wore heels and drank espressos around boardroom tables at midnight; I planned shoot schedules and wardrobes and sometimes flew across the country just to pick up the right lamp. There was always a character synopsis to work from: *John is a hardworking banker who likes good wine and good food. He works long hours but he surfs on the weekend and plays drums in a punk rock band.*

The client and I would discuss John like he was a real person who might have an opinion on the choices I was making. Would John really have a Chemex? Wouldn't he use a Nespresso machine instead? Might he have both? You could debate about fictitious John for hours, trying to get to the heart of his emotional complexity.

I was a natural. But then, I have always been good at inventing things. I met many people, received invitations to countless parties. For a while, I pulled off being that woman—the one who appears to have it all. On the surface, at least.

In Östermalm, I popped into a few designer boutiques. I bought two new dresses, a summer jacket, a pair of gold sandals. The baby watched me shop in silence while the sales assistant offered me different sizes and colors. I looked at myself in the mirror. Just the thing for Frank, I thought. Just stylish enough to rub it in, to remind her of her place.

Frank's style, no matter how far she rises in the world—Ivy League college, business school, holidays aboard a yacht—she's never managed to lose it. The sheen of a parvenu. Peasant stock, my mother would have said. She said it often enough about Carol.

In the Östermalm food hall, with its smells of cinnamon and citrus, I stopped for *kannelbulle* and a latte. I bought the baby a bun to suck between his gums. Sugar, I whispered, imagine what Daddy would say! He is using his left hand, the right arm he's keeping cradled to his side. I stroked it gently. There, there.

I ought to take him to the doctor, just in case. I considered it on the drive over. He also needs a series of shots. His six-month checkup, his nine-month checkup. I am supposed to have crossed these things off my long list of mothering duties. I told Sam that I did. It will catch up with me someday, I suppose. All of it.

Back home, after I had put the baby down for a nap, I found Sam in the living room. I sat myself on his lap.

Well, look at this handsome husband of mine, I said, straddling him, purring, pulling him close.

I kissed him on the lips; I pushed my tongue gently into his mouth, then not so gently. With my hand, I rubbed him through his shorts.

What's this, he said, taken aback at the sudden onslaught of affection.

Who are you and where is my wife? he joked.

Oh, I don't know, I said. I pulled his zip down, gripped my fingers around him, stroked and fondled. Why don't we just find out.

He kissed me, let his hands fall onto my breasts and down.

Guess what? I said. It's a red day today.

He moaned.

Afterward, I lay with my legs up, like you're supposed to do. The sperm trickles down; gravity helps everyone on their way. Sam touched a hand to my belly. Tender. No. Proprietary. He leaned over to kiss me where our baby would grow.

I read once about male cats, how their penises are barbed in order to scrape out any rival male's semen from the womb. It is excruciating for the female, an exercise in torture. But nature is not always designed for kindness.

Shhh, I say to the baby in the mornings when I slip the little birth control pill hurriedly into my mouth. Don't tell Daddy.

The baby watches me wide-eyed, thrilled to be part of another conspiracy.

I have a good feeling about this month, I purred. Sam held me and I did not pull away. I want him on my side. To leave Frank quite clear about the state of my marriage. My happiness.

All the things that are mine, mine, mine.

Later, the three of us took a long evening stroll, all the way through the woods to Sigtuna. On the way back, we walked through the housing estates and the stretch of fields that separate them from the reserve. On the side of the path, a pair of muddied pink panties lay winking in the afternoon sun. Neither Sam nor I commented. It reminded us too much of other events, I suppose. Things we're not meant to remember, or let on that we know.

Never again, Merry, he'd promised, more than once. He always seems more devastated by his infidelities than I am.

Funny, my father used to say just the opposite. I'll keep doing it, Maureen. I'll keep doing it until you let me go.

He'd bring divorce papers home every few months, which my mother would painstakingly tear into tiny squares of confetti. When he came through the door, she'd throw it over him, like a brideless groom on his wedding day. Once, she gave me a handful to throw too.

I can ruin you, she warned him. Whatever I don't know I can invent. And I'm very convincing, Gerald.

She had her ways, my mother.

You excited? Sam asked. For the visitor.

Oh yes, I said, pinching a small white flower off its stem with my nails.

You know what, he said, I am, too.

I felt something catch in my throat. I turned to look at him.

Yeah, Sam said. I've always liked Frank.

Frank

More than a year since I've seen Merry, and the moment I laid eyes on her it felt like yesterday. Oh, it's the same feeling as always. A rush of adrenal glands in action, excitement and anticipation. Wondering: How will it be this time? Who will she be now?

Mer-Bear, I said. She opened her arms and we hugged a long time, breathing in each other's scent. I felt her bones under my hands, the frailness of her. She looks exactly the same, always so strange and aloof, an ethereal being of shadows and sand. It makes her irresistible. An elusive beauty.

And now she is also bursting with health and happiness. Must be the fresh country air, all this wholesome living she's been telling me about. Oh, and the pictures she sends—every moment of her life framed and caught and captioned. Look! Look at all this good fortune!

Frank! It's so good to see you, she said.

Is it? I asked. I was wondering if maybe it was inconvenient for you.

She waved her hand. Oh, not in the slightest. The timing couldn't be better. Sweden is just glorious this time of year.

Late summer. Everything sunny and in bloom. You'll adore it. You'll see. We're just thrilled you're here.

We each took a bag and wheeled the luggage out toward the parking lot.

You're not exactly traveling light, she said.

I made a face: Well, you know me. Besides, I'm planning on a fairly long trip.

I watched her flinch.

Don't worry; I won't overstay my welcome. I just plan on making the most of my sabbatical.

You stay as long as you like, she said. We're delighted to have you.

I watched her movements, light, confident; floating through the scene. The day was beautiful, blue summer skies, the sun low but warm. I didn't feel jet-lagged. Only that familiar delight at being with Merry again.

At the car she turned to examine me. You look great, she said.

A lie.

Well *you* do, I said. But you always do.

We pulled out of the airport parking and she took the next exit. Everywhere was green, pastoral almost.

Are there really duck ponds on the highway? I said.

This place is something, she said.

So you're happy here, I said. You're good.

Oh, Frank. Life here is amazing.

She was radiant. I swallowed. I opened the window to let in some air.

Merry of the countryside, I said. Who would have ever thought?

Merry turned left and drove slowly along a dirt road, dense forest on either side.

This is the nature reserve, she said. Or, as we like to call it, home.

She pulled up onto a gravel drive and parked in front of a cabin of red wood and glass. I tried to take it all in, the setting, the lushness, the overwhelm of rustic charm.

Sam must have heard the car pull up outside. He came out of the house, the baby a little Buddha smiling in his arms.

The baby! I shrieked. Oh, let me see the baby.

Sam kissed my cheek hello. He tried to hand the baby over, but the child burrowed into Sam's armpit.

He's won over a little slowly, he said.

I settled on a foot and gave the baby's toes a tickle and Sam a playful punch on the arm.

You dark horse, you, I said. Look at all this. Look at what you have here.

Sam shrugged. Our humble abode, he said, and smiled as Merry sidled up to him.

Between us, we unloaded the bags and took them inside. The house was sparkling, spotlessly clean, immaculately arranged, as though cut from some Scandinavian lifestyle magazine. Flowers in a vase, the smell of something freshly baked in the oven. Was this really her?

It's a good thing you waited a year to visit, Sam said. We did a ton of work on the place.

Oh, Sam was incredible, Merry said. She touched his arm. *Mine.* He did everything. He transformed the house.

And you, too, it seems, I wanted to add. I bit my tongue.

They led me to the spare room, a sun-filled space beside the baby's room.

Merry went all out for your arrival, Sam said. Royal treatment. New sheets, new throws.

Oh, but you shouldn't have, I said. I didn't want to cause you any trouble.

The baby in Sam's arms clapped his hands.

It's wonderful, I said. A beautiful home.

I looked at the jolly trio. For a beautiful family, I added.

Merry in the kitchen was counting out knives and forks, carrying dishes outside to the table. I stole another look around the house. Everything is new—new furniture, new crockery, not a thing from their New York apartment aside from Sam's African masks. As though every part of their old lives has been discarded in a heap.

Well, typical Merry, I suppose.

What can I do to help? I said.

Not a thing, Merry sang out in that voice of hers. Just make yourself right at home,

I went outside to the garden and sat on the lawn, next to where they'd laid the baby on a blanket. I shielded my eyes from the sun and studied his face. Merry, but not Sam. Fat cheeks, alert, darting eyes the color of soft caramel. Perfect little creature. I gave him my finger and he tried to shove it in his mouth. I could feel sharp teeth gnawing against my skin.

★ ★ ★

Merry emerged with salads and a roast chicken, a loaf of bread. Sam carried out an ice bucket. The weather was glorious. We sat, passing the dishes around the table, swatting away the bees. The food was good. Everything delicious, well seasoned, beautifully presented. She has really outdone herself this time.

Sam poured from a bottle of chilled prosecco and raised his glass for a toast.

Welcome, he said.

To life in Sweden!

To new beginnings!

We all smiled and tilted back our heads and let the bubbles fill our throats. With the sun and the long flight, I was soon light-headed.

Has it really been a year?

More than that, I said.

And so much has happened.

Yes. I crossed my legs and leaned over into the dull ache.

Flight okay? Sam asked.

Long, I said.

But first class, no doubt. Merry smirked. Frank hasn't flown coach in years.

I held up my hands. The only way, right?

This is what we do, she and I. Pretend that I have somehow arrived. That everything I have managed to do and achieve is enough to impress her. That she has given me her blessing instead of withholding it all these many years.

★ ★ ★

The baby was gnawing on a chunk of cucumber.

Adorable, I said. He is the real prize, and we both know it.

Merry smiled. We couldn't be happier.

I can tell, I said, I can totally tell.

I watched her. I tried to read her smile, to see behind it.

She got up from the table and cleared away a stack of plates, returning outside with the dessert. It was an apple cake, delicate slices fanned out onto a pie crust, sticky with cinnamon and dusted with powdered sugar that had turned syrupy in the heat.

The bees landed on the cake; one found itself caught.

You made this, too? I said.

Let me tell you, Sam said, as Merry sliced through the pastry and the bee fought to escape. This woman is a domestic goddess. Housewife of the century.

Who would have known, I said.

Sam speared a piece of cake into his mouth. It's like she's found her true calling. Like she's the woman she was always meant to be.

He winked at his wife. Well, I knew she had it in her from the start.

I looked over at Merry. There was nothing I could read in her gaze.

Sam cut himself a second slice of cake while Merry walked me around the garden, showing off the thick patches of vegetables and herbs, carrots and coriander, bushels of thyme and basil. She lifted the leaves of the berry bushes so that I could see the plump fruits hanging in their flaming shades of red and blue. It seemed a marvel, to grow things and then eat them, to labor at something for so long only to devour it in a few bites.

Let her taste those strawberries, Sam called. Let her try them right off the bush.

Merry pinched off a handful of berries and held them out. I ate the fruit and licked the red juice that trickled down my fingers.

Wild, I said. I can't get over it. Your life. It's so.

She waited but I didn't finish.

Sam took the baby inside to put him down for a nap. The two of us sat back down at the table. Merry poured coffee. Again, her movements were careful, deliberate and slow. Like she'd studied it all, watched and learned.

Merry a wife and mother, I mused. I wouldn't have dreamed it.

She stiffened. You act so surprised that I'm happy here, she said. It's all about timing, isn't it? Certain point in your life, you're just ready.

I finished the last sip of coffee and licked the grounds around my mouth, rough and slightly bitter. My head was weighted with tiredness and wine, with the pills from earlier.

I'm happy for you, I said. That this life agrees with you.

Well, I'm happy to have you share it, she replied, her voice thick with smugness.

What's this? I said, glancing over at a framed photograph on the living room shelf. It was my mother.

Oh, Merry said, I've had that one for years.

I smiled. We really are sisters, aren't we, Mer?

It always fills me with a particular joy. All of what we share. All of what connects us, the roots of our friendship that run so deep.

Yes, Merry murmured. I suppose we are.

Sam

All weekend we showed Frank around, paraded her about the place, showed off the best of life in the Nordics. Took a nice long walk into Sigtuna through the forest, a trip to the lake for a quick dip in the cool water. Drove to Stockholm to stroll around the old town, escaped the tourist traps and found a place for a traditional *fika* at a café in Söder, where we sat with coffee and cardamom buns.

Look at you two, Frank said. Such locals. You've really settled in.

Merry held my hand in hers.

Frank wanted to see the Vasa Museum, the doomed seventeenth-century warship that sank before it ever left the harbor. We spent an hour walking around the wooden model, Conor in his stroller niggling to get out.

Later, we visited the *Moderna Museet,* an all-women exhibition with the usual feminist crap; bleeding vaginas and menstrual blood sewn into a canvas. There was one piece called *The Falling Women,* a larger-than-life video projection that showed a woman on a podium, standing proudly in first place. From offscreen, another woman shoved her off, and she fell down into a darkened abyss. Another woman took her place; another half-woman pushed her down. So it continued, a constant loop, a never-ending supply of angry women.

Like it? Frank asked me.

I rolled my eyes.

At a small café overlooking Lake Mälaren, we ate an early dinner.

So what's the plan, Frank asked. Will you get a job here, now that you're settled?

Merry gave her a dark look. I told you before, she said. Being a mother is my job now.

You don't need to work, that's great, Frank said.

I've got a few big projects coming up, I said. We're doing just fine.

The waiter came over to take the order. Frank and Merry asked for the same thing, down to the no onions, medium steak, dressing on the side.

I laughed. Christ, I said. You two are so similar. It's like watching twins. How you talk, the words you use. Even your gestures. I never noticed it so much before.

Merry smiled. I suppose that's what happens when you go way back.

It's like you're mimicking each other, I said. Monkey see, monkey do.

Frank looked at Merry. It's a form of empathy, she said. In evolutionary terms. Mimicry is how primates form emotional connections. Babies, too. It's how they learn emotions. You must be seeing it with Conor. How he mirrors what he sees in you.

Merry tore off a piece of bread and set it on her side plate.

And it's not always benign, Frank said. Look at cuckoos. The females mimic the sound of hawks to scare smaller birds away from their nests. Then they lay their own egg inside, an exact copy of the other eggs, so it will blend in. The other bird comes back to the nest, cares for the impostor egg, does all the real work.

What about when the eggs hatch? I asked.

Well, Frank said, the cuckoo hatches and destroys the other chicks. It makes sure to monopolize all the resources. It's simple Darwinism, a way to thrive.

Jesus, Merry said.

Brood parasitism, Frank said. That's what it's called.

Pretty heartless, Merry said.

Or maybe ingenious. Frank winked.

We both laughed.

Great having intelligent conversation again, I said. Feel a bit starved of it, being off campus and all.

Frank smiled. Glad that master's is coming in handy for something, then.

Merry was silent. She's sensitive around the topic, of course, since she never finished anything she started at college. But like I say to her—you don't need a degree to roast a chicken.

Feels good having Frank around. I like it. A breath of fresh air. Bit of titillation. She's great with Conor, too, a real natural. Right on the first day, she scooped him up and hoisted him on her hip like she's reared a dozen babies. She feeds him his lunch and crouches on the floor to play with him. His face lights up when she walks into the room; she knows how to make him laugh.

Didn't take you long to win him over, I told her.

She laughed. Maybe this should be my new demographic for the opposite sex.

Come on, Frank, I said. Who are you trying to kid?

She knows exactly what she's got. The way men are when they're in her orbit.

She burrowed her nose into Con's neck. If only they were all as charming as you Hurley men, she said.

The waiter brought over the food. Merry's steak was undercooked, but she wouldn't send it back.

I like bloody sometimes, she said.

What are your plans for this sabbatical? she asked Frank.

Frank shrugged. I want to travel. To see friends. Figure out what comes next.

How will the consulting world live without you? Merry asked, somewhat sarcastically, I thought.

Frank smiled. Well, maybe it's good to have a break from solving other people's problems.

I looked at the two women across the table, fair and dark, soft and sharp. Met them both the same night, more than seven years ago. I was twenty-eight. It was a Friday night in the King Cole Bar at the St. Regis. There'd been a faculty dinner, a celebration of the awarding of the Huxley Memorial Medal, the anthropological equivalent of the Nobel Prize. The department was in a frenzy of excitement.

I saw them standing by the bar. Drinking martinis. One

beautiful, hair blond and long and loose around her high cheekbones, eyes fierce blue and lips rounded into a soft red pout. High breasts, full and fleshy, a tight body poured into a black dress; the type you already know will be flawless when naked. The other, Merry, plainer, slightly asymmetrical in the face, not ugly but not entirely pretty, either. Body just a little too angular, awkward in its composition like the face.

Something about her, though, a vagueness or openness, a space to be filled. There was a purity to her, like she'd not yet been written in full. It makes you look twice, and then you find yourself unable to look away.

She's the one, I remember thinking. She's just the one.

I watched Frank now. All I had missed.

If you love Merry so much, why do you cheat on her? Malin often asks. She isn't angry. Just curious. She wants to understand, to make sense of it.

I don't know the answer. It's hard to explain.

Maybe the other women let me love Merry better. Because they are disposable and she is permanent. Because she is and always will be mine.

Frank

Well, Merry's life is perfect. I'm not sure why I expected anything less, though somehow I was sure I'd arrive and find it all in pieces. Or at least a very poor facade. I'd heard about Sam's dismissal from Columbia—not that Merry's letting on that she knows—and imagined somehow that between this and their strange exile to the middle of nowhere, she'd be miserable. Quite the opposite. She seems to be in her element. Wife and mother. Ha! My little shape-shifter friend. How she does it with such ease, I'll never know. It's something I might even admire in her, the ability to so convincingly—so seamlessly—transform herself. It's never come easily to me.

The handmade loaves of bread, the lovingly tended garden, the little pots of food crafted fresh for the baby. The sachets of lavender in the laundry cupboard, the lavish home-cooked dinners every night.

God, I said, can this really be you, Merry Crawford? City girl transformed.

Merry, Merry Strawberry. One day a hardened feminist, the next, the quintessential earth mother. Had she ever boiled an egg before? Had she ever so much as held a child?

Such a change, I said. I can hardly believe it's you.

It's just like they say, Frank. Motherhood makes you feel like you're fulfilling some greater purpose as a woman. I hope you find out for yourself someday, she said.

She removed a batch of banana muffins from the oven. Sugar-free, gluten-free.

This is all I've ever wanted, Frank.

Sam came up behind her and kissed her cheek. The baby clapped his pale, doughy hands.

The child. The baby. He is wonderful. Sam, too. Handsome and strapping. All hers. A happy family. Island of three. Man, wife, child. Self-sufficient and contained, as though in a snow globe. Shake, and the glitter will dance. Shimmer, shine; is there anything more beautiful than what's inside the glass?

What about you, Frank, Merry asked. Tell me what happened with Thomas.

Of course she knows already. It's always the same story.

Is that Carol's engagement ring? she said, looking at my hand.

Yes, I said. You remember.

She gave a little snicker. But wasn't that supposed to be saved for your engagement, wasn't that the plan? Wasn't that what Carol always said?

She does not lose it. The ability to shrink me down to size.

Still, I am happy she has found her place, her tribe. Merry, content. God knows it has taken long enough, those myriad lost years of searching for the thing, some essence to hold on to for dear life.

I want her to be happy. I have always wanted only this. Merry's happiness is like my happiness. It is enough for us both.

Merry

At the lake in the late-afternoon sun, I stole a look at her body. Frank is like always, toned and tanned, long and graceful limbs, curved and smooth and soft all at once. The body other women wish for. The body she must work at, long and hard. Her breasts are incredibly perky. She has no wrinkles around the eyes.

I wonder if she has started already with the first of the nips and needles, the staving off of age and decay. She would have learned well from my mother. Frank always seemed an eager student.

Yes. She is striking. Intoxicating. Frank the seductress, a woman who looks like she's aching for it, is how Sam described her once. She has never struggled to attract the attention of men. Still, it's never been quite enough to seal the deal. To make them stay. How that must enrage her. How that must remind her of her failure. And it is a failure, as a woman.

That and a barren womb. Poor Elsa, I thought. A cat at home with nine lives to spare; nine babies without one living to draw breath. Life can be cruel.

I smiled, or smirked. The familiar thrill, the pleasure of knowing that Frank will never get what she wants. In middle school, she was the first of the girls to allow a boy to finger her; soon after she was the girl who'd let them go all the way. Behind the stage in the drama room, that's where she lurked and waited. She thought they'd love her, but all they did was laugh and call her names. The other girls and I would snicker. Skanky Frankie, I think I might have started that one myself.

Oh, there are endless tales of Frank's thwarted happiness, not a few related to me.

I took Sam's hand. I lifted the baby into my arms.

Come, the loves of my life, I said. Let's go and take a little dip.

I could feel Frank's eyes on me. The longing. The hate.

Yes, I thought.

This is it.

This is what I have missed. This is just what I need.

The water was bracing to the skin as I waded in, too cold, even in high summer. Underfoot, the smooth algae-slicked pebbles shifted under my weight. I kissed the baby and handed him to Sam. I'm going under, I said.

I was feeling bold. Clear somehow. I looked back, Frank small and alone on the towel. My best friend. My other half. My measure of reality, of years and time and achievement.

I gave a little wave. Filled my lungs and sank myself under, relishing the sting of ice water on skin. I could feel every part of my body, in and out, flesh and organs, teeth and bone.

You don't need her. You don't need her in your life. Sometimes I have said these words to myself.

But they are not true.

I do need her. We do need each other. Sam tells me who I am. And Frank is my proof that what he tells me is real.

Why else would she envy me so?

I came to the surface and opened my eyes. Sam and Conor were on the towel with Frank. And I was alone in the water.

Frank

I opened and shut kitchen cabinets and drawers, looking for what I needed. Everything is alarmingly neat—equally spaced, arranged in tidy rows—not a jar or a tea cup out of place, as though everything has an invisible line around it, keeping it within its parameters. She is a meticulous housewife, my friend.

I set a little spoon for honey down on the tray and took it into Merry's bedroom.

Tea and toast and honey, I said.

Honey toast, she said, smiling. I remember that from your mom.

Yes, I said. Old Carol and her stash of home remedies. I passed Merry the tea. How are you feeling?

She made a face. She's been laid up in bed for days now, struck down with a vicious flu. Of course she can't be around the baby in her state, so I've stepped in. Conor doesn't seem to mind his substitute mother. He's a terrific boy, a bundle of smiles and drooly kisses for his Aunt Frank.

Aunt Frank! I love it. I think it fits. And I do adore him so. Those fat cheeks and dimples, his chubby thighs, always kicking at something. He loves having kisses blown onto his belly, and if I pretend to gobble him up, he's just in absolute hysterics.

You're so great with him, Sam said earlier. I can't get over what a natural you are.

I was feeding him breakfast, choo-choo-ing trainloads of porridge into his open mouth.

Oh, he's just the best child, I said. I'm absolutely in love.

Yes. It is true.

I handed Merry a pile of vitamins. Go on, I said.

Just when I thought we were too old to play doctors and nurses, she said.

I laughed. Oh, I remember those days! But really we just wanted to be housewives, didn't we. Married with two kids each.

I can see us clearly, two girls playing dress-up, taking turns to wear the single pair of high heels that my mother had in her possession—unfashionable silver peep-toes with a little strap across the ankle. We'd sit at the dining room table, drinking soda from coffee mugs and pretending they were cappuccinos.

We always brought notepads along as our daily planners. We'd sit and schedule manicures and PTA meetings and appointments with interior decorators.

Such were the lives we imagined lay ahead.

Merry swallowed and sank back down against the pillow. I'm going back to sleep now, she said. Thanks for looking after me.

I touched a hand to her forehead. She was burning up.

Come on, Sam said when I emerged from the room. No sense in all of us being cooped up today. I'll take you to another one of the lakes.

It was a splendid afternoon. Sam, Conor, and I, lying out on the soft grass in the twinkling sun. Taking long dips in the cool water. I slipped off my dress and watched as Sam's eyes worked their way down, surveying my body. Just his type, I suspect.

I smiled.

He shook his head, seemed to laugh at himself.

He lifted Conor and we waded together into the lake. Other families played and napped in the sun; as they passed us by, they smiled and said hello. We must have looked like a little family ourselves.

I liked that idea. I liked it a whole lot.

My cheeks were warm. There was a sense of lightness in my blood.

What a day, I said.

Well, you have to seize them, Sam said. Blink and the summer's gone. Only drawback.

We'd stopped at a market along the way to pick up some bread and cheese and fruit for our lunch. Sam had brought along baby food for Conor, which I fed him while he sat snug in my lap. At one point he took a hand to my bikini top and pulled on it. It shifted, exposing me. Sam pretended to cover his eyes while I readjusted the fabric to cover myself.

Nothing I haven't seen before, he said.

Oh, stop, I teased.

After lunch, Conor fell asleep, curled up against my side, breath warm and delicious against my skin. I lay myself down next to him and shivered with the pleasure of it. The longing.

Probably not the sabbatical you imagined, Sam said, all this childcare.

Better than I could have imagined, I said.

He laughed. Don't push it.

I'm serious, I protested. This place. I see why you're so happy here.

I rested a hand lightly against Conor's cheek. And this guy.

Sam stood up to go back into the water. I looked at his body. Solid. Strong. His shorts sat low. I could see the thickening of hair, the way it would get thicker still. I'd glimpsed him once before, naked, out of the shower one summer when we'd rented a place together in Maine, Merry and Sam, myself and Simon. I remember how Sam had looked at me then, looking at him, knowing, smiling. The look of a man who likes to play.

The look he's given me all day long. Twinkle in the eye, mischief in the smile.

It wasn't long after that vacation that Simon broke off our engagement. I didn't understand; I was devastated. A few days later, Merry announced that she was going to marry Sam.

But you said you were having doubts about him, I'd sobbed.

She'd laughed, oblivious to my tears and heartbreak. Or fueled by it.

No, she said, not anymore.

I suppose she cannot help the way she is.

Frank

Life and fortune really can change in an instant. I suppose this must have been what my father believed in—what he bet on—sitting for days straight at the casino, refusing to accept that his luck couldn't turn, even when he'd lost it all. The house, the cars, my college fund. Gone in a single night. He didn't even apologize, just shrugged his shoulders and said, That's how it goes.

But the point is, I can see it. How the picture can always change, often in the blink of an eye. How just like that, it can reveal a whole new set of possibilities.

Oh, breathe, Frank, breathe! I'm really quite giddy.

It's been a wonderful few days. Merry in bed, hot and sticky in the sheets, sweating out her fever. Sam and Conor and I, making the most of the glorious Swedish summer. Together. Just us. It is heady pleasure. The best tonic I could have hoped for. I feel better than I have in absolute months.

Sam took me for a walk through the forest and back down to the lake for another chilly swim. We picked vegetables from the garden and he showed me his film reels in the studio.

You're so talented, I said, and watched him beam. Reminds me a little of Herzog, how you work with character. Very compassionate, and yet quite obviously involved. Is that the intention? I asked.

Well, he just about passed out cold.

I cook and help him shop and straighten the pillows on the couch. I think I've embraced more domesticity in the last few days than I have in my entire life. I am lapping it up. I cannot get enough.

I take Merry glasses of water and lemon tea, trays of easily digestible food and vitamins doled out in a glass dish. For the first time in my life, I am my mother. The quintessence of a housewife, making and baking and doing. She'd never believe it was me, just as I never imagined she enjoyed it, all that service. Now I see how there is joy to be found in it all. It can be just the trick.

Get better, I say to Merry, but secretly I wish she would never leave the bed.

Oh, wicked me! I mustn't be cruel. But I am just enjoying this all too much. The beautiful house and garden, the fresh country air. Conor in my arms or at my feet, babbling and smiling and sweet; darling child, dear little boy. Luminous eyes, those strange deep eyes of his that lap up the world. He is so easy to make laugh, and to love. Oh, the love that pours from him—a fountain of joy and delight.

This must be unconditional love, the love for a child. The love a child gives back, so freely, with such unimaginable generosity. Why do we lose this ability, and when? Why do we cut love out and set it to so many conditions?

⋆ ⋆ ⋆

I won't lie. I am enjoying Sam, too. Too much, perhaps. It is treachery, isn't it? That golden rule of friendship: stay away from the man. But, but. I can feel his eyes on me. I watch how he laughs at my jokes, how he enjoys my conversation—starved as he is of intelligent company, as he says—how he smiles at my sweetness in caring for his son. This most of all is what astounds him.

We eat our dinners outside under the still-light sky. This evening I made an Ethiopian dish, a stew atop homemade *injera,* after Sam mentioned in passing a week spent at a conference in Addis Ababa and the sublime food they ate every night.

He was delighted. We broke off the bread with our hands and scooped up the steaming stew. We talked about art and politics and culture—or he talked, and I mostly listened, but either way.

You're a stimulating woman, Frank. He grinned.

Yes, stimulating. I smiled back, a little too tipsy, a little too fresh.

We stayed out past eleven o'clock, after the sky turned slowly dark. The stars blanketed the blackness along with the yellow half-moon, and in the reflection of the windows, I stole a quick glance. My best friend's husband. I cringed just a little. Because you could not miss it. We cut a handsome pair, he and I.

We make a good fit.

Merry

I find myself woken from a fever dream. No, I think I've awoken in the middle of one. My eyes are blurry. I wipe them. I try to clear the picture.

My house. My husband. My baby. But what's wrong with the picture?

The answer is everything.

Scratch that.

The answer is Frank.

Oh, look who's up!

She was draped on the couch, Sam beside her, blanket covering their knees. Two glasses of wine, an empty bottle on the coffee table, another on the kitchen counter. Dead of night. The sleeping hour. The witching hour.

What are you two doing? I asked.

Sam laughed. Frank was regaling me with tales of the corporate life. The wicked world of high-flying consultants. She's navigating million-dollar projects and the CEO is playing Angry Birds on an iPad. Ha! Can you imagine?

She laughed too, waved her hand. Anyway, we were just having a laugh.

They looked at each other, a smile, a wink. A private joke just for two.

Great, I said. I stood there in the doorway, not sure where to place myself in the house.

You feeling better? Sam asked.

I think so, I said.

Well, Frank here has been a terrific stand-in wife, he said with a grin, his hand on her knee, easy and familiar. She's taken care of everything.

Has she, I said. Lucky us.

Frank was smiling at me. Pleasure was all mine, she said. Truly.

I guess I'll go back to bed, I said.

Sam did not join me.

In the morning, I wrapped myself in my robe and went out to the kitchen.

Frank had the baby in his high chair, expertly spooning food into his mouth. He was laughing, generous with his smiles for her. Affectionate and responsive. Mirroring, I suppose. There were several pots atop the stove, busily simmering away.

Oh, look who's here, Frank cooed. The baby looked at me but did not smile.

Want to come uppy? Frank said, and the baby lifted his small fat arms to her. She rubbed her nose against his round belly and he roared with giddy laughter.

Ooh, Aunt Frank could eat you up, she said. Just eat you up.

Aunt Frank. I see they are good friends, Aunt Frank and the baby. She held him loosely on her hip, confident, motherly, entirely at ease. He sat snug in her arms, a cozy pouch made just for him.

Want to go to Mama? she sang into his ear. The baby turned away. Frank shrugged and laughed and kissed his cheek. A reward to him for playing along.

Who's my best guy? Who's my little prince? she cooed.

Where's Sam? I asked. I felt hot and sticky and irritable. My head ached.

Sam is in the studio today, Frank said. It's probably best if you don't disturb him. He's working on a big pitch for this week. Some massive NGO project.

She lifted a lid off one of the pots. The smell of wine and garlic filled the air.

Dinner, she said. *Boeuf bourguignon.*

Sam's favorite, she added, as though I might not know.

I tried to smile. I drank a glass of water and watched her move about the kitchen, my kitchen; saw the way she opened and closed cupboards and found things in the refrigerator. The way she was holding the baby. The way she was giving me instructions about my husband.

Coffee, she offered me.

Please, I said, and she poured. She is using the mugs I had packed away in a bottom cupboard. She has moved the bowls and glasses to different shelves.

Look at you, I said, nodding toward the baby so nonchalantly slung over her hip. Didn't take you long to get into the swing of things.

* * *

To take over, is what I wanted to say. Because this is Frank. This is what she does. She seeps in, like a very dangerous gas leak; she finds a way to lodge herself where she is not wanted. Roots herself so deep she cannot be excised.

Memories came in a flood. Snapshots of thirty years of friendship, or whatever this might be called. A confusion of lives and homes, me in hers, her in mine. Ponytails snipped off with garden shears, dolls stolen, tales told to get the other in trouble.

We brought out the worst in each other. Envy, anger, deceit. It's only later when you learn to hold the impulse to hurt with your fists. You discover words and silences are the real killer. The withdrawal of affection, the sly planting of rumors and half-truths, the deft salting of the wounds you know cut the deepest. This is where the power is. A different kind of violence.

But she's my friend. But I saw him first. Your clothes always look so cheap.

There were no rules. There are still none. I don't know who did what or worse. It was all interchangeable parts. Love and hate. So entwined you can't tell one from the other.

I watched as Frank twirled the baby in the air, whooshed him about like a kite, like a bird.

I love this little bundle, she said, just love him to bits. Her face was flushed, glowing, in fact. Maybe this was it. A mother's love. It looked good on her, anyone could see.

Yes, some women have it, don't they.

Sam emerged from the studio, coffee mug in hand. He gave

the baby's cheek a pinch and put his arm loosely around Frank's waist to give her a squeeze. He loves you right back, he said, and all the lights in her face went on at once.

In place of my heart, two angry fists beat at my chest.

I wanted to get out of the house. I should probably see to the garden, I mumbled.

I took care of that while you were sick, Frank said. I hope I didn't ruin the system. Step on your toes.

In the vegetable patches, I saw where she had plucked up fistfuls of under-ripened vegetables, ripping them out at the root and then leaving them forlornly in the soil to rot. Deliberate. Spiteful. Or was it all just in my head.

I gathered a few carrots and a head of lettuce that the slugs hadn't gotten to yet and brought them inside to rinse.

The baby looked up and stuck out his tongue. Baa, he said. Everything solid turned to water.

Frank

I am in the middle of a puzzle, and too many pieces do not belong.

I'm trying to make sense of it all, this curious reality that is revealing itself to me, piece by piece. The Japanese have a whole art form devoted to cracks. *Kintsugi,* it's called. They gild the broken pieces of porcelain and make the reconstructed whole precious—beauty in the brokenness and all that.

Well, perhaps the cracks I am seeing in Merry's life will reveal some beauty to me too.

She emerged from her week of convalescence in a foul mood. She's always been so ungracious. Not a *Thank you, Frank* for looking after things, for mothering her son, for keeping food in the fridge and dinner on the table.

Never mind; Sam is full of gratitude. Full of praise. I see him watching me in wonder, the way I am with Conor, the way the child is thriving under my care.

Naughty me! I stole Merry's copy of *The Ultimate Guide to Baby's First Year* from her bedside table while she was sick and read it cover to cover in an evening.

Some days later, I suggested to Sam that we do core strength exercises with the baby to help get him crawling.

It's just that now's when he should be reaching that milestone, I said. I noticed he's a little behind.

I didn't mean to be intrusive, but these developmental stages are crucial. Everyone knows this.

Sam looked slightly put out.

Sorry, I apologized. It's probably not my place.

No, he snapped. Merry should be better at this.

Well, now he and I sit cross-legged on the floor with the baby every morning, getting him to lift brightly colored balls out of a plastic bucket. This is supposed to strengthen his upper body, which will encourage him to try to crawl. It's too adorable to watch. Conor loves this game—and others. Hide-and-seek under a blanket; where's Bear? Or roly-poly—we play for hours.

Such a natural, Sam says to me, over and over again, and slowly I understand why.

Because Merry is not. No. She is the furthest thing from it.

She had me convinced for the first few days. But now I see it all. Remember those Where's Waldo? books, how hard it was to spot the first Waldo in those busy illustrations? And then once you did, you'd be able to find him anywhere. The beach, the zoo, the streets of Paris—he'd pop right out at you, the first face in the crowd. It's the same with Merry. Suddenly it is all blatantly obvious. I can see everything.

Merry, Merry, the unmerriest of them all. My poor, desperate friend. Her life is a ruse. She dials it up if Sam and I are around, but when I spy her alone with the child, it's a different story altogether. Nothing maternal, not even a flicker of it.

It's all an act. Or a trap. Merry playing at motherhood like she's played at everything else over the years. Merry the innocent, Merry the party girl. Merry the drama student, Merry the poet, Merry the yoga instructor, Merry who became Amira for a year after she went to Pune to take sannyas. Six different colleges she tried. Six! Two separate gap years, traveling the world with Gerald's credit card in her pocket, trying to find herself. What nonsense! As though there were ever anything to find.

And worse, the countless casualties along the way, the brokenhearted souls who fell for her act hook, line, and sinker, who took her at her word and believed she was who she said she was. I knew many of them, ran into a few in their post-Merry pain, saw the looks of devastation and ruin. How well I know the feeling. This is what happens when you play with people, isn't it? When you lead them on. When you allow them to believe that you are everything they have been looking for.

I shouldn't be angry. It's just how she is. This is her fuel. This is how she feels most alive, I suppose. In truth, it is more worthy of pity than rage.

Sam doesn't see any of it, or doesn't want to. But I know her too well. Inside out. How could I not after so many years?

This has always been a thorn in her side, that I of all people can see her with such clarity. Unmasked, no matter which one she is wearing. No matter how splendid the disguise, she can't hide from me. Anyone else might put her behavior down to some kind of postpartum depression. Of course it's not. This is just Merry. Merry being Merry.

The love inside her stuck. Trapped in a fist in the pit of her belly.

Or maybe that's wishful thinking. Maybe she doesn't have any love to give at all.

Certainly after today, I could believe it. We'd been sitting outside, eating lunch together. Merry took the baby inside to change, and I dashed in a few minutes later to use the bathroom. I passed the baby's room on my way, looked in. He was on the changing table, whining and kicking. He was having a bad day, poor lamb, sore and grumpy from the teething, as they get.

Merry I saw standing over him, watching him silently, stiff like stone. I stood in the doorway, mesmerized by the sight of her, by her coldness, by the sheer absence of warmth or maternal love. How she was looking at Conor with such loathing in her eyes. As though there was only ice in her veins. As though he was some monstrous, terrible aberration, and not her very flesh and blood.

I shuddered inside. But it took an even worse turn. As Conor cried, Merry held out a hand and hovered it over his naked belly. I watched as she clenched and unclenched her fist. He squirmed. Then she took the hand to his thighs.

The fingers tensed. He let out a cry. I held my hand over my mouth to stop myself from crying out too. Why, I don't know. I suppose I didn't yet know what I was seeing—how it could be real, this whole wretched scene unfolding nightmarishly before my eyes. Maybe somehow I thought if she were caught in the act, it would unleash even more violence.

So I did nothing but stand and watch. I watched as the fingers gripped his flesh, tensing, tightening, squeezing. Harder and harder, digging in, full force. My brain could not compute her intention to hurt him, to cause him suffering and pain. Her son! Her child!

My heart was breaking, my thoughts a scramble of why and how—you cannot make it logical or fathomable—you can do nothing but shatter inside. It was the dawning of the very worst truth, the collapse of all I know to be right and decent.

I watched the hand, still there, as his face pulled and twisted with hurt, as his little body writhed beneath the cruel fingers of his mother. Merry did not flinch.

At last I could take no more and walked silently away. In the bathroom, I splashed cold water on my cheeks, flushed the tears from my eyes. I tried to stop the shaking of my hands, but they would not hold. I looked at my face in the mirror. Stricken. It was one of the worst things I have ever witnessed.

By the time I returned outside to the sunny garden table, Merry was sitting with Conor on her lap, smiling and sipping her lemonade, just as carefree as you can imagine.

There you are. She smiled warmly.

Sam held up the wine. You look like you could do with another glass.

He turned to Merry. But none for the wife, he teased. We might have another Hurley on the way.

Merry held up the hand she'd just used to abuse her son.

Fingers crossed, she said.

I went cold.

Sam

The women. The women are in heat. It's pretty amusing, I won't lie. The pair of them vying for my attention like two bristling lionesses. At some point, I think I even laughed out loud.

Maybe it's the isolation that's heightening it all. The feeling that we're the last three grown-ups in the world. Course, there's only ever room for two.

I should be in my element. Merry, pliant like putty, falling all over herself to be wifely and obliging. Think she might actually be pregnant; last time around she had the same look about her in the early weeks. Something wild and uncontained, bordering on feral. Pregnant Merry. There's no better thing. Round and full, bursting with life. It's too soon for the test, she says, but it has to be. We've been at it long enough. Even more so now that Frank's around. Merry's pushing herself at me every chance she gets.

And Frank. Dear old Frank. All peeking nipples and miniskirts, always braless and scantily clad, showing off that body, every inch of it if she can help it. She's caught the sun, bronzed and ripened. She smells of citrus and sandalwood and that familiar scent of a woman longing to be consumed. The way she looks at me, as though I'm the messiah himself; shining eyes, quickened pulse. You feel it in the air, desire, hot and electric like a building storm. I don't discourage her. Old habits die hard.

She leaves her underwear to dry over the bath rail. Every night, I move them aside to climb in. Black and lacy, red and sheer.

Sometimes I pick up a pair to examine them more closely. Thin stains of white against the black lace; the smell is soap and salt. I breathe them in.

In the bed, Merry purrs against me. Sometimes I shift her over to her front, push her head down into the sheets; imagine she's not Merry but the woman in the other room. The voice in my head issues a warning. Everything else is happy to play along.

I should probably know better than to engage in any more of these games. They have their inevitable endings. It's always the same. Already I can imagine Malin's face. Merry's, too, crumpling with betrayal. The wife always feels it as her own shame. *If I were enough, he wouldn't need to go elsewhere.* They're not always wrong.

I know, I know. I shouldn't, especially with Frank. Too close. Like a sister.

I won't. I wouldn't.

I'll just play. No harm, no foul. She's enjoying it too. Of course she is.

At night, after Merry goes to bed, the pair of us sit out under the stars, share a cigarette, maybe another bottle of wine. Stolen pleasures. Why not, we say, why not.

I flirt, I tease. Tell her things she wants to hear. Look at her in the way she wants to be seen. She laps it up; milk for a thirsty kitten. I dish out more. Here, and here's some more.

Touch her sometimes, feel the current hit my skin. Her eyes, they're begging for it, her whole body is, arched towards me and just waiting for the cue.

Desire is there for me but it's only part of it. It's the tease. The torture of the tease. So comfortable, like an old pair of slippers. This again.

Tess, I remember, her naked limbs wrapped into mine. She told me my goal was to punish women.

You're a misogynist, she said, disguising yourself as a player.

I'd laughed, put my hands under the sheets, into dark and warm places.

Nonsense, I adore women. Can't you tell?

She moaned; she could tell.

She blamed my mother, whom I'd only spoken of once in her company.

If every woman is a bad woman, you'll always be hers. Classic, she said.

Jesus, Tess.

It's true, Sam. It's a common pathology.

She was doing a double major, anthropology and psychology. She was intense; she'd had herself sterilized at twenty-one, made her mother drive her to the clinic to do it.

I'm not like other women, she said. You don't have to play with me like you play with the others.

I love my wife, I told her at the end, and she shook her head sadly.

No, Sam, you despise us all.

Maybe this is why she reported me to the dean.

I imagine Frank's an animal. Nothing she won't do. Beautiful women aren't always the best to fuck. You fuck them anyway, for the conquest. The vindication of being the one to close the deal. But Frank I bet would be a pleasant surprise.

I try to reel it in, shake it off. Lift some of those free weights I've got lying around in the barn. Five sets, ten repetitions. Burn, hurt. Come on, it's just playing. I'm restless. Bored.

I need the distraction.

Sorry, Malin. Old dogs, new tricks.

I told Merry I booked another job. She gave me a kiss.

Making it work, didn't I say I would.

She nodded. Proud of her husband. Suitably reassured.

What she doesn't know won't hurt her.

Merry

Orla in Donegal leaves the cupboard with the bleach and the oven cleaner unlocked. Eloise in Bordeaux makes sure to fold back a small corner of the pool cover and leave it untied.

What's wrong with you, Sam asked this morning when he saw me fetch a box of tampons from the cupboard.

I don't know, I said.

Last month, I invented a visit to the gynecologist. All clear, I reported. It will happen soon.

I suppose it must eventually. This is what he wants from me. This is what he needs me to be.

Another email from Christopher received and deleted. No subject line, just the same three words inside. I ought to block him but I don't. It's that flicker of something every time I see his name on the screen. A reminder of something I once had. Power, perhaps. I can't bring myself to excise it altogether, least of all now, with Frank here and everything thrown into disarray; upside down and wrong way around.

We all took a late-morning walk to Sigtuna. On the return, we ran into Elsa and Karl on the trail.

Oh, we must get together, Frank said. I really want to get to know some real live Swedes.

Now they are here for a light dinner. Sam is grilling meat on the barbecue. Frank is inside making her potato salad, which is famous around the world. She regaled us with a story of a New Year's trip with friends to Sri Lanka, how she absolutely had to make the potato salad and absolutely managed to track down capers for the recipe, despite no one on the island knowing what a caper might be.

Her life as she describes it is very colorful. Friends, so many friends. So many exotic trips. Headhunted left and right. Everyone wants Frank's head. It is a perfect life, to hear her describe it. And still she is intent on inserting herself here.

I'm reminded of that feeling I had once before, after Frank's father lost everything. They had to sell the house in Brentwood and move out to her grandmother's two-bedroom place between Mid-City and Koreatown. Frank was mortified; she hated it there. So she got herself out.

She'd take the bus to my house, arrive on the doorstep, win my mother over by telling her how great she was looking, how glamorous her hair was, how fashionable her shoes. She would stay for days on end, weeks, it sometimes felt like, with me sulking in my bedroom and Frank a smiling surrogate daughter my mother could take on shopping trips and spa days. I was always invited. They knew I'd say no.

It felt like Frank was always there. Taking up space. Trying to be a better version of me. Maybe she is.

★ ★ ★

There is music playing, some African jazz Frank picked up on a trip to Ghana.

Oh, it's just wonderful over there, she said earlier, before she and Sam and Karl discussed at length the fascinating burial traditions and elaborate carved coffins. Of course she went to a funeral; of course she has a very good friend living in Accra who showed her the best of his country. No run-of-the-mill sightseeing for Frank. Seventy-two countries she's visited. Always room for more, she adds.

She brings out the potato salad as Karl is telling us about an incident at one of the refugee centers in Gotland. Right-wing extremists setting fire to a young woman in a hijab.

Jesus, Sam says. Didn't think that could happen here.

Well, Karl says, the Swedish people have a right to protect their way of life.

Elsa nods solemnly, and I wonder if I should say something in defense of the charred Muslim woman on life support. I study Karl. His eyes are on Frank's cleavage, amply displayed in a tight, crimson-colored dress that looks vaguely familiar.

I am holding the baby awkwardly in my lap. Elsa is watching him closely. She is less beautiful today. I notice fine lines at her mouth, a dryness to her skin. When she bends down to pick up a napkin she's dropped, I see a patch on her scalp where a clump of hair must have fallen out.

I touch a hand to my own face.

You'll see, my mother always said. It goes quickly.

Or maybe all women pale next to Frank.

I watch her entertain my guests, my husband. In my twenties, I dated a choreographer for the San Francisco Ballet. His prima ballerina was injured before opening night, and as the understudy curtsied to thunderous applause during the curtain call, I watched her face, transfixed by her reaction to the adoration that had been meant for her all along.

I take the baby every day and I run. Farther and farther. As far away as I can get. I breathe in the air of freedom, great gasps of it into my shocked lungs. I try to take it with me, to keep it close. This feeling, this feeling. It will not stay. Frank offers sometimes to watch the baby, but I make a great pretense at bonding. Mommy-son time, I say, to deter her from coming along, to stop her from taking even more away from me.

When the baby is in front of me, helpless and pink and angry, weak with need and his endless demands, I cannot help myself. I pinch. I twist. A dark shadow over his small frame. He feels something and I stay numb. The blue bruises on his flesh are another set of eyes; they watch me and I watch them back. My life. My lies. My punishment. He smells of soured milk and tears. Everything is all wrong.

Elsa was saying something about the nature school down the road closing.

Not enough children.

Yes, Karl adds. Birth rates in the Scandinavian countries are notoriously low.

Catastrophically so, actually. We're a dying breed.

I jiggle the baby. I hold a carrot to his mouth to suck on, to ease the soreness of the teething gums that keep him awake at night.

Well, of course, Karl continues. Women have much wider options these days than motherhood.

Yes, Elsa nods. She looks wounded by this fact.

Sam announces that the meat is ready, and we sit down around the table. Elsa eats even less than before. The bones of her tiny wrists look like they may snap at any moment. I have a sudden vision of Karl setting her alight. A punishment for her barrenness, perhaps.

Where is Freja today? I ask.

She is visiting her grandmother, Karl replies. In Katrineholm.

Frank, playing hostess, titters about passing food and topping up drinks. The potato salad is ruled a success. Karl asks Elsa to get the recipe.

Looks like you're really part of the family, Elsa tells Frank.

She sure is, I smile, and the taste of her potatoes rises up in my throat.

In the kitchen, Frank and I stack the plates. She's been strangely aloof from me the last few days, watching me closely but saying little. Perhaps she is confused too, by this topsy-turvy state of affairs. Tonight she seems in better spirits. Maybe it is all the applause.

I feel like a fifties housewife over here, she laughs. And you know something, I love it.

Are you wearing my dress? I ask. Now I see it's one of the new dresses I bought in Stockholm. I haven't worn it yet. In the places where it gaped on my body, it sits tightly across hers, as though her flesh has been poured in and stitched up, like stuffing in a doll.

Oh, she says. I'm all out of clean clothes. I didn't think you'd mind.

I load the last few glasses into the dishwasher and lift the door shut.

Oh—Frank says, clicking her fingers. I totally forgot to mention it before.

Christopher, she says.

Who? I ask.

Christopher Atwood. You met him at that Christmas dinner I threw right before I moved to London.

I nod vaguely. Sure.

Funniest thing, she says. I bumped into him in the Starbucks line at Heathrow. I was heading here and he was on his way back to New York after a business trip.

I busy myself rinsing the blades of the food processor. What a coincidence, I say lightly.

Well, I told him I was off to see you in Sweden—he was very surprised to hear you'd moved. And had a baby.

We weren't friends, I say. I just met him that one time.

Well, Frank smiles. Anyway, I promised to send him pictures of everything. He's never been to Sweden.

In the sink, the water is suddenly stained red.

Merry, Frank cries, you've cut yourself.

Later, after everything's been bandaged up and packed away, the baby on the living room floor rolls himself over onto his belly. He heaves himself up on all fours. He rocks back and forth, back and forth. Then he reaches out an arm and begins to crawl.

Sam jumps up from where he's been sitting, Frank shrieks and applauds.

They hug each other. They cheer the baby as though he has taken mankind's first steps on the moon.

Look, Frank cries, we did it.

The we, like most things these days, does not include me.

Frank

At the self-development retreat I attended a few years ago—you know, yoga and morning meditation and little shots of green juice—Krisha, the woman who ran the seminars, spoke to us about presence. The perfection in the now. You aren't supposed to wish for anything beyond what you have and are, in any moment. Anything else, she warned, and you doom yourself to a fruitless search for a happiness you won't find.

I can't help but think of her now, and I can't stop myself from wishing for everything she warned against.

I know it's a ludicrous thought, the very idea of it—madness—and yet I can't stop it. The idea that Merry doesn't want her life; that I want it more than anything in the world. I have been playing house here, this I know. Playing as though this might be my house and my life, my husband and my child. Why not? It is easy and familiar, as though it has always been this way or ought to have been. Cooking dinner, playing with the baby, seeing Sam soak it all in.

And then Sam at night, almost every night, hand on my arm, eyes on my eyes, sometimes stealing a quick look down to my braless and beautiful breasts. Desire there, but something else, too. He sees it; I know he does. He sees that I should be the one.

Yes, madness, but also not.

Because it fits. It works.

It would set things right.

I could slip in and she could slip out, a trading of places so seamless and smooth, you wouldn't even notice a ripple. Mine for hers. A simple switch. Surely stranger things have happened. And Merry—my poor Merry. How my heart aches for her. She is miserable. A prisoner of this life who longs for her freedom. Really, I have seen too much now to believe otherwise.

Every day since she's recovered from her flu, Merry has gone out for a hike with Conor. They are always gone a long time. She always comes back smiling.

I don't know what it was that raised my suspicions. Maybe when I asked her if I could join and she balked at the suggestion. Maybe just a feeling in the gut, a wave of something not quite right. I have been on high alert since I first saw her hurting Conor. Well, she bundled him up this morning and the two of them left around nine. Sam was out for the day, off in Gothenburg for a meeting. I have introduced him to a few contacts I thought might be useful; this is one of them. Aren't I a tremendous help? He is very grateful, he tells me. So very grateful. The least I can do, I reply.

I put on my sneakers and followed behind Merry. She moved quickly, pushing the stroller over the stones at a brisk pace.

I hung back while she readjusted something in the stroller. Then she crossed over the path and made for the trail. I walked slowly behind, and hid a moment while she climbed the hill.

When enough time had passed, I climbed it myself. In the clearing at the top, I stopped. I looked at the sight before my eyes—a puzzling one for sure—and went behind a tree to observe. It was Conor's stroller, abandoned in the middle of the trees. I could see the child inside, very still or possibly asleep, his blue blanket tucked into his lower half.

Merry was nowhere. Vanished. Conor had been left all alone in the woods.

I waited by the tree, assuming she was peeing behind a bush or, I don't know, foraging for berries. I waited and waited, tried to rationalize the scene, but she did not return. Twenty minutes, then thirty passed. Eventually I went over to the stroller and peered inside. Conor was awake, watching alertly.

Oh, Conor, I cried. You've been left all alone!

My little lamb, those fat cheeks, that button of a nose planted in the center of his face—I touched a hand to him and felt his cold skin.

He was unperturbed, and I was struck with the idea that this might be nothing new for him. I picked him up and planted kisses all over his face, tickled under his arms—tried to show him that the world was not a cruel place. My heart sank, thinking of what I'd seen only a few days ago. And in between.

And what about this? Dear God, I thought, who knows how far she will go.

I kept him cradled safely in my arms, his plump cheeks pressed to mine. It was maybe an hour or so later when I heard the rustling of trees and the pounding of feet over ground. I put Conor back down and crouched again behind the tree. Casual, easy, not a care in the world, Merry gave her son a brief glance and then wheeled him home.

I waited some minutes in the shade, stilling my heart, gathering my thoughts.

She does not deserve him. She does not even want him. This was confirmed.

I walked slowly back to the house, seeing it all in reverse now. Not beautiful. Not the place of longing. Just a set piece.

Merry appeared surprised when I came in the door behind her.

Where have you been? she asked.

Just took a little walk. Fresh air and all.

She looked at me sharply. Whereabouts did you go?

I waved my hand in the general direction of the woods. Around the trails. The lower one, I said, and watched her relax. She had removed Conor from the stroller. She had him awkwardly in her grip as he wriggled to get free.

Darling boy. How much cruelty can he be expected to endure?

We spent the rest of the day pottering about the house. Merry in the garden pulling up weeds and planting rows of broad beans, me playing on the lawn with Conor, trying to shower him with an abundance of love. God knows he needs it.

I helped Merry make his next batch of baby food, and later,

a simple salad and grilled lemon chicken for our dinner, which we ate at the kitchen counter.

This really is the life, I said.

Yes, we're very lucky.

You are happy here, aren't you, Merry? I asked, hoping to coax something more truthful from her. To help her at least share her pain, if not solve it.

I'm your best friend, I said. You can tell me anything. I'm always here for you.

She only gave me that fixed smile. What's not to be happy about? she said.

Well, all these other lives you've lived, I said. They couldn't have been more different from this.

I didn't know what I was looking for then. I didn't know what fit.

And this?

This is it. This is me.

Right. I nodded. I had opened a bottle of wine and poured a single glass. Now Merry fetched one for herself from the cupboard.

Sorry, I said, I thought you were trying for a baby. I sipped my wine and watched her fill a generous glass.

She gave a sort of grimace. Oh, I'm not pregnant.

You can be so sure?

She laughed. Yes, Frank. It's really quite simple.

Well then. I refilled my glass, and together we finished the bottle.

In the night, I heard the baby cry out. I slipped quietly back into his room and picked him up in my arms. I held him close and shushed him gently. Shhh, shhh, back to sleep, lullabies in the dark, a comforting rock in the big armchair. I inhaled his sleepy smell, milky and soapy and soft, the excruciating perfection of new life, like the best things achingly fragile and too easily lost. When he was in my arms, sleeping soundly, safe and happy, it was easy to forget that he was not mine.

Merry

Freja in our living room was playing with the baby, pulling him back by his legs when he crawled off toward danger. He is a permanent blur of motion now, gaining speed and agility by the day. Frank and Sam could not be more pleased. I have been told to be more vigilant with where I leave things.

I found one of your hairclips in his mouth the other day, Frank chastised me over dinner. And the day before, she said, I picked a button up from off the living room carpet.

You'll need to be more careful, Sam said, irritated. These things are choking hazards.

Yes, hazards. Potentially fatal hazards. Tiny objects that can steal life away in a few seconds.

Freja is a sweet child, curious, polite. She has Karl's piercing gaze, a little unnerving, a little too blue, like the children in those Hitler Youth propaganda posters. I offered her a cup of apple juice, which she drank carefully, using both hands. She is learning English at school, but she is shy to speak it in front of me. To the baby, she speaks in Swedish.

Frank was on a Skype call with some friends in Paris or Dubai or Hong Kong. Every so often, loud peals of laughter sounded from her room. I imagined she was entertaining her friends with tales of our provincial ways, stories of quaint Sigtuna relayed to the good people of the world's more thrilling metropolises. I wonder how she acts around them, what kind of woman they imagine she is. Popular, successful, ambitious. Maybe. Maybe she is all of these things in the world. A woman to be admired. A woman who has achieved significant and impressive things. Made something of herself—that most curious of notions.

I don't know this Frank.

I know only the woman who is no woman at all, but a girl. The girl who will always be outside looking in. Desperate. Ruthless. While she was in the other room, I snuck a peek at her phone. It was full of photos of freshly baked breakfast muffins and the views of the lake from the kitchen window, pictures with the baby, a few with Sam. Just the sort of photographs I used to send her. But I am in none of these pictures. It is as though I do not exist at all.

I enlarged one picture of Frank, Sam, and the baby. A dazzling sight—an overload of good looks and white-toothed smiles. You almost cannot look away.

My stomach lurched. Sam's arm around her. Sam, who cannot keep his hands to himself.

It couldn't be. She wouldn't dare. But the way she drapes herself on the sofa. The way she looks at Sam, touches his arm, his hand, anything she can, any chance she gets. The way she picks up the baby and slings him onto her arm. Who loves you, my little Con? Who wants to gobble you all up?

Like it is all hers. Like the guest in this house is me.

And Sam. I see how he looks at her. How they sit and

talk late into the night. So close. Almost touching. Sometimes touching (I have stood at the window some nights to watch, breathing into the folds of the curtains, trying to stay hidden from view). I see how they have private jokes and gestures. How they closet themselves in the studio to talk about his work—because isn't Frank just full of ideas!

No. No. Anyone but her. I can take anything—I have taken plenty already. But I could not bear that. If Frank took what was mine.

If it ever came to be that Frank got what she wanted. No. Never. I would not survive it.

I looked at the photo one last time, zooming in on the baby's smiling face. Brushing away the other thought, unwelcome and distracting.

Outside, it was raining again, a faint, damp drizzle. Already the weather is getting a little chillier, the days cool and prone to downpours. You can feel the seasons slowly changing, the light giving way to the inevitable and desperate darkness to come. A second winter here looms, black and cold; the elements conspiring with Sam to keep me locked away inside. The baby will soon be a year old, another milestone, another marker of time. One whole year.

We will need to throw a party. Sam will want to celebrate the occasion in fitting style; cake and candles. For my first birthday party, my mother hired a pony and a clown. My father did not attend. I cried the whole way through and stopped only when the last guest had left. My father is seven years dead and I cannot think of a single memory of him that is a fond one. Three weeks before my wedding, that's when he chose to do it. There was no one to walk me down the aisle on the day. I gave myself away.

★ ★ ★

From the kitchen, I watched Freja playing with the baby. Elsa had come to the door this morning, looking terribly anxious. I thought it might have been something to do with the baby again, but since Frank has been here there is a lot less crying for her to complain about.

Merry, I need your help, she said. I am sorry to impose.

She had an urgent doctor's appointment. She did not say what for. She had a little blue cooler box in her hands; she clutched it tightly. Her eyes were wild with panic.

Please say nothing to Karl. He mustn't know.

Of course, I said.

He'll only worry, she added, forcing a smile. That's the only reason for it.

I nodded. I smiled. I touched a reassuring hand to her arm. She flinched and pulled the cooler out of my reach.

She waved Freja hurriedly over to our house and drove away in her silver sedan.

Well, Freja, I said. What do you want to do?

She pointed to the baby on his play mat.

Terrific, I said.

She went and sat down beside him on the floor.

Jag är din mamma nu, she told him. I am your mother now.

Where is Freja's real mother, I wonder. Did she leave them? Did Karl send her away?

When we were little, any time Frank visited my house, she would go home with something of mine secreted away in her pockets. I'd notice the missing thing after she left—a Barbie handbag, a pretty pen with glitter stars inside that danced as you tilted it to write. The next time I was in her bedroom, I might even see the pilfered objects among her things.

That's mine, I'd say, but she'd just look at me and smile.

Oh no it isn't. It's mine.

You stole it! I'd cry.

She'd laugh and shrug and say, No, Merry, you must be mistaken. I've always had that.

I checked the vegetables simmering on the stove, and tried to make out what Frank was saying over Skype. When she emerged from the bedroom, she was still laughing.

My friend Will, she said, he's hilarious.

I poured her a glass of water, trying to be hospitable, trying to keep it all under control. Play nice. Wasn't that what I was taught? Play nice, girls. Yes. That is how they want you.

Where's Sam? she asked.

In the studio, I said. Editing footage for that Gothenburg project.

I'll just go and see how he's getting on, she said, and wandered off, leaving me to my vomit-colored vegetables.

I want her to leave. I need her gone. She is too much. It is too unnerving. That she might send this whole house of cards tumbling down, everything I have worked to build. Everything from which she has always been excluded. It cannot be otherwise.

I will need to think of a way to do it, something that doesn't make me seem overly childish, petulant for being left out.

Otherwise, Sam will tease me. Oh, someone is jealous, he'll say. He'll be thrilled. He'll be vindicated.

You women, he'll say.

He thinks women need to be held in check. Guided, he calls it, because women are no good at making up their minds. I'm never sure if he means all of us. Or just me.

I heard Freja call out from the living room. Conor has made a poo-poo, she said.

I went over to where they were playing and picked him up. He was angry at being removed from his toys and started to cry.

Freja looked up at me and laughed. Ha-ha, she said, and made a face. See, he doesn't like you.

Sam

Outside, under the stars. After a few chilly days, those first signs of autumn, this evening's sky was clear. Pink and wide and magnificent.

Merry had stayed awhile on the lawn, before Con started to cry. This teething, she said. Frank looked at her and smiled. She did not get up.

The two of us were left outside alone. Something hot in the air between her and me, daring, dancing on the edge. I've been a naughty boy. Not playing fair. Too many lingering looks, lingering hands. She has the idea in her head. That this is something.

A few nights ago, I saw her passing through to the bathroom, nightgown open, naked beneath. She is shaved everywhere, smooth as stone and white. Beautiful breasts, high and full, dark nipples, the rest of her lithe like a dancer, the muscles clear under the surface, like an anatomical illustration. A woman waiting to be devoured.

Oh, sorry, she said, making as if to cover up. But her movements were slow, reluctant. She wanted me to see. To know.

She smiled. I smiled. What've you got there, I teased.

I shouldn't.

I shouldn't, but I do. I've been ignoring Malin's texts. I failed to show up at her place this week. Last time we saw each other, we'd had an argument. I told her I was trying to get Merry pregnant, which probably wasn't the right thing to say.

She shook her head, disapproval or disbelief.

I made some comment about how long it's taking to happen, and she seemed to snap.

Not everything has to be everyone else's fault, she said. What if the problem is with you for once?

I guess she wanted to have her little dig. Can't blame her, I suppose.

Now she must be feeling bad. She's texted twice already. No response from me.

Not fair to her, but some things I don't want to deal with right now.

Maybe I'm a coward. Like my mother says, all men are when it comes down to it. She sent more money. At least she's good for something.

Frank's eyes, holding mine. Smiling; a secret, knowing smile. How many I've seen before just like that. The moment before the prize.

I've probably pushed this too far. Should have drawn a line. Pulled back, pulled out. This is what I was thinking when she leaned in, her lips on my mouth, the softest kiss.

Jesus, she was like something sweet and melting on the tongue, warm breath, warm everything. Old pleasures, the forbidden kind. I felt myself surrender. She pushed closer, panting, pawing, my hands were pulling at her, under fabric, into flesh. Urgent, hungry.

Then the scream.

Piercing the dark, shattering the moment.

Conor. My son.

Like a cold shower. Like a rude awakening. My son.

Stop, I hissed, pushing Frank away.

She held on. Sam, but Sam.

I gripped her hands. Stop, I said. Stop.

Her face crumpled. She didn't understand. Sam, it's okay. It's what we both want.

Hideous now, pleading and begging.

The spell was broken.

You're not making sense, Frank, I said.

No, Sam, she said, the only thing that doesn't make sense is you and Merry. Look at her. Look at her with Conor. Sam, listen—she doesn't want this. It's all wrong, it's all—she's.

I held her face in my hands. Firm, too firm, perhaps. She tried to pull away.

Frank, listen.

She squirmed. I held her in place.

Merry and Conor are the only things I'll ever care about. Not you.

Understand? Never you.

She looked at me like I'd cut her with a knife, a fatal wound. Her cheeks shocked red and wet.

In the kitchen, I poured a glass of water, looked out toward Frank still on the lawn, lying on her back, staring at the stars, lit by the moon.

Fuck, I said. Idiot.

The house was in darkness. The crying had stopped. I slipped into Conor's room to see if Merry was with him, soothing his tears. He was alone, already fast asleep, the heaving chest slow and steady under his little gray romper. My son, my heart. All that matters.

In my pocket, my phone beeped.

Malin again. Not letting up.

Come by tomorrow?

I touched a hand to Conor's forehead and went back out to the kitchen.

Outside, Frank lay motionless, a discarded pool toy left on the lawn to fade and crack in the elements.

I spat into the sink. Whore. Trying to seduce a married man. A man with a family.

Another text came from Malin. *10 a.m.?*

I thought of her face, that soft smile, her eyes the color of chocolate and just as warm. The smell of fresh-cut flowers and hot coffee, her perfume and her laugh and everything about her that feels like an embrace.

No. Enough. They are all the same. My head throbbed with blood and panic.

I texted back. *Can't. Sorry.*

I stood in the dark a while longer.

I'm trying, I said to myself. At least I'm trying.

Sam

A new day. A new day. I reconsidered what Malin said. I made an appointment for myself at a fertility clinic in Uppsala. Just in case.

I'm tired of waiting. Of wanting and not getting it. It's time to take responsibility for my life, to stop blaming everyone else. Malin's said this to me more than once, in that way she has that makes it all sound reasonable and gentle. She is a rare one. I probably owe her more than I let on. Maybe that needs to change too.

After I made the appointment, I booked a hotel for Merry and me. Anniversary celebrations. I want to go all out. To fix it. To set it all right again.

Frank wasn't even up by the time I was ready to leave. Merry had Conor in his high chair. She was cool toward me. Borderline hostile. Maybe she saw something last night. Maybe she got the wrong idea.

I love you, I said. You know that, right?

I pulled her close. I kissed her mouth, put my hands on her, under her.

We should really work on this baby some more, I said. Seems we've not been trying hard enough lately.

She smiled. This is what she wanted to hear.

There's my girl, I said. That's how I like you.

Samson Hurley, I told the receptionist at the front desk as she handed me a form to complete.

Taking charge. That's what needs to be done. No more weakness, but action.

Yes. This is how you do it.

Frank was only a distraction. Noise. Nothing that matters.

I handed the form back to the receptionist and she pointed me to the dimly lit room.

Frank. Frank. Her tits, the feel of them under my hand, and her cunt, tight and wet, so fucking wet—I'd pushed my way in, two fingers, three, and she'd moaned, grabbed for my cock, over my jeans, bursting out, wanting, wanting, imagining already how it would feel to be deep inside and she was imagining it, too, wasn't she, writhing and pushing and forcing my hand deeper, all the way, far as it could go.

Frank, Frank, dirty bitch.

Quietly, in the darkened cubicle, I came into the little plastic cup.

Frank

All is lost. Perhaps it was too soon. I should have waited. Or I should have said more. Given Sam something more solid on Merry and what she's been up to.

Oh, I don't know, it's all too much of a mess now. He's acting like I made the whole thing up. I'm wondering if I did.

But how could I? I'm not blind. I have eyes that have seen things. Too many things.

My only consolation is that dear, beautiful child. Conor, son of my heart, if not my flesh.

Yes, I'll say it. I am a better mother to him than she'll ever be. I love him, with every fiber of my being. And I thought there was a way for— Well, no use now.

Silly, silly me.

Sam is being deliberately cruel. Making his point. He can't take his hands off his wife. He's arranged elaborate anniversary celebrations in the city. And I am to babysit. Nothing more than the hired help.

I'm sure you won't mind, Frank, he said. You're great pals, you and Con.

They left in the early afternoon, to make the most of it. He booked them a fancy dinner, a night in a hotel. Merry wrote up a list and stuck it on the fridge. Meal times, meal combinations, bottles, different medication for different ailments, favorite toys, bedtime routine.

Like I don't already know it all. Like I haven't been doing it for weeks.

I was feeling spiteful. After they left, I rifled through the drawers and wardrobes in the house. What did I find but birth control pills, hidden in a pouch in the very back of Merry's underwear drawer. Another titbit Sam surely knows nothing about.

I pawed through her underwear and bras. Plain, cotton, mostly faded from the wash. No wonder Sam is so easily led astray. She has a box with letters and a few photographs in a bottom drawer. A photo of her with her father, a photo of Sam as a student, somewhere overly exotic-looking, posed beside a man covered in white ash or mud. A photo of her mother, from some professional shoot she had done, by the looks of it.

My other daughter, Maureen always called me; the daughter I ought to have had.

She was easy to win over. All you needed to do was tell her how good she was looking that day.

Oh, you are a dear, she would say, feigning embarrassment, acting as though she hadn't laid it all out for you on a platter with her titivating and preening and never-ending nips and tucks.

Not too much? Not too young?

Oh, no, Maureen, that miniskirt is splendid on you, what with those legs for days.

★ ★ ★

You learn the tricks, then soon enough they come naturally; your default setting. Flatter, fawn, find your way in.

You're a leech, Frances.

I can remember Merry saying that to me over and over again when we were teenagers.

No, I said, I just know how to get what I want.

I always thought that was a good thing. A true life skill. But Merry's never known what it means to want. To long for something that's out of reach. How could she, when all of life has been handed to her on a platter? Anything she's ever wanted, or toyed with the idea of wanting.

Anniversary dinner. I pictured the two of them, celebrating their idyllic life in the woods. How can she fool him so? How can he fool himself?

Well, I've decided. I have no choice but to tell Sam everything I know, everything I've seen these past weeks, the strangest and most seductive of my life.

Conor deserves this, if nothing else. Someone to look out for him. Poor mistreated boy. Yes, I'll deliver a full report. Let them find all their secrets revealed. Let them drown in a sea of truth. Let it rise up slowly and wash away all this murky falsehood, the great facade of their lives. It will be better for everyone.

I stood in front of her bedroom mirror. I had found her wedding dress, stashed in the back of the wardrobe and covered in plastic. Strange that she carted it all the way over here when she left so much else behind. I remember how she looked in it, the corseted body pinching in her waist, the wide lace skirt billowing out all the way to the floor.

A princess dress, the one I dreamed of for years. I put a picture of it on the dream boards we made once—the things you do at seventeen—cutouts of houses and cars and baby strollers, the engagement rings we'd be adorned with, the beaches where we'd vacation with our handsome husbands. The dresses we would wear on our wedding days. It was mine. She had stolen it and worn it and walked down the aisle in it, beguiling, ethereal Merry with her painted-on smile, while I stood in the corner in my apricot-colored bridesmaid dress and tried not to burst with rage.

I slipped the dress out of the plastic. Felt the material in my fingers, the stiff bone of the scalloped bodice. I pulled off my clothes. I stepped into the dress. It was difficult to get to the buttons at the back, I swiveled the dress around so that it was backwards and fastened up three-quarters of the buttons. Then I shifted it slowly back. The bone of the corset was pressed too tight, constricting around my rib cage, forcing out the air. I held my breath.

I looked at myself in the mirror. No. I was not beautiful in the dress. I was not anyone's bride.

Conor began to scream from his bedroom. He had woken from his nap. I tried the buttons to remove the dress but they were too finicky.

I went to Conor's room. He was standing in the crib. He beat his hands against the bars, angry and urgent. Uppy, I said, and he held up his arms.

It's okay, I said. Aunt Frank is here. Aunt Frank loves you.

Loves you loves you loves you, I said again, into his belly to make him laugh.

The sound was a tonic for the soul, a reminder of all that remains good and beautiful, even in such darkness.

How lucky they are. How many blessings they have been dealt.

Conor grabbed at the beads on the dress and pulled.

Isn't it a silly dress? I said. It was too tight. I could feel the sharpness of the metal fasteners digging into my side, cutting at the flesh.

In the kitchen, I reached up to grab one of Conor's bottles out of the cupboard. I felt a tear of fabric.

Oh dear, I said. These things happen, don't they?

It was easier to breathe. I found a bottle of wine for myself and poured a glass. I checked the time. I set Conor on the rug and brought him a stack of his wooden blocks.

Let's build a house, I said.

He was soon bored, and a little cranky. I hauled out some pots from the kitchen cupboard and let him bang them with a spoon. He liked that. I removed one of Merry's little jars of baby food from the fridge and heated it up. I tucked a dish towel into the top of the wedding dress and fed Conor with a spoon. He watched me and smiled, waiting for me to make the noises of the trucks and the planes and the rocket ships.

How natural it felt, just us. He looked at me with great love.

The phone rang as I was lifting Conor out of the bath. It was Merry.

Just checking in, she said, full of sweetness and cheer. How is everything going? All okay?

Yes, I said. We're just peachy. Enjoying the celebrations?

You know, she said. We're having a great time. A really great time.

I hung up the phone. I caught a glimpse of my reflection in the big glass window. Woman in a twice-stolen dress. I did not recognize myself.

I looked down at the baby, naked on his back. Staring up at me with those fiercely trusting eyes. Wondering what I'd do.

I stared a long time, in a daze I think, a delirium of rejection and injustice. Conor was tired, rubbing his eyes, yawning. The fat belly, the chubby thighs, the kneeless legs that kicked at the air. His feet, familiar feet belonging to Merry. Long toes, narrow and tapered. He kicked at me. He wanted to move, to be lifted up and loved.

What possessed me, I'll never know. Maybe it was her. Merry. I looked at Conor and I held his legs. I held them down. I squeezed. The flesh in between my fingers was squishy, boneless, almost. All fat.

I was in a trance, a somnambulist. A woman outside her body.

I clenched and he cried out and I clenched harder, briefly—only a brief moment—and then pulled my hands away; shaking, weak. The skin was red. The child was screeching. My heart pounded frantically as I lifted him up.

He swatted at my face and I welcomed it. Oh God oh God, what monstrous thing did I do. I wept and wept, I bounced and rocked and hushed and kissed.

You're okay; you're okay. Conor's heart was racing, too; I felt it against me, like the batting wings of a moth caught under a glass.

Oh baby, oh baby. A rush of too much love and endless regret.

I checked his legs for bruises. I kissed him all over and rocked him in the chair until he fell safely to sleep.

I must have slept too, curled on the soft carpet at the foot of his crib.

In the morning, I woke to the sound of crying. I was still in the dress. At the place between two of my ribs, a thin gash of blood had leaked out and stained the fabric red.

Merry

I feel like a new me. Or the old me, perhaps. Lighter, happier, more clearly defined. Restored. Because everything is going to go back to how it was before.

Our anniversary celebrations went surprisingly well. They were even fun.

We'd driven to Stockholm and checked in to the hotel. The room was clean and simple, nothing overly plush. Sam lay down on the bed, patted the duvet. Come over here and test this out with me.

He has been overly affectionate, tender and attentive, these past few days. Trying hard. Or making amends.

No. It doesn't matter. His focus is back where it belongs.

At six o'clock, we took a shower and got dressed.

You look fantastic, he said. I was wearing a new dress, black and lace, a delicate sheath that hung softly to my ankles.

The restaurant was a few minutes' walk away. The streets were full of tourists, boatloads of them off the cruise ships, set loose to buy Viking trinkets and plastic trolls. We headed away from the crowds and found the restaurant nestled up a cobbled side street. Inside, it was more charming than I'd imagined, all low lighting and carved art nouveau wooden booths.

The waiter was a young man with a thick Spanish accent. He brought us menus and a tray of amuse-bouche.

We ordered our starters and mains and Sam took my hand.

This is nice.

Yes.

You're happy.

Yes.

That's what I want. That's the reason I do everything I do.

I nodded. I looked at my husband, my too-handsome husband. Too handsome for me, I know that's what people must think. But he chose me, didn't he. Of everyone, me.

To my wife, Sam toasted. To our beautiful family. To expanding it, too. He smiled.

I felt a wave of guilt, shame low in the belly, at the root of me. Mild panic, too. There was an email just before we left the house. For once, different words inside. This time only two: *I know.*

I swallowed.

To our beautiful life, I said.

The food arrived, wooden boards with three kinds of herring and tiny glass pots of mustard. The waiter brought over a small basket of fresh bread rolls. The food was delicious, flavorful and delicate.

The chef uses only local ingredients, Sam said. Apparently he goes foraging in the forest for a lot of it. Berries, mushrooms. The herbs.

Those Swedes, I said. They really do take it to the extreme.

There was a couple seated across from us. The man looked exactly like my father. Sam looked over. A Swedish Gerald, he said.

I nodded.

You miss him.

No, I said. You can't miss what you didn't have.

Don't know, Sam said. I missed my father. I felt his absence.

It was a rare moment of vulnerability. Sam showing his cracks. I took his hand. I wanted to do better at being his wife. At being his.

The waiter came over with the mains, put down the plates, and arranged the little dishes of sides between us. Spinach, roasted carrots, sweet potato fries.

Everything all right? he asked, and we nodded, yes, wonderful, thank you.

You're beautiful, Sam said. I don't tell you enough what you mean to me.

I nodded. I know, I know.

And still, I have wronged him in unthinkable ways.

Merry, he said. About Frank.

What about Frank, I snapped. I did not want to think about Frank.

He took a bite of his food. Nothing, nothing serious, it's just. I really think it's time for her to go.

Why? I said. What's happened?

What has she done. What have you done, I thought.

He shook his head. No, nothing. It's just been almost a month.

Over a month, I said.

Yes, too long. I want our space back. I want you back all to myself. The way it's best.

He flashed that smile. I let out a breath.

I'm so happy you mentioned it, I said. I feel exactly the same way.

Good, he said. Then you'll talk to her.

I took a bite of food. I chewed slowly.

This is nice, Sam said. You and me. Time alone.

He'd finished his food. From under the table, his hands found my lap, pried me open, forged ahead.

Feels good, doesn't it.

The second bottle of wine was almost finished. I lifted my glass and emptied it. My head floating, my body singing. The thrum of music from the hotel bar, the hands pressing me, burrowing into flesh.

Yes, I said. It feels good.

It did. Like the old days, the early weeks and months when it was all new and thrilling. A new kind of life with a man who looked at me like he knew exactly what was in store.

It was just us two then, and that was more than enough. Sam and Merry. Two halves made whole. Two halves, nothing else. No one else in the picture to confuse things.

The dessert came, little rounds of chocolate mousse with basil ice cream and honey wafers. I dropped the fork on the floor and Sam substituted with his finger, chocolate into mouth, harder than it looks. We laughed and hid behind the napkins. I wiped mousse onto my lips and gave him a chocolate smile.

We finished off dinner with double espressos and the bill; Sam tipped handsomely and the waiter wished us a good night.

There was a bar a few doors past the hotel, down a winding staircase and into a tiny, cramped basement. The barman wore a suit and stood behind an old wooden bar, pouring gimlets into crystal glasses. We ordered a couple of drinks and settled into the velvet-upholstered sofa; hands on thighs, tongues loose, smiles largely unforced. The freedom was heady; I think I must have felt happy. The relief of Frank leaving, the relief of knowing that when it was Sam and me, it was all just right. It would all be just right again. I would make sure of it.

The email, the words, they faded into the haze of smoke and candlelight, fine as gossamer, and then altogether vanished. Yes, I thought, I would make all of that go away.

In the hotel room, Sam and I fell onto the bed, fumbled, kissed, partially undressed, made love or attempted to do so. We slipped heavily and quickly into sleep, the pair of us lying cupped against each other like two soup bowls on the shelf.

You forgive me, he mumbled, almost incoherent, into my ear.

What?

You forgive me for bringing you here, and we're happy. The three of us. We're happy.

Mm, I said, or nodded, or groaned. Some passable sound came from me and he squeezed me further into his knees so that I was pinned in place.

I'm trying, he murmured. I'm going to be a better man, I promise.

We'd returned home the next day smiling.

It would all be good again. I knew how to make it so. To clear the slate. To start over. No secrets. No mysteries. No doubt.

I looked at the house against the trees as we pulled up in the car. Beautiful. Wonderful. The day was overcast, but it looked as though the rain would hold off for a few hours yet. I took in a few deep breaths, the mossy smell of the damp woods. The end-of-summer rot, as the leaves started to fall and the last of the summer berries grew fat and sweet on their branches. I made a note to do a final berry picking, to stock up on blackberries to turn into the jam that Sam likes with his morning toast.

I thought of Frank leaving.

I smiled.

Merry

The baby was on the bed. I had the windows open, the day outside was all pastels and hazy light, like a watercolor. John Coltrane was playing in the background; Sam's favorite. Earlier, I'd poached him eggs, made hollandaise from scratch, and buttered thick slices of sourdough toast. Frank stayed in her bedroom, out of the way. Perhaps she senses that she has overstayed her welcome.

I looked at the baby on the bed, studied his face and form. I traced his features with a finger while he watched, big eyes following my movements. Suspicious. Always suspicious.

I suppose he ought to be.

I put my head to his belly, inhaled the smell of newly changed child, talcum powder and soap and innocence all blended together.

A wave of dread, a flicker of doubt.

I'm sorry.

I'm sorry. He didn't ask for this.

In the kitchen, Frank was making coffee, still in a robe.

Day off? I teased.

She looked up. She rubbed her head. I couldn't sleep last night, she said. I have a lot on my mind, I guess.

She looked awful. I thought about the way the air prickled when she and Sam were in the same room yesterday and shook my head. What does it matter? She will be leaving soon.

I cleared my throat. Frank, I started. Sam and I were talking the other night.

She set down her mug, her face searching mine.

It's great you visited, I said. But now it feels like time to get our space back. To return to our regular routine. We think it will be better for all of us.

We think it's time.

We think you need to leave.

She looked at me, the hurt registering in her eyes.

I see, she said. You want me to go.

No, Sam and I. Both of us, I said. We both want it.

I watched her expression. That look. Wanting. Yes, this was how it was meant to be. Frank wanting.

I stood taller, held my head high.

I felt good. Powerful in the way I can only ever feel around Frank. Whatever might have happened, I am the one who has won.

She was picking at her nails, frowning. She shook her head. I know what you're doing, Merry. I know—

I was enjoying it too much. I was being cruel. For old time's sake, I said it. Because I'd said it before.

You don't belong here, Frank.

You don't belong anywhere, I almost added. Her face was twisted, the hurt spreading like a rash, red and raging. Woman in flames. Burn, I thought, burn.

Inside, I felt alive.

Frank

He was on top of me, grunting his pleasure, trying to contain it so he wouldn't come. We were in the barn; around us the smell of untreated pine, the feel of cold wood. Like animals, I thought.

And why not. Why not go all the way. Make it even more base and sordid than it is already. Naked bodies entwined, a dirty secret in the dark.

This is my go-to remedy at times like these. When feeling at my lowest, I always like to go lower still. Numb the pain with shame. I like the sting of it. The loathsomeness is my only comfort.

But you're married, I had protested, as though such a thought was shocking to me.

Yes, he breathed in my ear, hot and urgent, and when has that ever stopped anyone before?

His hands were on me, squeezing everywhere, pushing and prodding with his fingers and tongue. Yes, oh yes.

Lust, I have realized over the years, makes men horribly unattractive. It's just the same repetition of primal urges. Insert here, press this, pound that. All roads lead to Rome. We'd met out at the recycling bins; he was disposing of the week's plastic.

Come with me, he pleaded.

I didn't require much persuasion.

I closed my eyes. I felt neither pleasure nor pain. I didn't want to feel much at all.

This has always been my problem. Heightened emotions.

Feeling too much.

Loving too much.

Merry wants me gone. No, correction—Sam and Merry. We, she made sure to say. We. Us.

To be expected, I suppose. And she is right. I don't belong here. She doesn't either, but that isn't any of my business. Everyone has made this crystal clear.

Sam, well, I can't blame him for wanting his little family to stay intact. If I had a family, it's all I'd want too. Perhaps he was just bored. Perhaps I am as irresistible as I've been told. Men who say that don't mean it as a compliment. It's more of an accusation. For leading them astray. For stealing them from their wives.

Fuckable. That's the word. The kind of woman a man wants to have sex with. Not marry, mind you. Just fuck.

Yes. I am good at sexiness, the performance of it. Pout, pose, push it up into their faces. Tease them with an illusion of the pleasure that awaits.

He was hurting me now, aggressive with his movements. Rough was how he liked it. No surprises there. That's usually the way with married men. A gentleman with the wife between the Egyptian cotton sheets, and a sadist with the mistress.

How many married men does this make it? It doesn't really matter. I once worried that it would. That karma would find me out and do the same thing to me, make me the woman whose husband cheats or leaves. But there is no husband. And the men always leave.

They'd stay if you weren't so needy, Frank. That's what Merry told me a few years back.

You suffocate them with the ferocity of your need. Of course they want to run a mile.

She was trying to be helpful, I think. Or spiteful. She has always been good at the latter. Reminding me of what I'll never have. How I'll always be deficient. Maybe this is the marker of the truest friend, the teller of all the things you don't want to hear.

It was cold in the barn. Pitch dark, too. I could make out only the whites of eyes and teeth. Vampiric was how he looked.

I wondered about spiders. Nests of wasps in the rafters. Rats in the corners. I shuddered against him. Perhaps he thought it was an orgasm.

Yes, oh yes. He had my hair in his fist, pulling my face away from his, gaining speed; he'd be done soon.

Merry and I in high school, how we'd laughed over the diagrams of the female body during sex education classes. Look, here is where the eggs are; here is where the baby grows.

Ejaculation, erections; we blushed at those words, imagining the boys we knew, trying and trying not to picture their penises. They didn't even teach us girls that we had a way to our own pleasure. That we might fuck for any other reason than to procreate or please a man.

Look, Merry had said, snickering at the splayed female torso, legless and truncated, just a great red gaping hole. It's like an open mouth, she said. Like someone screaming for help.

Mrs. Foster shushed us and pulled the baby out of the plastic woman on her desk.

It is settled: I will leave Merry and Sam to their island paradise. I will return to the life I have waiting for me, the life I have built and made beautiful with nothing but sheer force of will. I've achieved, haven't I? More than most. Brown University, Harvard, one covetable role after the next. A partner in the firm, a life in London—well, it can't get better, can it? This is the stuff of dreams.

And what has Merry done with her life? Found a husband and given birth. As though that qualifies as success!

I am not Merry. This is not my life. And my God—after the other night, that awful and indelible moment when I felt what she must feel and revel in every time she mistreats her son—well, if that is what it means to be Merry Hurley, I thank the heavens I am not, nor will ever be, her.

His body convulsed against me. He pulled out and came quickly over my chest in thick bursts.

I could hear the ferocious beating of his heart, the exertion required for his pleasure.

I imagine your wife doesn't let you do that, I said coolly.

In the dark he found his clothes. I heard the zipper of his jeans.

You're right about that, he said.

He bent down to kiss me on the mouth. So we'll need to do this again.

He grabbed his jacket from off the floor and left. I wiped myself with my shirt and slipped on my coat. I walked back across the field, naked underneath, the soft echo of birds in the dawn, the tickle of grass under my feet.

Yes, I will leave. But first, I will see to it that she cannot hurt Conor again.

Sam

Italy, Frank was saying. We were sitting in the kitchen, each of us standing with a mug of coffee in hand. She was smiling, more chipper than she's been in days. Like nothing happened and we're just a couple of old friends having a chat.

Good, good.

Well, I leave on Friday, she said. The flight takes me directly to Florence and from there I'll pick up a car. I hear it's the best time to visit, after the crowds.

Merry was nodding.

Anyway, Frank continued, I have had a wonderful time here, and I hope I haven't overstayed my welcome too much. I really didn't want to cause any trouble, she said.

Merry said nothing.

It's been good to have you, I chimed in.

I left the women and headed outside to the barn, pretending to look for tools, but really just needing a drink. Something bothering me. An idea not yet fully formed.

The doctor had called a few days back.

Simple issue, he said, relatively easy to solve with a prescription. Should fix the problem.

It's not a big issue, he reiterated, to be reassuring.

I took a long drink and left the barn. I looked back into the house, saw the women standing very close, their heads bent together, as though in conspiracy.

Oligospermia. Low sperm count.

Not a big deal. Not a big deal at all.

Karl's front door burst open across the way. Freja came running out as though she was being chased.

What's happening? I called.

She ran over, breathless, shining with excitement.

Ebba, she said, Ebba is getting her baby.

She took my hand and pulled me along with her. We ran across the fields, down to Mr. Nilssen's place. Come, she urged.

I followed her around the back to the stables, where Nilssen was crouched down a short distance from one of his mares. She was on the ground, calm and unmoving, as a slippery white membrane made its way slowly out of her body.

Ebba, I said. Now I understood.

Karl arrived with Elsa, said something in Swedish to Nilssen, who nodded.

She has been desperate to watch a birth, Elsa explained, nodding to Freja.

The stables smelled of rust and hay and blood, animal smells and human. It reminded me of something from childhood, which I pushed away.

The horse reared up suddenly onto her legs. She stood a few moments, then eased herself gently back to the ground, this time rolling onto her back. She was groaning now, a low moan of pain. Inside the membrane, blood and liquid and a dark shadow of a foal's hoof.

Freja was riveted to the spot, neither particularly afraid or repulsed. My stomach churned. Ebba was stiff, waiting. From her udders, milk trickled slowly out. More of the membrane had pushed through, two forelegs now. One had pierced its white covering.

Nilssen had done this many times before. He moved behind Ebba and put his hands gently to the encased foal, pulling at the legs. His overalls were slicked already with the secretions of birth and suffering.

Out, out it came. Human and animal, up close it's all the same. Merry giving birth was primal and monstrous, crying and grunting. But out of her stormed life. My son. Mine, harbored inside like a secret that grows and moves until it takes on a life of its own.

Freja gasped, a little cry that echoed against the concrete walls of the stables. The foal was born. Limp and murky, a pile of bones and flesh blanketed under the remains of the white membrane.

Nilssen observed, waited for signs of breath or life. He touched a hand to the foal's body, felt for something, muttered in Swedish, tried again.

Elsa had tears in her eyes. Karl took Freja's hand in his. All was quiet.

Ebba turned her head to look, to nudge at the body of her newborn foal.

A nagging question popped into my mind just as Nilssen pronounced it.

The foal was stillborn.

Frank

I folded the letter I'd written to Sam and slipped it into an envelope, which I wedged between the pages of a book beside my bed. There, something for the final day. I've written down everything I know. How Merry deliberately hurts Conor. How she leaves him alone in the middle of the woods while she runs off. I've warned him as best I can. What happens next is a matter for him, not me.

I am glad to be leaving soon. We are all relieved, and me most of all. I let myself get carried away. I lost myself for a while, didn't I, in shimmering, silly mirages. From far away they look like what you want, but up close it's only a trick of light and water. Nothing is real.

Merry's life, she can believe in it perhaps, but I know the truth. And maybe that's enough. Maybe that's all I need. I will wish her well. I will wish her happiness. But I will leave.

Earlier, I spoke to my father on the phone. It's about that time; he's worked through the last of the money I sent him a few months ago.

You're a good girl, Frances, he said. Your mother would have been proud.

He only says this to make me more generous with the amounts I transfer to his account. Well, I've never needed much from him. Hardly the father figure a girl hopes for. But he did teach me a few tricks.

Merry in the hallway was tying her shoelaces, getting ready for her hike. She's been attached to Conor for several days now, keeping him to herself. Putting on a great show for us all. Every time I reach for him she sweeps him up and says, No no, Mama needs her hugs. She really is too much sometimes. I ache for him, the feel of his plump skin, smooth and soft, his smell, the way he smiles and melts all of my insides.

Well. I'll get used to it. I'll fill the empty space with other things. Italy will be a glorious start. And from there—the whole world awaits. What more could I ask for?

We'll be off now, Merry said.

She was in a peculiar mood suddenly, quite distracted.

Or nervous. Maybe that was it.

Sam, off today in Stockholm, he seemed preoccupied too. I didn't dare ask why.

I must give up trying to understand them. I must leave them to their uneasy universe of make-believe and find my way in another.

Some hours later, packing the last of my things into my suitcase, I heard the scream as it shattered the silence and sent the birds scattering into the heavens. The sound of unimaginable despair. Relentless as it echoed back and forth, back and forth, a reverberation of horror, a cry without end.

I ran to the front door. There was Merry, charging wildly out through the trees.

Frank, she screamed, Frank, oh God, Frank, something has happened.

Something terrible has happened.

Sam

I left my appointment and went straight to the nearest bar.

Double, I said.

I held in my hands the page that had been printed out for me. Looked like ink blotches from a faulty printer.

This is accurate.

Yes, sir. It's pretty definitive.

Same again, I said to the barman.

It took the edge off but nothing more. Still it raged.

I'd lied and said I was going to be in Stockholm today for a pitch presentation. I'd kissed Merry goodbye and said it. I love you.

Looking into her eyes, trying to see behind them.

I love you, Sam, she said. I love you more than anything.

Love. What is love but the prelude to betrayal?

I told you so, my mother will hiss. And she's the worst of them all.

Son, son, you're all I have. You're the only man I need.

Lying on her bed in her negligee, everything visible, everything outlined in the soft light, curves and peaks, all the mysterious parts you only know in two dimensions, from screens and pages, and now here before your eyes. A teenage boy, confused and lost.

Come here. She'd pat the blanket. Come here and comfort your mother.

Bile is the taste in my mouth, the smell and the feeling all over. Just bile. Revulsion. I'd picked up the prescription, those little yellow portals to success. And then.

I'd thought about it for a few days and called the doctor back.

But how did it happen the first time? I asked.

You weren't on medication then?

An awkward silence on the other end.

I'm sure there's an explanation, he said, to fill the space.

Suddenly it was obvious. How could it be anything else?

In my hands, I balled the doctor's printout into my fist.

I ran to the bathroom and vomited out my insides; other men's piss wetting my knees. My phone fell out of my pocket onto the tiles. I wiped it. Sixteen missed calls. All from Merry.

I vomited twice more and drove home. As I approached, I saw the flashing lights. Ambulance. Two police cars.

The front door was open. Merry on the sofa, a policewoman opposite her, taking notes. Frank was in the kitchen, making coffee for the police.

Merry held a hand over her mouth when she saw me. She stood up, came toward me, her face stricken and white. I saw her register my state, my smell—vomit and booze, but she just shook her head.

He's gone, Sam, he's gone.

In the bedroom, Conor was on the bed. Pale and small.

Blue. Cold. Dead.

★ ★ ★

Death makes humans small, babies smaller still. Doll-like and otherworldly, the humanness all but vanished. I was reminded of the death masks of the Middle Ages, of the cabinet of shrunken heads I'd seen as a student at the British Museum, the collector Henry Wellcome's personal stash of morbid and grotesque curiosities from around the world. I'd gone to the museum on a date. The girl was called Sinead—she came from Cork and played the bodhrán.

Jesus. Jesus Christ.

Conor, I said, like he might wake up. Conor.

Merry was on the bed, dazed, unable to focus. Her eyes were glazed; her words made no sense.

She had taken him for a hike, she said. Just like always. Somewhere on the way back, she had stopped; she noticed that Bear had dropped. She had picked him up. She had looked inside and seen Conor. Then she knew that something was wrong, that he was not breathing or moving.

But, but, she stammered. I tried to resuscitate him, I tried to—I tried to revive him, but.

I think he was already dead, she said. Dead. He was cold. He was—his skin was weird, like wax. I—I ran home and called the ambulance, but. I don't know, I don't know what's happening.

I looked at the baby on the bed and had the urge to throw up again. I held my mouth.

In the living room, the police or paramedics. Frederick and Linda, their names marked on little badges pinned to their red uniforms. Linda smelled of eucalyptus and old coffee. She had copper hair tied in two braids.

We are very sorry for your loss, she said.

Yes. Frederick nodded. It is hard to understand something like this. As we were discussing with your wife, it is very possible that it is sudden infant death syndrome. This is unfortunately quite common. Or, even a fever is a serious thing for a baby, a virus of some kind. These are the most likely scenarios, but of course we will need to investigate this further.

Linda nodded. To rule out all possibilities for the death.

She looked at all three of us and tucked her notebook away into her jacket pocket.

I was still drunk or stone cold sober, I couldn't tell. All the voices were a blur, all the actions, too, moving parts but nothing in a way that made any sense.

Son, my son.

I was only numb.

Frank

I am broken.

All of us are. I am trying to make myself invisible, trying to offer tea and food and tissues and otherwise stay out of sight. I am afraid to make too much noise, afraid to take up space here, when the house is so full of grief. Terrible, unthinkable grief.

I am inconsolable. I cannot stop the tears.

Conor is gone. Conor is dead.

Merry is strangely silent—numb, I'm sure, although . . . well. She is how she is. She has always been strange around emotion. Disconnected from it. Now she is trancelike. Mostly just sitting cross-legged on the couch or curled in a ball on the bed in her room, motionless and staring into the abyss. I brought her a cup of mint tea and set it down. She hardly flinched.

I'm sorry. I'm so sorry, I said.

Nothing.

Sam's outside, he's pacing back and forth, smoking in full view, taking a swig of whiskey from the bottle. Letting all his secrets out. What does it matter now? What could possibly matter.

I took him a black coffee, how he likes it. I didn't say anything and neither did he. He drank from the cup and stared out at the lake where we had swum not too many weeks ago. There is no more sun. No more warmth.

Everyone else has left the house. The paramedics took the baby, little Conor—the worst thing I've ever seen—they wrapped him in a blanket and walked him to the ambulance parked outside. They opened the back doors but we did not see anything more. Whether they strapped him to something or set him in a bed or a box. I shudder to think, but they hurried him away, vanished him into thin air as though he might have only ever been a dream.

Oh, that beautiful, dear little boy. Light and love, the purest incarnation of joy. How I loved him. How I loved him so.

My hands, my hands will not stop trembling.

Merry

The house is silent, every day, nothing but silence. The inside of the house the same as when you lie floating on your back in the ocean, ears under and eyes open; nothing to hear but the sound of breath and cold hearts beating. Empty and bereft. There's been a heat wave, a few strange days of baking sticky heat, cooking us inside the walls, sweating out the juices and the tears. The glass traps the heat, the sunlight floods into the rooms but the feeling isn't lightness, it's dark. The worst dark you can imagine.

All is numb. Dead inside, dead out.

It is done.

The baby is gone.

How is it possible.

No.

What did I do.

What did I do to our boy?

I am sick with it. The guilt. The awfulness.

I don't deserve to live.

The first time I held him, I felt certain it could not be human. Dark, withered little thing, pink and wriggling and scaled.

He's beautiful, Sam said, but he wasn't. Newborns are terrifying, feral and squirming, animal-like, eyeless creatures in search of a teat. He came early, charging his way out of my body, cutting and tearing as he went. The violence is unthinkable, but they refuse to call it anything but a miracle. The midwife pulled him headfirst from my split-open self and placed him on my breast. He was tiny, held in two cupped hands; sum of all our parts. Life the miracle and then death, the end of it all.

He is lost. We have lost him.

The thoughts float but won't settle. Why won't they? Why can't I remember? The last days morph into shapes and colors, smiles and winks; the feeling of happiness and certainty—a way forward, a plan—but now. This. Only this.

But did I? Could I? Was it possible? The statement I gave to the police officer and watched her scratch into her notepad. Written in blood, sins of the flesh, secrets and lies. Lies, so many lies.

I had no choice. I willed it and made it happen.

Did I. Didn't I.

The baby, the baby. Warm and then cold. Here and then not. Alive and then vanished. As if by magic, as if by some dark magic. Witches in the forest, a curse upon your head, a hex to make you suffer. A split second, and the scene is changed, forever and irrevocably.

I was outside myself.

I am always there, it seems.

Parts displaced. A broken woman.

Now I am broken all the way through. All the king's horses and all the king's men couldn't put Merry together again.

I did it. I did it.

* * *

Please, no, I begged the dead body. I screamed, but the trees stood stiff and unmoved. In my body, an ache, profound and guttural; something is missing. Something is lost. Something will undo me. It will all come crashing down.

Sam! Sam! Everything holding me together is gone.

I can hardly breathe. I cannot stop throwing up, nothing there but yellow and air, but out it comes, every time I think of it. Every time I think of the moment.

Sam will not touch me. He is in shock, literally, as if it is electricity in his veins. He is an animal. Pacing, furious, waiting to attack, to set his grief in motion.

I don't get it, he says, I don't.

Fever, he says. Could he have had a cold? That you didn't notice. A temperature. Should he have been outside in the— Was it too cold? Too hot? Was the— Did he get jolted somehow too violently, over the path while you— His voice breaks and he shakes his head. He bites his fist.

Me, I bite down on my lip. I taste the blood. I suck it back in.

We won't know anything for a few days, that's all they said, that's all we know. We can only wait. Exist in the hollow space.

We will always be here now.

Sam

Karl visited today. Elsa, too. They brought a basket of food: a roasted chicken, a loaf of fresh bread, a bag of red grapes from the market. They'd seen the ambulance, the police cars. Someone must have broken the news.

Mr. Nilssen dropped by with a small spruce tree in a green plastic bucket.

Perhaps you could plant this for the baby, he said. It is what I did for my wife, when she passed.

I invited him to have a coffee with me and we sat together in silence, the tree in my lap where Conor once might have sat.

We were married fifty-two years, he said sadly.

The house is a tomb for the dead. The doors are closed. The curtains drawn. No light let in or out. I can't think. Can't feel. He's gone, but I don't know if what this is counts as grief. Devastating loss. Or something else.

Loss. It's loss, because all is lost. Everything that was good and right turned unthinkable and horrifying.

I have been betrayed.

Frank said she would take the car and shop for our groceries.

She returned and set a plate in front of me, cleared it again hours later, mostly untouched. She brought coffee. She set out sleeping pills in little dishes I didn't know we owned, and drew shut the curtains when it turned dark.

I can't eat. Can't sleep. Can't cry. Sometimes I lie still long enough for the exhaustion to wash over me, something between sleep and waking. I see in this fog Conor, Conor calling for me, Da da da, and me running to find his crib empty, his body stiff on the shelf above the bed; a taxidermy baby next to the stuffed giraffe and a sad-looking Bear and Biscuit.

Worse yet, the waking dream that is no dream at all. An empty crib. A pile of diapers on the changing table, folded and forever to remain unused. Son. Child. Gone.

All of it voided.

I feel robbed. Of everything that was supposed to be ahead.

Love. Family. A perfect Swedish childhood for my son, enveloped in goodness and shine. Tricycles and then bicycles and fishing in the lake, Legos, and playing ball and licking ice-cream cones by the cold gray Baltic Sea. Boat trips around the archipelago, island hopping and dips into the cool water from the sunbaked rocks. Campfires and ski trips and sledding in the winter snow, popcorn at the movies and dinosaur collections lining the windowsill of his room, and midsummer picnics in the park, dancing around a maypole with fair-headed friends whose sisters he would later love. Three Christmas stockings, or maybe four, filled with knickknacks, initialed and identical and hanging in a row; Easter egg hunts and first teeth kept in a little box and exchanged for coins. Grazed knees and first dates and first kisses, boys' trips and fishing trips and always and forever the solidness of that one unbreakable thing. Father and son.

My heart is cut in two.

★ ★ ★

Merry, Merry. I walk around her. I can't bring myself to touch her skin. I clench and unclench my fist.

Not yet. Not yet.

I haven't called my mother. I sat with my phone in my hands and found her number. I stared at it but did not press call.

Your grandson is dead.

Conor is gone.

I have some terrible news.

My mind is a cloud. Too many moving parts, too many questions without answers.

I loved him, he was mine and I loved him.

Son. My son. And now, no more.

A double blow. And which is worse?

Natural causes. Sudden infant death, the paramedics said, but what is natural about a baby turning up dead?

It is all a confusion.

And where were you, sir?

I lied without hesitation; this is how easy it is. The instinct to cover up the truth. The refusal to name your shame.

There was a noise—ringing, screeching bells. Furious and shrill.

I looked up. Through the glass, I saw two policemen outside the front door.

Frank

They came for Merry. They took her away.

They did not cuff her as they ushered her into the back seat of the waiting car. She did not scream or resist.

What's happening, Sam said, what's going on?

We need to talk to your wife, they said. In connection with your son's death.

But why are you—

Sir, they said. You can follow us to the station.

Now we are here. My hand on Sam's arm, gentle and reassuring.

We'll get to the bottom of this. We'll figure this out.

He is reeling in shock; of course he is. We all are.

As if what happened with Conor wasn't wretched enough. Now this. Devastating. Unthinkable. The most inconceivable information to process. No, it is not to be understood. Not at all.

I watch Sam's hand, clenching and unclenching into a tight fist, knuckles white, veins throbbing, wanting to shatter something. Someone.

Let me go and get you a coffee, I offer.

I don't want a fucking coffee. He pulls his arm away, stands and paces the floor, click clack of flip-flops on the linoleum; he'd grabbed the first pair of shoes he could find in the hallway when the police came to the door.

It isn't as bad as one imagines, the police station. Well lit and recently refurbished. Clean. Modern. Absent of shrieking hookers and bleeding addicts. A poster calls for new members to join the Swedish Police Choir.

I watch the other people in the waiting area. An elderly woman, laughing into her phone. A young couple whispering as they fill out an official form.

Another poster, *Sweden Welcomes Refugees*. Earlier, a policeman hauled in a drunken man clad in leathers. He had a swastika tattooed on his neck, and wore dark glasses as though he were blind.

Sam sits back down again. Jesus, he says. It's like the fucking Twilight Zone, the last few days.

I think I know a lawyer I could call, I say.

He shakes his head. I don't need a lawyer. I need some fucking answers.

They won't tell us a thing. They have Merry somewhere, locked in a room. They won't let Sam see her yet. Perhaps that's for the best.

A policeman passes by the waiting area and Sam calls out to him.

Officer, please. Can someone explain to me—

I'm sorry, sir, he says. They will come to you as soon as they are able to give you more information.

He sits. He reeks of alcohol, cigarettes. His clothes are pungent with sweat, his breath foul. I pity him. Even after the way he has treated me, I pity this man.

His whole world has been shattered.

The bubble is burst.

Merry

The detective asked one of her colleagues to fetch her a bottle of water. When it arrived, she set it down in front of me. She smiled kindly. She had very short nails, no wedding band, no jewelry.

It can be very difficult, can't it?

What?

Motherhood.

I watched her.

Alone, so isolated over in Sigtuna, a new baby. Yes. Very hard indeed.

I swallowed a sip of water. I looked up at the fluorescent lights.

Cancer, I said. These lights will give you cancer.

The detective opened a file. New York, she said. That's where you and your husband moved from, before you came to Sweden.

Yes.

It's a wonderful city, New York. Very vibrant. Always something to do. The city that never sleeps, right?

I nodded.

Well, Sigtuna must be quite the change, I'm sure. Maybe not the best choice.

She sighed. There are not so many Americans who move

here, she said. Not many at all. Culturally, I imagine it is just too strange. We are very different people, the Swedes and the Americans. Chalk and cheese. Day and night.

She shuddered slightly. I couldn't live in the States, she said. I know I would absolutely hate it. I would want to run away any chance I could get.

She looked at me. She read something in her file.

Do you feel strange here, Merry? Lonely. Depressed. Desperate?

I looked at her.

It would be completely understandable if you did. It would be absolutely normal.

The room was silent, not the slightest interference from the outside world. I wondered if Sam was on the other side of the walls. Waiting. Worrying. Fuming. What had they told him? What did he know?

The truth will set you free. This is what they say. But what is the truth? I cannot even recall.

I don't want a lawyer, I told the detective when she asked. She looked surprised, but not displeased.

She sighed now. Mrs. Hurley. It will really be in your favor to talk to me.

What did you say your name was? I said.

Detective Bergstrom.

Yes, now I remember. Detective Bergstrom.

Merry, she said. I want to help you. Understand?

I shook my head. I was cold. I was shivering. I wanted to go back home.

Home. Where the heart is. Where you belong.

Merry, she said.

I looked up. I don't understand at all. My son has just died. I don't know why I'm here in a police station.

My mother slapped me across the face every time she caught me out with a lie.

I hate liars, Merry.

Well, you married one, I said, or sometimes, if I really wanted to be cruel: Your whole face is a lie.

I didn't mean it. I didn't mean it. I didn't really mean it.

The detective was watching me, the way they do, sizing me up from all angles. Making judgments about what I might be capable of doing. I doubt she could tell. You seldom can.

The baby, dead and cold, in my arms, his breath extinguished. Just like that, he doesn't exist. Problem solved. I think that was my first thought.

Be careful what you wish for, you just might get it. Was that my mother too?

I was shaking.

I had gone for a hike. A run. I was happy. It was a good day, wasn't it? Wasn't I feeling good? Frank. Frank would leave. I would stay. I had won. I had Sam. Me and Sam. Just us, always better when it was just us.

A clean slate, a do-over. No more secrets.

It was not possible. It could not be. In my mind, there was the forest clearing, but it would not clear. I ran hard. Felt the muscles stretch and burn, running away, running toward. From above, I'd looked down at the lake, a ghostly mirror to the overcast sky, no line to separate one from the other, water from horizon, beginning from end, good from bad. A dance of light and matter; a shimmering horizon that's so close, almost within reach and yet so unbearably far away. Always retreating.

Hiraeth, that's the word, Welsh in origin and untranslatable in English. *Hiraeth,* a poem on the tongue, beautiful and wretched. Homesickness for a home you can never return to, or that never was. Yes, yes, this is the feeling. I was trying to get back, wasn't I, to some earlier version of me. Of us. The emptiness would go.

Once more I would exist. Me. Me!

Yes, that was it.

Wasn't it?

The detective leaned forward. Merry, she said. Listen very carefully.

Why was she still talking? Why did she have so many questions?

Merry, she said. You're here because we think that your baby was murdered.

Sam

The police have asked me for names and numbers to confirm my whereabouts at the time of death. I showed them my parking receipts.

Sir, we'd still like those names.

Murder. The autopsy points to a possible murder. *Autopsy, murder.* These are words now. These are words in my vocabulary.

Homicidal smothering. Death by suffocation. This is what they say. A pillow, a hand. More than likely, the blue baby blanket that was in Conor's stroller, keeping him warm in the woods.

What are you saying?

Mr. Hurley, when it comes to infant deaths of this nature, it is very difficult to distinguish sudden infant death syndrome from deliberate suffocation.

Deliberate, I said.

The medical examiner has found evidence of petechial hemorraghing, which in itself is not necessarily enough to rule your son's death a murder. But it is also enough to warrant further investigation.

Murder, I said again.

We think someone may have intentionally killed your son.

How many hours had passed? Was it the same day or the one after? I looked at my shoes. My feet were cold. My breath was rancid. Things in my brain floated, collided, shattered on impact. Nothing would stick.

From the other side of the table, the questions kept coming.

Sir, was your wife, to your knowledge, depressed?

Sir, was she on any medication?

Has she had any issues in the past? Depressive episodes. Psychotic breakdowns. History of violence. History of mental illness. Was she bonded to the baby?

Was it unusual for her to take him into the forest?

What was her behavior in the days leading up to?

What were her words when she called?

Merry, Merry is a suspect. The one who was with him at the time of his death. Also: something about evidence of prior abuse. Merry. Perfect maternity incarnate. Everything I wanted. Everything I thought I had.

The last few days morph into one horror after the next, a kaleidoscope of too many terrible things.

The policeman left the room.

Hello, I am Detective Bergstrom.

A woman came in, shook my hand. She was wearing a gray pantsuit. She did not smile.

I'd like to ask you some questions, she said.

I've just answered a whole fucking load of questions.

I have only a few more.

She sat down opposite me. The chair creaked.

You do understand what's happening here, Mr. Hurley.

No, I said. I really fucking don't.

Right, she said. Okay. Well, we have reason to suspect that your son, Conor, might not have died from natural causes. We think he might have been murdered.

Son. Every time they say it I wince.

You said you were out of Sigtuna at the time, she said. And you were where?

At a meeting. For work.

She looked at me. She made a note.

Your wife was the one who was looking after your son. This is what she said.

Yes.

So you understand why we're questioning her about your son's death. Your son's suspicious death, she added.

I waited. She was watching me, tracking every movement, every flicker of the eye, every twitch of the facial muscles. Eyes up and to the left, a lie. Eyes down and to the left, a memory. Nonverbal communication, the truest kind. The body can't lie. It hasn't got a chance.

Mr. Hurley, she said, can you think of any reason why Merry might have wanted to harm your son?

I clenched my fist, shook my head.

Was there any behavior you noticed that was suspicious? Was she doing anything strange or unusual, anything that concerned you? Were there ever any signs that she was deliberately hurting your son?

I shook my head. I could not speak.

Did you ever notice any bruises, any signs he was injured?

Jesus, I said, I think I'm going to be sick.

One final question, sir. Would your wife have had any reason to want your son out of the way?

Merry

Do you see how we're confused, Merry?

The detective is exasperated. She wants me to say it. She wants to go home.

I do too. There is a lot to do. Today must be a laundry day. It's time to sow the seeds for the turnips and the radishes. I think Frank has her flight booked to leave.

Detective Bergstrom pushes a file in front of me. An X-ray.

Let's talk about this. This is your son's arm. His right arm.

See here. She points with her pen. It's a slight hairline fracture to the bone of the right ulna.

I wince. I look away.

No, please look at it, Detective Bergstrom says.

This is old. The medical examiner thinks it goes back a few months. Is there anything you can think of that might explain it? An injury. A day he got hurt, a day he fell. Off the bed, out of his crib. These things happen, of course.

I shudder; I shake my head. I feel that familiar twist inside. Poor baby. Poor little boy.

Merry, Detective Bergstrom says, there were other things the medical examiner discovered during the investigation.

★ ★ ★

She looks at a photograph on the table and then turns it over.

I won't show you, she says. There is no need, perhaps.

He found bruising, Merry. Signs of trauma. Again, these were inflicted some time before his death. They appear to be . . . deliberate. Beyond the usual childhood scratches and scrapes. Something done with the intention to hurt.

She leans in close, too close. I smell her lunch. Onions and fish.

Merry. I'm sure you see where I am going with this. What this looks like for us. The conclusions we are drawing. I'm sure you can see why I need to hear the truth from you.

Hold it together. Do not crack. Do not break. Do not let anyone inside.

She takes a sip of coffee. She offers to have someone fetch me a cup.

No, thank you.

They are so civilized here. Even in a police station. The room is small and bright; table, chairs, no windows for a desperate person to throw themselves out of, no pens left lying about to launch into a jugular. A box. A coffin, throbbing with white noise and questions.

Let's go back, she says. To the beginning. Your move here, what was it—a year ago?

A little more than that.

You were pregnant.

Yes.

You wanted to move here.

I swallow. No.

Your husband's idea.

Yes.

He had talked about it for a while—this was something he always planned to do?

No.

So it was because he lost his job at the university.

No, I say. He wanted to leave. To do something else.

She shakes her head. He was fired. Dismissed for—what does it say here?—repeated misconduct with female students . . . sexual harassment, accusations of inappropriate sexual relations.

Does this sound about right?

I open my palms and stare. A short heart line, I was told once. I don't recall what it means. I pull on the skin to lengthen it; a different fortune now.

This is the official statement from Columbia University, she insists.

I say nothing.

The wife always knows, right? The wife always has that sixth sense.

Still I say nothing.

You have friends here? A job?

I shake my head.

And your husband. He works. Travels a lot, he said. It wasn't unusual, was it, that you were left alone with Conor?

I guess.

She makes a note. Might he be having an affair over here?

I bite my lip.

So, husband has an affair, loses his career, packs you off to a new life somewhere far, far away. You have no friends, no job, no family around—correct? No one else is here in Sweden?

I don't need anyone. I don't need more.

She ignores this.

So you're alone. Stuck out on that reserve—which, let's be honest, is okay in the summer, but God help you come the winter months. Well, even the best of us would go a little crazy, don't you think? So isolated. So cut off from everything and everyone.

I say nothing.

Detective Bergstrom nods.

I would. I would for sure. And I think maybe you did too.

Crazy. A madwoman who needs to be locked away. A woman who harms her child. Filicide. Infanticide. Which is it? What will it be called? Monster Mom! No doubt that will be the headline. They like alliteration, in these cases. Something catchy.

Did you, Merry? Did you love your baby? Did you want him?

That squeezing in the gut. Yes, yes, I say, I love my son. I love him.

Liar liar, a voice says. *Pants on fire.*

It is too hot in the room. I pull at my sweater, try to let in some air. My stomach groans. I need to eat.

Of course you loved him, she says. Of course.

We are quiet a moment. I sip some water.

Funny thing about love, though, she says. It isn't always enough, is it.

She is watching me, eyes boring into my being. I wonder what darkness she sees.

★ ★ ★

Sometimes it feels like a trap, doesn't it? she says. Love. Marriage. Motherhood. It takes so much. It leaves so little.

My mother's face, frozen in a grotesque plastic mask. My father's, desperate and pleading. Let me go, Maureen, let me leave.

Some of the greatest cruelties are the ones married people inflict upon each other.

I hate you, I screamed, I hate you both.

His brains splattered over the study lamp—why did she make me look? Marriage, she'd said. This is what you get for thirty years of marriage.

What is it they say? The opposite of love isn't hate, but indifference. Hate is what you feel when love betrays you.

I never wanted to be a mother, Maureen said. It was your father who wanted a child—but he was imagining that it would be a son.

Oh, Conor, oh, Conor, whatever did I do?

Please stop now, I say. Please.

I can't stop, Merry, Detective Bergstrom says. A child is dead. Your child.

My whole body, shaking with tears and terror.

Some women just aren't meant to be mothers.

Or don't deserve it.

Opposite me, Detective Bergstrom waits.

He wasn't sick, Merry. He didn't die of natural causes. But you know that, don't you?

Yes, yes. The blanket at his head. Bear, Biscuit, a pillow. My own full body weight—yes, yes, how many times hadn't I dared it. Willed it. The things I did to that boy, that baby.

Think it, will it, make it so. From the start, child unwanted, willed out of existence, a secret wrapped in a blanket. I had planned him dead and now it was so.

Merry, Detective Bergstrom says again. You know that.

No.

You do. You do. You know because you were there.

No.

Do it. Do it.

The dare and then the deed. Baby in arms, one last time. Solve it. Make it go away.

That way we could start over. That way it could go back to before. Before Christopher. Before the lies. *I know,* he'd written, but what did that mean? I needed it to be fixed.

Just us.

Sam and Merry. Merry and Sam.

Merry, Detective Bergstrom says. We both know you were there. And we both know you killed him.

Sam

Frank drove us back home from the police station. I didn't speak and neither did she. I held my fists. I clenched my jaw, ground down on my teeth. I pinched my skin, felt the sting. Still there, I thought, but only just.

At home, I went straight to the barn, drank back a few shots of whiskey from the bottle, felt the slow burn of warmth and obliteration.

Merry's face as they bundled her off in the police car. Murder, they said. We think your son was murdered.

Frank put her head around the door of the barn. Anything I can do, you just say.

I shook my head. Just leave me alone.

I sank to the floor, held the bottle against me. On my phone, a message.

Where were you today?

Malin.

My head swam; the floor danced beneath my feet.

I must have drunk myself to sleep. In the morning, there was a blanket covering me and a pillow under my head. Frank. I got up, too fast. My head was pounding, loud and angry. My fingers were frozen stiff. I went inside. I put on the coffee. I looked around the house. A mausoleum. That's what it is now. Death inside walls. A memorial to the dead and the death of dreams. There is no point to the house now. No point to any of it.

I burned the coffee and drank it anyway. I sat and stared at a photograph stuck up on the fridge with a magnet shaped like a pretzel. Merry, Conor, and me, a shot from this last summer. A trip to the Gothenburg Archipelagos. Ferries and lakes and ice creams in the sun. We rode the ferry to Donsö, walked around the little fishing village and stopped for coffee and pastries on the pier. In Styrsö we ate oysters, in Brännö, it was swimming at the beach, dunking Conor's toes in the water, laughing as his face scrunched up in delight at the cold.

Smiling, happy faces.

It feels so pure here, I said to Karl once. Like nothing bad ever happens or could happen.

He laughed. You know how many people here are depressed or alcoholics? he said. Or depressed alcoholics.

Come on, I said.

And the weather, he said. That alone is enough to kill you.

I thought it was a dream come true.

I took the empty coffee mug and hurled it at the window. The mug broke, but the window did not.

Frank ran into the room. Are you all right, Sam?

I'm great, I said. Just great.

She offered to make some eggs. You need it, she said. You really need to eat.

She set a plate down on the counter, knife, fork, napkin. She poured more coffee, then smelled it and threw it out.

I'll make a fresh pot, she said.

She found a broom and swept up the remnants of the broken mug.

You don't have to do it, I said. Leave it.

She swept anyway. She emptied the pan into the trash and washed her hands.

Weren't you supposed to leave yesterday? I said. She nodded.

You missed your flight.

Didn't seem like a good time to go, she said. Merry needs me.

I snorted.

She served up the eggs, a slice of buttered rye toast. She set out a jar of blueberry jam. I stared at Merry's handwriting on the label. Another of her homemade feats.

A woman who makes her own goddamn jam, and she's suspected of killing her child.

I watched Frank move around the house, straightening up, trying to restore some kind of order. Felt a kick of something, maybe regret. I could hear her behind the bathroom door. Sobbing. I think of her with Conor, a natural like I've never seen. As though she were born to mother and love.

The doorbell rang. Karl.

I can come back, he said. If it's a bad time.

It's all a bad time, I said.

He sighed. I understand. I just thought maybe you'd like some company. A walk or something. A distraction.

Hold on, I said. I ducked out of the house and slipped into the barn.

I held up the bottle of whiskey.

Even better, he said.

We walked along the dirt road that links our properties, then off the reserve and across the road toward the forest trails.

I know a spot, he said. Elsa and I go there often.

We walked briskly, the half-empty bottle swinging in my hands.

There are no words, really, he said.

No.

We are so sorry. So sorry for this terrible loss.

We came to a hilltop, a clearing that overlooks the lake. Shielded by a circle of trees, soft moss underfoot, blueberries popping as you stepped over them.

We sat on a log, dead wood from a tree, rotted or felled. I handed Karl the bottle and he took a swig. He was unshaven, rugged-looking. It suited him and I wondered why I noticed.

He handed the bottle back to me and I swallowed.

They came for Merry yesterday, I said.

Merry?

They're saying the death was suspicious. That it looks like Conor might have been murdered. Smothered.

My God, Sam.

I shook my head. They found signs of petechiae— Christ. I can't even say it. Makes me want to throw up.

But Merry, he said, incredulous because of course he'd witnessed it too. Mother of the fucking year.

She was the one looking after him when it happened, I said.

I took another sip, long and slow this time. The day was cold; a thick fog hung over the lake. I shivered. I thought about telling him the other news.

No, not yet.

Take another drink, Karl said, and I did, grateful for the lubrication to the brain, the soft blur of thoughts and time. I saw a flash of Merry on our wedding day, promising herself to me. Merry in New York, coming home at strange hours. Big shoot, she'd explain, her face flushed. Then pregnant, a dream come true. A child, a chance. Family and happiness.

Taken now. She has taken it all.

Who would hurt a child? I said. Who would be so sick?

Still I couldn't imagine it.

Karl said nothing.

I took another sip. I coughed. I swallowed; spit and whiskey, all down the same hole.

They found other stuff, I said. Evidence of prior harm, they called it. Suspicious bruises, a fracture.

Bruises, I thought, suddenly remembering.

Karl cracked his knuckles. He leaned over and picked up the bottle, took a long drink.

Sam, he said. It's not my business. But a few times, Elsa mentioned something to me. About overhearing a lot of crying coming from your place. The afternoons that she was home early.

I waited.

He shrugged. I don't know. I'm only saying what she said. That there are cries and then there are cries. Different sounds. Different... causes. She said it a few times. How Conor was always crying. How it sounded like... Like it wasn't just teething. Like something bad was happening.

I looked at my hands. Clenched and unclenched.

Slowly, it is sinking in. I am sick to my stomach. So sick I want to reach in there with my bare hands like those Filipino faith healers I went once to Laguna to observe. Yes, I want to dig into the flesh with my fingers and pull out every strand of the bloody rot, the pain and the grief and the burning red rage that's lodged deep in the pit of my gut, sitting, sitting, marinating in the juices of Merry's betrayal.

Which is worse, the murder or the lie? In my mind, they are one.

Karl and I got back to the house just after the police had arrived.

Search warrant, Frank said. They came straight in.

Back and forth they went, officers with cameras and evidence bags, shoes booted with plastic covers to stop any transfer of evidence. Clip, snap. Cameras and flashes; the sum of our lives bagged and sent away for analysis.

I went into the bedroom. A man was pulling something out of one of Merry's drawers.

What is that? I demanded.

Looks like birth control, he said. He opened a plastic evidence bag and dropped the little wheel of pills inside.

Birth control. All those red days, those dewy-eyed

discussions of our baker's dozen—oh, Sam, I can't wait, the more the merrier.

It's all been a game. Everything. Nothing but Merry pretending. Putting on a show. Making me believe that all this was real.

Frank

I'm doing whatever I can to be useful. To stay out of the way, to be around if Sam decides that he needs me. Poor man. He is grieving twice. First for the dead child, now for the murderous wife. A shocking turn of events, an awful and tragic revelation. A woman hurting a child. It goes against all the laws of nature, doesn't it? An aberration.

I still cannot believe that he is gone, that beautiful, magical child.

He is everywhere in the house. His smell, his clothes, his little blocks of brightly colored wood. In the fridge, neat rows of uneaten baby meals, green and orange, pureed and ready to be spooned into his mouth. Vroom vroom, chuck-a-choo. The train or the fighter jet his favorite; he'd always open wide for those.

In the bathroom, plastic toys wait patiently on the rim of the tub, three big-eyed ducks that squeak and the blue elephant that squeezes soapy water from its trunk. Quack quack. Splish splash.

His socks, pulled off his toes, hidden in the cracks in the couch. His bottles, sterilized and stacked in a line in the cupboard, the brown teats overchewed and ready to be replaced. The board books, the bath books, the attachment for the stroller and the car seat, the activity mat on the floor, the soft smell of a half-eaten digestive biscuit spit up and abandoned somewhere only he could know. In the glass door, a line of handprints reflected in the sunlight, along with slobbery kisses planted and not yet washed away. There's not a corner of the house that does not contain him. Oh, it is agony, the cruelty of him being vanished from this world.

I cooked dinner tonight, a roast and vegetables—the last of the greens and carrots still salvageable from the garden. A big green salad, homemade vinaigrette.

As I tied Merry's striped red apron around my waist, I shuddered.

Where was she now? In a cell, in another interrogation. I know what she is accused of—I know the crimes of which she is guilty—and yet I pity her. My dearest friend. A desperate woman. A woman trapped by her own lies.

A lie is like a snowball, my mother always warned. The further you roll it, the bigger it will grow.

I doubt Carol uttered a single untrue word her entire life.

Sam came into the kitchen. What's this?

Sometimes a good meal helps, I said. Even just a little.

I lit the candles, I poured him a whiskey.

He sat down and I served up a plate of food. He took a bite. He chewed and swallowed, and the walls echoed back the sounds.

After a while he spoke. You know her.

I sighed. I thought I did.

★ ★ ★

He looked up sharply. You know her secrets, he said. He pointed at me with his knife. You know what she's been up to.

I must have looked as startled as I felt.

Yes, he spat, you knew, didn't you.

I swallowed, shook my head. I'm so sorry, Sam. I'm so sorry. I didn't want to interfere. I didn't—

She's my best friend.

Tell me, he spat. Tell me everything.

I took another breath.

All right, I said. It was soon after I arrived. One day, I walked past the room as she was changing Conor. She had him on his back. She stood over him a long time looking at him, and then she took his legs and she squeezed, she pinched. She was hurting him, it was clear; she was hurting him on purpose.

Sam said nothing, and I continued.

Conor cried, I said, and she pulled her hands back, and I walked away, because I couldn't believe what I had seen.

I was going to tell you, Sam—I was going to tell you everything, I swear. I wrote you a letter; I was planning to give it to you before I left. So you'd know. So you'd know it all.

He looked down at his fists, shaking his head. No, no, he muttered, you don't get it. I'm not talking about—

I'm so sorry, I said. About everything that's happened. I keep thinking if I'd said something sooner, well, maybe things would be different. Maybe Conor would still be here. Maybe the outcome of all this would have been something else.

He gave a cold laugh. He pushed away the plate. Your best friend, he said. Strangest fucking friendship I ever saw.

He stood up to fetch the whiskey. Thanks for a great dinner. He sneered. He took the bottle and stormed outside into the night, back to the barn like a bear to his den.

I scraped the uneaten food into the trash and slipped into my bedroom. I retrieved the letter I'd written to Sam, secreted away between the pages of my book. I opened it and scanned over what I'd written.

The physical abuse. The forest runs.

I walked back out to the table, where the candles still flickered, where the place settings still lay; the remnants of a cozy dinner for two. I held the letter over the glowing flame and waited for it to catch and burn.

Sam

I don't know how to contain it. It is consuming me. Relentless.

I bite down on my fist until the teeth crack the skin; bite and bite, teeth on shocked white bone. Yes. Pain is the singular comfort. When it feels too good, I stop.

In my childhood, Ida brought me back gifts of picture books when she and my grandfather visited her homeland, English translations of the Swedish classics. *Peter in Blueberry Land, The Children in the Forest, 100 Swedish Folk Tales.* They were magical adventures in snow and pine; intricate full-color illustrations of smiling children and woodland creatures. Occasionally there was a story of something frightening—the evil trolls or Huldra, the conniving forest wife. But mostly the fairy tales ended with a reassuring happily-ever-after. The blueberry boys and the blueberry king, helpful and playful and kind.

Oh, you will love Sweden, Ida used to say, in her lovely staccato way. It is very beautiful; it is a very wonderful place.

Can I go there someday? I asked her, and she kissed me and patted my hand.

Of course, dear boy, of course.

I loved Ida. So different from my mother, so warm and soft and kind. No ulterior motives in the doling out of her love.

★ ★ ★

Sweden, I said to Merry. Let's go to Sweden.

We'd just found out about the baby. There was a house waiting, a country full of strangers. Brave new world; we would make ourselves over and better.

I was suddenly excruciatingly aware of her body, the delicateness of her bones and the places she was softest and most vulnerable. Here, let me; no, don't lift that. A choreography of roles and purposes. Husband, wife, parents-to-be. I bought her the vitamins and the books, printed out from the internet the lists of things to be avoided: tuna, salmon, toxic detergents.

Like Ida's fairy tales, I built us a house of wood and stone, planted a garden of flowers and vines. We hatched our oracle child and imagined long lives ahead. Everything done wrong to us we would do right by him.

My mother always told me that my father beat me—I didn't remember it, but she insisted it was true. That's why I sent him away, she said.

She relented and gave me his full name on the morning of my twenty-first birthday, my hand pushing her head down into the pillows. I met him at a steakhouse off Michigan Avenue. Didn't need to ask if we were father and son.

She tricked me, he said. Got pregnant so I'd leave Beth.

He didn't leave Beth, or their three sons. And he didn't want to get to know me.

Nothing personal, he said, as we shook hands, then made for opposite ends of the DuSable Bridge.

He was nowhere for me, but I would be a constant for my own son. This is how I would be a better man.

* * *

I wanted to believe the Swedes were rubbing off on us. Wholesome. Everything in order, nice and civilized. Everything in moderation.

Lagom, as they say, just enough. Even at the airport, catching sight of a middle-aged pair of Swedes decanting bottles of spirits into their flasks first thing in the morning, or hearing the chants of neo-Nazi protests outside the Swedish parliament, or reading about men found with their daughters chained up in their basements, I refused to believe in anything but the good. I brought us here so we could be the people I wanted us to be, away from the city and its temptations, its memories and its relentless need to suck you in.

She could be the wife I needed. The mother my son deserved. Blank slate. That's what it was.

No, something else, too. A way to contain her. To keep her focused on what mattered.

All alone. No friends. No job. Just me.

Just us. Better that way.

I walked around the house, in and out of the rooms, a hamster in a maze. At the doorway of Conor's room, I stood. I could not go in. Instead, I locked myself away in the studio, watching hours and hours of my old unedited footage. Files marked by date, some just *Conor,* some going back all the way to his arrival in the world.

Day-old Conor, week-old Conor, Conor smiling and crying and sleeping. Older Conor laughing and clapping his hands, lying outside on the lawn, he and Merry side by side, the baby nestled against the crook of her soft body. In one clip, she tickles him under his chin to make him laugh for the camera. Good boy, she says, who's my good boy.

Another clip, I'm spooning food into his mouth—his first solids, a milestone. Then my birthday, Conor in my lap, chocolate cake baked by Merry in front of us with a candle waiting to be used up on a wish.

I blow; Conor cries because the flame is gone.

There is loads of footage. Conor ages before me on the screen, a life rapidly evolving. He looks happy, most of the time, a baby boy like any other, unblemished by the world. We look happy, too. She made me believe we were.

The final clip I watch is marked *Lake,* from the early days of this last spring. Merry is in a floral one-piece swimsuit. Conor, four months or so, is smiling in her arms, sun hat on his head, fat belly naked, arms flapping.

Isn't this the life, I hear myself say, and Merry does not move to respond, her smile a smile that's painted on, her head held stiff. But there it is. I catch it, I see it now. On camera it's hard to miss. The tensing of her arm muscles, the clenching of her fingers around his fat white thighs. He screams, an angry scream, and then the camera goes off.

I play it again. Then a third time. Zooming in. Watching the fingers grip the flesh, digging in, squeezing, hurting.

I switched off the screen and sat in the dark a long time.

She has made a fool of me. Of everything I built for us. Of my dreams.

She has done nothing but lie and deceive.

Treacherous.

All along she was treacherous.

I remembered the little wheel of birth control pills. But why, if she knew that—

Maybe she doesn't know. Maybe she could only guess.

Is that why she did it? Conor's face, frozen on the screen, smiling out at me. I could hardly bear to look, to see. His face no longer my face but a stranger.

I am not sorry he is gone.

Merry

How many days since I have seen light. Or slept, or washed. I could hardly hold my head up. My hair itched. When I dug at it with a fingernail, I drew blood.

I'm telling you the truth, I said.

I don't think you've said one word of the truth, Merry. Just a whole lot of lies.

I shook my head. No, you don't understand. It wasn't me. I'm certain it wasn't. Frank, I almost said, maybe she could have— But what was the point? All her perfect mothering of him these past weeks, all that natural maternal wisdom and care. It would only make me look worse.

You want to be the victim here, she said. The bereaved mother.

I am the bereaved mother.

No. You are a woman who killed her child.

What day is it?

Thursday.

When did I get here?

Tuesday morning.

Where is my husband?

He went home.

When can I see him?

He does not wish to see you.

Someone brought me fresh coffee and a cinnamon roll. I was ravenous. My teeth were coated in fur.

Detective Bergstrom came back into the room. She had changed clothes. A fresh shirt, a navy pantsuit. She was wearing white sneakers. She set a fresh bottle of water down in front of me. Still, she said. They're out of sparkling.

She sat down.

Merry, she said. You are far away from home. But in this case, it is a good thing.

Swedish justice is not like American justice. We do not look to punish, but to rehabilitate.

She lifted her arms above her head and stretched. I imagine she is good at yoga. Flexible. I taught yoga for a few months, ran a studio out in Colorado while I lived with Matt, the snowboarding instructor.

Why am I telling you this? she went on. I am telling you because I want, genuinely, to help you. To get you the help that you maybe have needed for a long time. Do you understand?

I would not look at her.

I have been a detective a long time. So long that I have seen more than a few cases just like this. A desperate and depressed mother, unable to cope. An absent father. A child caught up in between. The outcome is tragedy, but we do try to help these women because— Merry, look at me.

I let her lock me in her gaze.

Because we know they are not bad women, she said. They are only women who have been pushed to the absolute edge of what they can bear. They do a very, very bad thing. But they can be helped. They can be forgiven. But this must always start with the truth.

She had more papers in her file. She opened it and found what she wanted.

Your father. He committed suicide.

Why are we talking about my father?

We are talking about state of mind. In 2014, your mother passed. Is that correct?

It is.

And how did she die?

With her tits cut open and her nipples in a surgical bowl beside her. Is that irony or satire? I remember the call, Esmerelda, her housekeeper, phoning to break the news.

She died during a plastic surgery procedure, I told the detective.

She had a number of surgeries?

Yes.

Was she on any medication for depression?

I don't know. She took a lot of painkillers.

You had a good relationship with her? she asked.

I shrugged. She was my mother.

Someone knocked on the door, and Detective Bergstrom jumped up to open it. She said something in Swedish and closed the door quickly behind the man who'd interrupted.

Unbelievable, she said. A sign says, *Do Not Disturb,* and still, someone always knocks.

What about Sam? You consider it a happy marriage. He is a good husband to you?

I'm very tired, I said.

We have only a little more to get through. Sam. What kind of a man is he?

He's a good husband, I said.

Violent.

No.

Possessive.

No.

Are you sure? He didn't bring you here to keep you locked up all alone?

No.

He seems to be the one in charge. Move here, do this. Have a baby, stay at home. He's the one who makes all the decisions. Who decides what your life will be.

No, I said, no.

She searched my eyes.

She made another note. She drank from her water bottle.

Merry, you know what I think. I think it's like this. Sam messes around, loses his job. He packs you up and ships you off to godforsaken Sweden. And then he leaves you alone all day with a new baby. No friends, no support system. Nothing familiar or friendly. The baby is a trap. You can't leave. Sam won't let you, will he?

Her eyes were shining. The underarms of her jacket were stained wet. She had sweated all the way through her clean shirt.

So you know what you have there? she said.

She leaned forward, put her face up close to mine.

What you have, she said, is motive.

Sam

I want her to suffer. I want her to pay.

In the studio, I edited the clip of Merry hurting Conor, cut it so it would be just that scene, playing on a loop. All the evidence you could need.

I grabbed my keys from the kitchen counter. Frank had just woken up.

I'm going to the police station, I said.

I handed the disc to the detective, sat down beside her while she watched it. She shook her head. She played it again. She sighed.

You have it now, don't you? I said. Proof she did it.

She shook her head.

No, she said. Your wife has not confessed to anything. She insists she did not kill your son.

She's a great fucking actress, I said. I'll give her that.

The detective stood and paced the room. I wonder, she said. Maybe she will talk to you. Maybe you're the person to get something out of her.

I can't, I said. I might kill her.

No, Detective Bergstrom said. But you might force her to tell the truth.

★ ★ ★

In the room, Merry looked up and saw me. Her face fell.

Sam, I didn't do it. You have to believe me.

I believe nothing you say, Merry. It was all a lie.

She shook her head. No, no. Please.

They'd loaned me a laptop. I turned it to Merry so she could see the screen. I played the footage for her. Her own face reflected back at her, her smile that wasn't a smile. The embrace of her son that was no embrace.

Watch, I said.

She clutched at her waist and moaned. Sick bitch. I wanted to hit her, slap her, make her bleed. Bam. One strike of her head against the corner of the table, her skull would split clean in two. Her brain would leak out, dribble from her nose. Her eyes would roll back in her head, whites to the front, vacant and unseeing.

This is your wife. For better or worse. Worse could not get lower than this. Revulsion, a sourness the whole body can taste. Do it, I thought, why not? What is there to lose that is not already lost? I leaned forward and she flinched.

I'll tell you, Sam, she said. I'll tell you everything.

I sat back in the chair.

She wiped at her eyes. She was hideous. Not even human.

I waited.

You're right, Sam, she said.

I'm guilty.

Merry

I did it, Sam.

You're right. I hurt him. I'm guilty of hurting him. I pinched him or squeezed him too hard. I—I made him cry. I don't know why. I can't explain. I can't understand myself. I just felt, I don't know. So angry. So trapped. It felt like I was suffocating here. Like it wasn't my life anymore.

Like it never had been, I said.

He was watching me, face twisted in a snarl. Hate, so much hate in those eyes.

I don't know why I took it out on him. I just—he was there. So innocent and pure, and inside of me, it felt so rotten. So empty. You won't understand.

You lied, Merry. You lied about everything. It was all an act.

No.

Yes.

I'm so sorry, Sam. I don't know how to be more sorry.

You want forgiveness, he said.

No.

You want me to understand.

You lied to me, too, Sam.

Bullshit.

★ ★ ★

You did. Pretended we moved here for some big change. You thought I wouldn't find out that you got fired. That you had yet another affair with yet another student.

Like it mattered, like it made any difference at all.

He gave a cold laugh. Affairs. He sneered. Do you really want to talk about my affairs?

I covered my face. I didn't do it, Sam. You have to believe me.

You were with him, Merry. He was smothered.

I shook my head.

No, Sam. It was. It was another thing I did. I would leave him, you see. I would take him into the woods and then I'd leave him there so I could run. I just wanted—

Jesus, Merry, you really are something.

I just needed to run, Sam. I needed to be alone. To move. To feel like there was something just for me. To feel alive. You were always gone; I was always alone. You know I hate to be by myself, you know.

You loved him too much! I wanted to scream. *There was no room left for me.*

Sam looked at me the way you look at a rabid animal. Horror and revulsion. And who could blame him?

You hurt him, he said. You left him. You wanted him gone.

No, Sam, no. I loved him, I said. I loved our son.

Suddenly his hands gripped my throat, squeezing tight, forcing the breath out, the blood up. I gasped for air.

Our son, he bellowed in my face. Don't you dare utter those fucking words to me.

Sam

After the detective pulled me off of Merry and before she sent me home, she sat me down on one of the gray plastic chairs in the waiting area of the station. She had someone fetch me a paper cup of water from the cooler.

In your statement, she said, you told us you were at a work meeting the day of the murder. You lied.

I pulled at the rough beard taking over my face. I said nothing.

Where were you? Detective Bergstrom asked.

I finished the water and crushed the white cup into my fist.

Doctor's appointment, I said. You can check.

We will. But why lie about it, Mr. Hurley?

I shrugged. It's kind of a personal matter, I said.

Doctor-patient confidentiality, they won't tell her a thing. Can't say why it matters. A feeling, maybe, that I need to be the one to tell Merry the truth. That way it will really hurt. Looking her square in the eyes: Game over, you're dead.

I drove from the police station directly to Malin's place. Pressed on the buzzer until she opened up.

Sam, I can't.

Please, I begged. I needed her. I needed to be in her presence, to feel the warmth of another human. Some faint connection with something other than pain.

She let me inside and prepared two espressos from the red machine in the kitchenette. Into my cup, she dropped two cubes of sugar.

I told her everything.

Back home, the house was too much, sucking everything dry, making it hard to think, to breathe. I walked over the field to Karl's place and knocked on the door.

Elsa opened up. Karl's in the back, she said. He's going out hunting today.

I went to the shed to find him.

Can I join you? I asked.

Have you been drinking?

No, I lied.

He packed up the rest of the gear and we got into the car. We drove, an hour or maybe two, heading west, deep into the mountains.

Thank you, I said. I need this.

They practice humane hunting here in Sweden; single-shot kills that deliver a quick death. The animals don't suffer. All the meat is eaten. It's the least amount of cruelty you can inflict, which I suppose in some instances is the best way.

We spent most of the day in the woods, beautiful, crisp mountain air, hundred-year-old trees, silence and endless sky beyond the pines. We crouched low, tracking two mature female elk. The animals were slow, methodical in their grazing. Every now and then, they tensed, prickling at our scent, at the sound of the grass breaking under our boots.

Karl had loaned me a gun. He didn't take his eyes off the elk. He signaled with his hand to show I had a clean shot. I watched the animal, the thick ripple of muscle and flesh, the steady gaze, the breath visible in the cold. In the silence, everything was heightened, the wings of a bird taking off into the air, the furious rustling of beetles against the bark.

The shot rang out, clipped, clear. It echoed through the trees, overruling any other sound. And then the stampede, the beating hearts, the scrambling hooves; the other animals taking flight, running for their lives. Life. Life and then death. This is all it takes.

She was massive up close. An expanse of once-living creature, the hind legs collapsed in the fall. The tongue lolled out, the eyes staring, accusatory. Why me? they seemed to beg.

We need to get her home, Karl said.

Together we tied the legs with twine and heaved the dead animal onto our shoulders, Karl in front, me bringing up the rear. The elk was heavy. Dead weight. I had to stop and shift position, easing the bulk toward my shoulders.

That was a good kill, Karl said.

Was it?

We drove home to Sigtuna with the elk tied onto the roof of the car, secured by Karl with the thick rope he'd brought along.

Did you enjoy it? he asked.

I'm not sure, I said.

★ ★ ★

He asked after Merry.

I hate her, I said. I hate her so much, I want to kill her.

He sucked in his cheeks, shook his head. Either in disapproval or empathy.

I'm not kidding, I said. Women. They're so good at lying. We don't stand a chance.

He looked at me. But men lie.

Maybe, I said.

Come on. We've all done it. Maybe not lying outright, but for sure not telling the whole truth. Omissions. Revisions.

You, I said. The ultimate Swedish alpha male.

He gave a cold laugh. Things are not always what they seem, Sam. Even here, he said.

Especially here, I thought.

It was pitch dark by the time we returned home. Karl pulled the car up outside the larger of his two barns. He left the lights on to illuminate our way, and hopped out to prop open the barn door with a log of wood.

Now it's carving time, he said.

We maneuvered the elk from the roof and hauled her into the barn. We had to turn the carcass sideways to drag it through the door. The cold had all but frozen her stiff. Or maybe it was just the fact of her death, the slow and precise shutting down of the system. Beating heart, pumping blood; everything that separates the living from the dead.

I couldn't help but recall the image of Conor on the bed, laid out on his back as though he was doing nothing less benign than taking a nap. His stiffened corpse, his face white and blank and cast forever in expressionless, cold death. How was it possible to fit so much horror into just one day?

A few strands of golden-brown hair stolen from Conor's hairbrush and secreted away inside a plastic bag. A doctor in Stockholm who offered same-day results for paternity screening. That very day. A confirmation that he was not mine.

And then, just like that: dead. Child no more. I could see why Merry would have wanted him gone. That day I wished him gone too.

Inside the barn, Karl had meat hooks, saws, a giant freezer, a plastic-lined table for carving the animal into pieces.

Looks like a serial killer's dream, I said.

Karl flashed me a smile. The trick, he said, is removing the innards first. It's less bloody. Better for the meat, too.

He set to it, carving, scraping, a surgeon at work. When the guts were out, he handed me the knife. Here, he said.

I hesitated. The knife was heavy in my hand, slicked with blood and death.

Start here, Karl said, then follow this direction. He showed me with his hands.

I sank the blade in, felt the resistance of the flesh, the click of metal on bone. Slowly I carved, piece by piece, through fat and sinew and muscle, reducing her down to a sum of bloody parts. Karl used a saw to cut through the rib cage, divvying up the carcass into steaks for the grill.

When we were done, we used the vacuum sealer to package the meat, enough for the whole winter. As we were cleaning up the last of the blood, Freja came to the door to see what was happening. She did not flinch at the sight of the entrails and bones. Karl said something to her in Swedish and she smiled and nodded.

She wants elk burgers for dinner, he said.

He loaded up a bag and handed it to me.

If you need more, you know where to find it, he said.

I was filthy. Exhausted. I could taste the blood. I reeked of slaughter.

In the kitchen, Frank sat under the dim light of the oven, drinking a mug of tea. She startled when she saw me.

I looked down. Everywhere stained with red.

Let me help you, she said.

She lifted my arms to pull off my bloodied T-shirt. She ran water in the sink and used the soap to scrub my hands. Her hands in mine, rubbing against the water, working her fingers around my own. Standing close, smelling the way she smells, her long hair in my face, brushing against me back and forth, back and forth.

She was in a nightgown, skin barely covered. I could see everything through the satin. I could see even more when she leaned forward.

They are all the same. All of them. You turn to them to be filled, you leave emptier than before.

I could still smell the dead elk on me. Heat was in the air, and daggers. Sharp and lethal. I recalled those nights under the stars. Frank and her longing. What did she want? What did I want?

I gripped her to me, pressed my mouth into hers. Her eyes were dark pools. You could not see the bottom. Hands on her flesh, the warmth and smoothness. I wanted more. I wanted to go back to before.

Wordlessly, Frank stepped away from my grasp. She wiped her mouth with the back of her hand and retreated slowly back into the darkened house.

Merry

Lior in Tel Aviv, the pediatric nurse who leaves her toddler alone in the bath. Verity in Perth, who keeps the balcony door open just a crack.

If not you, then who? The detective is trying. Maybe she doesn't want to believe in murderous mothers after all.

I don't know, I said. I just don't know.

Think, Detective Bergstrom said. Who you know? Who knows you?

I shook my head. The people around the baby had only love for him, cuddles and kisses. Daddy and Aunt Frank, the friendly neighbors, Karl and Elsa and little Freja. Pure devotion. It was only me and my broken parts.

I don't know, I said again.

I can't think of anyone but me who would've wanted him gone.

Detective Bergstrom was not taking any notes. But she did appear to be listening.

I had confessed everything to Sam. Well. Not everything. Some things. Only what I had to. Now I was repeating myself for the benefit of the detective.

I told her how I sometimes felt alone and frustrated and isolated, like I was a prisoner in Sigtuna, like it was some form of punishment. I told her that sometimes I had suicidal thoughts (you have to throw that in, don't you) and that, from time to time, I had thoughts of leaving Sam and the baby. I told her that once or twice, I squeezed him a little too hard out of frustration, to try to get him to stop screaming, that I had felt so terrible it made me think he'd be better off without me.

She nodded as I was speaking. It was what she wanted to hear. I always know what people want to hear.

She mentioned the forum. They'd checked the laptop, the browser history.

Yes, I said. Because I felt so alone. Like I was a defective woman.

She looked at me with something like sympathy.

I repeated the part about leaving the baby by himself in the clearing while I ran. That's what happened the day he died, I told her. I returned from the run to find him cold and unmoving and already dead. I told her that I had picked him up and tried to resuscitate him, that it was all in vain.

It was the worst moment of my life, I said. The worst.

This part was true.

Yes, it was clearer now. I had remembered; separated things into their proper boxes.

I told her I had thought at first it was my fault, that he'd been ill or feverish or that he'd caught a chill. I didn't want Sam to know how I left him alone; I didn't want the police to know, either.

So I lied, I said. I lied because I didn't know what else to do.

So what you're saying, Merry, she said, is that someone else murdered your son.

Yes.

Not you.

No.

It was true, wasn't it? This was it. Lies. Lies but not murder.

Maybe.

You didn't do this, she repeated.

No.

All the evidence, all we've discussed. And you are denying that it was you.

It wasn't me, I whispered. It wasn't.

She sighed. I want to believe you, but you're making it very difficult. You lied once to the police. You lied to your husband. How do I know you're telling the truth now?

Because I have to, I said. Because I was a neglectful, terrible mother. Yes. Yes. I'll take that. I'll own it. I'll burn on a stake for it. But I did not murder my son.

She studied me a long time, saying nothing, just looking.

I appeared distraught. Yes, I thought, the performance of a lifetime. But weren't they all? With Christopher it had been too much. It had pushed him over the edge.

Detective Bergstrom nodded. She left the room. When she returned, she had a map of Sigtuna.

Show me, she said. Where you ran. Where you were. Show me where he was found.

I looked at the map. I'm not good with this sort of thing.

Try, she said.

I marked it with a pen. Here, from our house. To around this spot. Maybe here. There's a cabin. It's boarded up.

What time, she said. What time did you leave home? What time did you find Conor?

What else, she said. Anyone who saw you. Anyone you talked to. Anyone who might have seen something else.

I shook my head. No one, I said. No.

She opened the file. She checked a few pages.

This might help, she said. We have a time of death. A small window. If we can place you well enough away from him at this time, you may have something.

But think. Something, anything that might be useful.

She snapped her fingers. One of those heart rate monitors, she said, the ones that track you while you run.

I shook my head.

Phone? Tracking on your phone?

I don't know, I said. I had it with me.

Good, she said. Good. We'll check that.

She looked up at me. Merry, she said. This is a long shot. I'm going out on a limb here. Understand?

I nodded. She was being kind. Showing mercy. She bought it, the broken-down mother, the cruelty that seeps out of desperate, lonely women. It didn't seem right, to be forgiven, or understood. To escape punishment.

Who would hurt a child?

Me.

The answer had been me.

Merry, she said. You'd better not be lying again. Do you hear me? Because then I'll come after you with full force. And it won't be so friendly. It won't be friendly at all.

Frank

I'm growing tired of our nocturnal trysts, Karl and I, alone in his cold and dusty barn. He is thrusting vigorously away, himself a little distracted this evening, though knowing him, he won't want to stop until it's done.

Regrettable, that this is now a thing. The first time served its purpose, but now it's only tiresome.

Yes, yes, I cry, to hurry things along. I stick a finger where he likes it. I fold my breasts into his face and shift myself so that it's less uncomfortable.

I try to picture Merry behind bars. A criminal. Being punished for her crimes. How curious life can be, the places it can take you. Sam the other night, pawing at me with his bloodied hands and stale breath. I did not notice it before, how rough around the edges he is. How unappealingly bullish and common. I am accustomed to a better-caliber man than that.

What was I thinking? Really, my judgment is sometimes quite flawed. Well. I have been through my own traumas, haven't I, these recent months, with their cruel blows. Some nights when I cannot sleep, I wander into Conor's room, smell his blankets, trace a finger over the place where he once lay. Feel the pang of grief in my heart.

★ ★ ★

There was a night when Sam had arrived home late. I'd been rocking Conor back to sleep in the old armchair in his room. Aunt Frank, Sam had whispered, the fairy godmother. I smiled at the idea then. Now I can think only of the godmothers who cast spells and curses. The ones who send children into hundred-year slumbers, or steal them away altogether.

Karl takes me by the throat, pulls, holds. My thighs ache but I dare not stop. Yes, yes, yes. He finally comes, inside me this time.

It's okay, I lie. I'm on birth control.

Elsa suffered another miscarriage a few days ago, he sighs.

She is distraught.

I have to hold myself steady, to keep from slapping his face.

He zips his trousers and leaves me on the cold cement floor.

Merry

Merry. Merry, do you hear me?

I longed to close my eyes. To disappear, cell by cell, fading into nothingness, allowing everything to give way to obliteration.

I'd had this thought before, once or twice, in New York. To just lie down in the street, or on the tracks of the subway, lie down and close my eyes and let it happen. Swoosh. A surrender. Not death or suicide. Only a way to give up the fight, the exhausting business of being alive.

I looked up and tried to focus.

Merry.

It was Detective Bergstrom, neatly groomed as always. Hair cropped and dyed a ferocious platinum blond. Had it been like that since I'd arrived? She was chewing gum. I could smell mint. Her breath must be stale. I cupped my hands to check my own. Wretched.

Merry, she said. We are withdrawing the charges against you.

What?

You will be free to go, she said.

I don't understand.

We were able to track down a witness. Someone to corroborate your story.

How? There was no one—there was no one I saw.

Yes, she said. There was. The cabin you mentioned. We found the owner. We went to interview him. Turns out he has a son, a teenager who'd decided to use the cabin as a meeting place for his girlfriend and himself. On the day of Conor's death. He had a stash of weed with him, some alcohol he'd stolen from his father's bar—that's why he didn't want to come forward. But he saw what happened. Or at least, enough to get you out of here.

He saw, he saw who killed the baby? He was there? I said.

She shook her head. No, unfortunately—or possibly fortunately for him, not.

When we talked with him, he told us that he arrived at the cabin shortly before you did. He saw you come up to the stroller, he saw you pick up the stuffed toy—like you said. He saw you scream, and lift the baby, and try to perform mouth-to-mouth. He saw you crying and hysterical, in shock. He wanted to help, he says, only he was afraid of his father finding out about the cabin.

Detective Bergstrom was looking at me, not smiling, not scowling.

This is good news for you, she said.

It felt like the opposite. An injustice. How could it be anything else?

Did he see anyone else in the woods? I said.

No. He didn't get to the cabin too long before you did. And he must have come from the other direction. The girlfriend, too. They saw nothing.

She did that stretch again, arms up above her head. I heard her shoulders click.

The team looked at your phone, too. They traced your location using the photos you took; the times and places match everything that you told me. Given the estimated time of death, there's enough room to suggest that you wouldn't have been able to do it.

The photographs, I said. I had forgotten. The light and colors of the lake, the enchanting mystery of a shimmering world below. I had stood there a long time, quite transfixed.

Merry, Detective Bergstrom said. I believe you. I believe that you did not kill your son.

I nodded. I shuddered. I'm free to go, I repeated.

Yes.

But it doesn't solve anything, does it?

It solves a lot for you. For the case, we are looking into some other possible scenarios. Now that we have a potential crime scene. The forensics team is working the area around the clearing and the cabin. They'll find something. Trace evidence, fibers. Something will turn up. And we will find out if someone did this to your son.

I sat looking at her.

So I just go home.

Yes, you are free to go home.

Home. Sam. Sam and his monstrous rage, let loose upon me. The wife who deceived him. The wife who hurt his son. It would be his right. It would be his revenge. Unstoppable, he would be.

Perhaps you will manage to work out a way forward with your husband, Detective Bergstrom said, as though reading my hesitation. Together, or not together.

She stacked her files. She slipped her handbag over her arm. She seemed eager to leave, or be rid of me.

I was so tired. I felt small and foul, something stuck on the bottom of a shoe.

I'm a monster, I said, aren't I? Even if I didn't kill him.

She stood up and opened the door. No, Merry, she said. I think you are a woman like many others.

Frank

Merry is back. I woke up and found her in the kitchen, casually brewing the morning coffee like nothing has happened. Like the past few days have been voided.

You're home, I said.

I was not sure whether to hug her or run from her.

Hello, Frank.

What happened? How is it that you are back?

You seem disappointed, she said. Her hair was wet; she was dripping little puddles onto the floor.

God, no, I said. It's great you're home. I just mean, what happened that they let you go? We heard nothing, Sam and I, we just thought they were still busy with the questioning, the, you know, how it was possible it was deliberate, trying to figure out what happened—

I'm innocent, she said. That's what happened. You believe me, Frank, don't you? You believe it wasn't me.

Of course, I said. Of course. There was never a doubt in my mind that you could be capable of such a thing. Oh, Merry, what an awful, unimaginable thing. Isn't it. Isn't it just beyond sense. The shock of Con's death—and then this. This terrible, terrible news that it was—

I could hardly bring myself to say the word. *Murder. Murderess*.

She slowly sipped her coffee. She poured more from the pot. She looked too thin, too pale. Haggard, but of course she would be. She seemed lost in thought for a while, and then looked at me again. She poured a mug of coffee and held it out for me to take. As I did, I stepped in the water pooled at her feet from her wet hair, felt the cold seep into my socks.

There was a witness, she said. A man came forward. He saw what happened.

Witness, I said. Where? What did he say? What did he see?

I felt more wetness dripping onto my toes. The coffee. I had spilled it.

Merry observed me. Careful, she said.

My hands were burning. I moved to set down the mug.

You must be exhausted, I said. I bent to wipe the tiles, bowed at her feet. She didn't move. I could feel her eyes on me.

Where's Sam? she asked over my head.

Probably the barn, I replied. He's been sleeping out there. It's freezing, but I guess that's what he wants. Cold. Hard floors.

I looked up at her and she regarded me carefully.

You're still here, Frank, she said.

Merry

Sam in the barn was curled up into a tight ball, pillow wedged between two boxes, blankets over his head to fight against the cold. There was a bottle next to him, a pack of cigarettes. So much for our wholesome Swedish ways. So much for any of it.

I crouched down. He smelled awful. There was spit dried white in the corner of his mouth, a slick of oil on his face. He opened one eye.

What the fuck are you doing here?

Sam, it wasn't me. They let me go.

He turned from me. He reeked of last night's booze, of days of unwashed man.

Liar, he said. Fucking liar.

No, I said. There's a witness. There's proof I didn't do it.

Liar, he said again.

I left the barn and closed the door behind me. I went back inside the house.

In the baby's room, I put my face against his blankets and breathed in, sniffed at the stuffed toys still coated with his drool and kisses. Bear and Biscuit, forlorn from overuse, ears chewed and fur matted. I inhaled the smell of him; I sucked at the corner of the wool to taste him and imagined him in my arms, cradled against me.

I opened the fridge and looked inside. The rows of baby food still sat unopened on the top shelf. Broccoli and carrots. Zucchini and red peppers. Potato and peas, his favorite. I felt the familiar stab of pain to the gut. Dead. Gone. You did this. You deserve this. Someday, Merry, it's all going to catch up with you. All your lies.

Who said that? I can't even place the face.

I took a garbage bag and held it open as I threw in the pots of food, one by one, dinners and lunches that would never be eaten. I thought of the days I'd left him hungry. The days I gave up trying to feed him after one or two mouthfuls. I saw his face, that open, trusting face, the way he watched the world through those dark-lashed eyes, searching out information, seeking smiles, wanting nothing from me but that most instinctive thing: a mother's love.

Mother's love. Mother's unconditional love. Where was it? Where had it been? I'm sorry; I'm sorry, Conor. Forgive me, son. I wanted to vomit. I wanted to scream.

I bundled up the trash and took it outside to the recycling bins at the end of the road.

Elsa was closing the lid of the brown waste bin, her winter coat pulled tightly against her tiny frame.

Hello, I said.

She shook her head at me, a nervous, quivering bird. Merry, she said. I just can't speak to you.

I nodded. I moved aside and let her pass.

⋆ ⋆ ⋆

I walked slowly back toward the house. It was an effort to move, to lift one foot in front of the other. I was bone-tired, cell-tired; everything wanted only to surrender. To the exhaustion, to the grief, to the great black void waiting to swallow me into the depths.

It is all gone. All you had is gone. Emptiness like before, but worse. Deeper, darker.

I deserve no sympathy. No mercy, either.

From outside, I glanced into the house, to see if Sam was inside. I saw Frank instead, in the kitchen, washing dishes, stirring something on top of the stove. This is what I would have looked like a few weeks ago, I thought. This would have been the picture of me. I liked the scene, the gentle domesticity, the pleasure of simple pursuits. Homemaking. Making a house a home.

Who might have wanted your son dead, Merry? Who might have benefited?

I had gone through the list of people we know in Sweden—a handful, if that. Detective Bergstrom had written them all down.

But they loved him. Everyone loved him.

A pang, a punch.

Everyone loved him but me.

Frank, so maternal and instinctive and tender. That photo of her and Sam and the baby lodged in my memory: a merry little trio. I wonder if this is the picture she sent to Christopher.

★ ★ ★

I watched now, from the outside looking in. You see it all differently like this. The perspective switched around, like a pair of binoculars used backwards.

Frank in my house, framed in glass. Frank in my house, looking terribly at home. Why did it feel like she was always finding ways to intrude in my life?

Frank. Frank and her ways. The way her hurt has always turned so quickly to rage. Boyfriends who scorned her, men who turned her down, husbands who failed to leave their wives for her after all they promised. Colleagues who got promoted ahead of her. I'd watched the bloody aftermath. She could be ruthless. Phone calls to the wives at dinner, underwear left behind for girlfriends to uncover, brown envelopes of incriminating photos sent to the Board of Directors. She always got her way.

I have to be like this, she told me once. It's the only way to get ahead.

Perhaps this is what a childhood of scarcity will do to a person.

But a child.

My child.

I kept watching her through the glass. Beautiful. She has always been too beautiful. But only on the surface. Really, it's all smoke and mirrors.

I love you, Mer-Bear.

I love you, Frankincense.

We are so good at pretending, aren't we?

A lifetime you spend entwined in someone's world, the cord that connects you thick and ropy and impermeable to the storms. Me, you, us, we. Two lives and two people, knotted together in a tight fist like the gnarled roots of ancient trees, so deep and twisted that you cannot distinguish one from the other, that you cannot uproot the one without killing both. Part you, part me. Best friends.

Things stolen from one another over the years, not to possess but only to hurt. Boyfriends I managed to turn against her. I was not very kind. Mario, the Italian, her great college romance. It didn't take much to orchestrate that little drama. He just stopped answering her calls. With Simon, too, the almost-husband. I had seen to it that the engagement ended quickly. I don't know why. I suppose she was just too happy. Too pleased with herself to need me. And that never feels right.

Be careful, I told Simon. She's prone to being overly possessive with the people she loves.

It was a sore point for him, Frank had mentioned to me once before. All I needed to do was stoke the flames. Invented tales of Frank's post-breakup overdose attempts—only for the attention, I explained—a restraining order, a slow cutting-off of all friends and family so that she could be the sole focus.

Just so you're aware, I said, as though I were being a good friend.

But these cruelties were unknown to her. Others, perhaps not.

Payback.

Revenge.

Or the same old games.

Mine.

No, mine.

Leave, I'd said, and watched with glee as her face fell. The singular pleasure, the never-disappointing thrill of poking her wounds. Betrayed, cast aside. All the things Frank cannot bear.

But this. A child.

She looked up suddenly from inside the house and held a hand to her heart.

She had seen me. And I had startled her.

Sam

I looked at Merry in front of me. Not speaking. Not moving. Waiting for me to do whatever I chose. I deserve it. That's what she was saying. That's what she would be saying if she could speak. I want it. I want the punishment, Sam. I want it to hurt.

I want you to do it. Do it all. Make me suffer.

The feeling inside is rage, burning, fiery, so hot it's like someone's stoking coal in my gut, the heat working up through the belly, into the chest, up up up and holding in the throat, strangling the breath out of me, holding it all inside.

I was shaking, my fists, those fists, tight and red and hot, throbbing, itching to do it, to send the hate out through the knuckles, to deliver it all to my wife, a strike, a blow, a shock of blood and bone.

Yes, said the voice, do it.

Do it.

The fists. The fists.

Now, Sam. Do it. For all the pain. All the hurt. For all the women who have done you wrong.

So many women. Manipulative. Cruel.

Liars.

All of them such good liars.

★ ★ ★

I heaved my full force into my hand and threw the first punch. It sank into her; she crumpled.

Another, said the voice. Really do it this time. Really feel it.

I leaned back, I lunged forward, I hit her. Again and again; my knuckles ached from the impact. There was screaming, terrified and brutal and urgent, but I ignored it and carried on.

Take it, take it, fucking whore, fucking bitch.

More, Sam, more.

Liar! Cunt! Miserable fucking bitch of a mother. Hideous woman. Cruel, terrible woman, you don't deserve to live.

The screams had intensified. There was blood on my hands and I paused to wipe tears and spit from my face. I was out of breath, sweating with the exertion. Shaking. The screams had been from me.

I looked at Merry, wife no more. Just a forlorn heap in the corner, bloodstained and collapsed.

Good, said the voice. You did great, Sam. Really great.

I wiped my eyes. I took a deep breath. Tried to find my focus. Still my heart.

Thank you, I said at last. I think I'm done with this now.

In the car on the way home, I thought about the conversation with Karl. The secrets we keep. But this is all on her. All of it.

You are so angry, Malin had said, and that was before all this had happened.

What use was it trying to understand? To unpack the story, as they say.

You go back, all the way. You go deep. Feel the pain. This is good, the shrink says.

Live in your truth. Own your pain.

Bullshit.

I'd tried it, after it all fell apart in New York. Tess on her high horse insisting that I pay for what I'd done—I thought, something has to change. Let me change. Let me try. Nothing changes.

Nothing ever changes.

How can it, when the women are all the same. It's in their DNA.

Frank

Things are awful around here. Sam and Merry thundering about the house, him in a half-drunk stupor, her in another kind of daze.

He was out most of yesterday afternoon, took the car and drove off, leaving Merry and me alone at home. She barely said a word, spent almost eighteen hours fast asleep. I popped my head in the bedroom door at one point to check up on her. She was under the covers, dead to the world.

She's not yet told me a thing. Witness. Witness. I cannot imagine who it might be.

I made some lunch and checked my options for flights. There's no doubt it's time to leave. Now that Merry has been cleared. Now that she is free. Honestly, I can't wait to go. To shrug off all this sadness, the great perversity of their lives. How different it all looks now, the curtain lifted, the masks off.

I suppose I'll stick with the plan and go to Italy. Though I could go anywhere, really.

There are other friends in other parts of the world, many of them. They always say, Come and visit. You really must, Frank. And so I will.

Alain in Paris, Oren in Brussels, newly divorced Nicolai in his high-rise in Hong Kong.

Yes, it will be a new chapter, a whole new world of possibility ahead. I am really quite excited.

Pick up a shovel and dig yourself out. That was one of my mother's maxims. You could never forget she was a farm girl. But she was right. I have always been skilled with the shovel. Making my own luck, setting my life on the right course.

You could be my daughter, Frances, Gerald said, but I put my finger to his lips and shook my head. I was sixteen.

I want this too, I whispered softly, an attempt at seduction. I was wearing new underwear, red and cheap. Merry's father liked them young; everyone knew that. I kissed him and put my hand down his trousers like I'd seen the women do in the movies. I rubbed until he was hard against my palm. He bit at my breasts and pushed me down with one hand until I was spread out flat on the kitchen counter.

Afterward, his face was stricken. He looked at me, pale and naked and painfully childlike; he trembled. What have I done?

I don't need to tell Maureen or Merry, I said. I wouldn't dream of it.

I wanted to go to college, that was all. The next morning, the first of several generous payments was deposited into my account.

Resilient old Frank. Yes, that's always been me.

My phone rang. Elias in Shanghai, an old friend from business school. He read a book on radical honesty two years ago and he's practiced it ever since.

I don't love you anymore, he told his wife. I find you repulsive. She divorced him and he moved to China.

What are you doing in the arse end of nowhere? he said.

Visiting an old friend, I replied.

And how's that working out for you?

It's a little dull, to be honest. I grimaced. And it was, wasn't it. How amusing now, to think I coveted it all.

I filled the rest of the day with napping and reading. I did some yoga. I finished a box of rye crackers and soft cheese. I looked around the guest room, which seemed sparse and cold and unwelcoming now.

How did you like Sweden? they'll ask, the London set and the New Yorkers, catching up on our lives over dinners and champagne brunches. I can see myself already, replying with a dismissive wave of the hand and a playful roll of the eyes.

Oh, you know how it is, I'll say, quaint but terrifically dull. We'll laugh and relief will wash over us, that we have been spared such parochial little lives and boredoms.

Around seven o'clock, I heard the front door open. Sam was home. I stayed in the room, listening for the sounds of his shoes. I thought he'd be straight back out to the barn, but I heard another door opening. The bedroom.

I got up and stood in the doorway. I heard voices. I crept closer.

I've apologized, Sam. I'm on my knees. I can't say it anymore. I can't be any sorrier for what happened.

Merry, trying another angle.

He was quiet.

I didn't do it, Sam. The police wouldn't have let me go if I had. So you go ahead and hate me. You throw me out, you punish me; you do whatever you need to do. But all I want is to find out who did this. I think you want to do the same.

He mumbled something in reply, but I couldn't hear what it was.

There was silence. And then Merry spoke once more.

I think it was Frank, she said. I think she might have followed me into the woods. I know it's crazy, but I think it was her.

In the dark, I stood, stunned. I felt sick, my heart in my throat. Unbelievable. After everything I've done. After the friend I have tried to be.

I moved very carefully away from the door and slipped out of the house, still in my socks. I pulled the door quietly behind me and sat myself outside. I scratched around for the pack of cigarettes Sam keeps under one of the flowerpots, and blew wisps of white smoke into the cool night air. My hands were shaking, fury and shock. The injustice of it all. But why am I surprised?

She's never hesitated to throw me under the bus. If only she could see. If only she could know.

We are the same. We are all we have to depend on.

I shivered, spying Karl's front door across the field, illuminated by the red-tinged lamp hanging overhead. A Christmas wreath had been hung on the door, probably handmade by Elsa and Freja; a cheery afternoon's craft project. Karl doesn't deserve them.

Elsa, he'd said. Another miscarriage.

Implying many before.

Poor woman. These really are the things that can destroy you. The feeling that no matter what you do, life will always find a way to deny you the things you covet most.

I looked up at the sky. It was a beautiful night. Biting but clear. The stars were luminous, the moon a pure circle of light. The end of a cycle. A good time for a big change, isn't that what they say?

I sat awhile longer, a lone shadow in a dark night. A girl a very long way from home. A girl without a home.

Poor Elsa, I thought once more, before creeping back inside.

Merry

The house chills you to the bone. Still, the windows stay open. No one has turned on the heating. There is no wood chopped for the fire. The cold is bracing, a slap, a punishment. Soon it will hurt more, it will be painful to breathe, painful to shift about. Every day is colder and darker than the last, less and less light; in a month or so there will be none at all, just a handful of daylight hours to break the blackened sky.

I took my morning coffee outside, sat gazing at the garden. Everything is succumbing to our neglect. Vegetables dying on their stems, branches fallen, grass overgrown, weeds everywhere, pushing their way in.

All of it rotting.

Bugs, tiny white flecks on the leaves, hustling their way through the green. Snails with their houses waterlogged, hiding under leaves. Collapsed produce, given up on life. Much of it already surrendered to the cold.

Decay is taking over.

Still, the birds are leaving for the south. The rest of the animals are preparing for their months underground. Nothing has stopped: time or season, growth or its opposite. It's just us, paused like a broken clock in the eternal moment of our doom.

In the chair, I felt the stiffness of my body. I bent over and stretched my arms, heard the hardened parts of me click and resist. I looked out toward the forest. The familiar trail. I'd not been back since that day. I finished the coffee and slipped inside to change into my running clothes.

I started walking toward the woods, still not entirely sure why. I walked and stopped. Walked and stopped.

I'm a free woman, I told myself, but I felt only guilt.

At the start of the trail, I looked back toward the houses.

Elsa and Karl on the left. Sam and I on the right. Two wooden homes, framed in view. Two vantage points from which to watch the goings-on of the reserve.

I walked on. I looked behind me. I couldn't shake the strangeness of the feeling, of doing this without the stroller. Without the baby. Never again with the baby.

As I approached the clearing, I felt it all come back. The terror of that day. The sickening realization that he was gone. That I would be found out. And I was found out, wasn't I? I suppose I had it coming.

Perhaps there is more. Perhaps this is only the beginning.

The blue and white police tape cordoning off the area has been broken and discarded. Some parts remained stuck to the entrance of the cabin. I walked up to it and tried the door. It opened. I went inside. It was tiny, dusty, and mostly empty. A wooden bench that probably served as a bed, a table, a shelf with some tinned food and an enamel bowl and plate. Not much of a love nest for the teenagers.

I stood at the window and looked out. The clearing, the trees. The rock on the right-hand side, the big tree on the left; perfect for hiding behind. For watching, for waiting. Someone was there. Someone had followed me. I felt my stomach turn into a knot. *And you left him all alone.*

Crimes like this, Detective Bergstrom had said, they tend to be personal. Intimate. Someone in the family. Someone wanting to frame me.

To take what was mine.

To punish me.

Friends. Sisters. Two parts of the same whole.

I looked out at the place where the baby would have died. Smothered. His own blanket, held to his mouth, held until he could no longer breathe. Blue, the color of the little fish printed on the cloth. The color of his face when I found him.

His head would have been swaddled tightly inside. Swaddling. That's what the maternity nurses teach you to do at the hospital. So that the child feels safe. So that the child knows there's nothing to fear from the post-womb world. Only love. Only love.

But you wanted him dead. You wished he'd never existed at all.

His face, always looking back at you, always threatening to spill another secret. I was going to make it right.

I know, Christopher had written. Not *I need you,* like every time before. This is why he wanted Frank to send him a photograph. He saw what I never did. What I never wanted to believe.

But I had a plan. I was going to reply, just this once. *He's not yours.* I'd pretend to be certain, imply I'd had tests done, irrefutable proof.

Perhaps I'd threaten him with something shameful if he ever contacted me again.

Who is Christopher? the detective had asked. We found over two hundred deleted emails from him on your laptop.

I'd swallowed. An old friend. He's not well, I said. Mentally unstable.

Seems a little obsessed with you, she said. Is there a reason for that?

I shook my head. He's not well, I repeated.

It was true. He wasn't well when I met him and I'd only made it worse. Pretending that the intoxicating love he felt was reciprocated. Pretending to be just like him.

It's like we're the only two people on the planet who get what it all means, he told me.

Yes, I'd enthused, just you and I.

He was an engineer by day, all numbers and measurements; by night, a manic poet yearning for a muse. I loved how he looked at me. I loved how vivid I felt, reflected through his eyes.

I need you, I'd said. I love you, I'd promised.

I never did. Maybe I never do.

It was only ever a salve to something else. A taste of a life less small. A way to be anyone else.

And then it was a curse.

* * *

There was a rustling outside, a sudden intrusion upon the silence, a pounding of shoes over ground. A woman emerged from the trees, her back to the cabin. She wore a cap covering her hair. She stopped, out of breath, in the middle of the clearing. The very place. She looked up, into the sky, into the invisible tops of the pines. She looked around, held her hands over her face and let out a cry, loud and sudden and shrill.

The sound of pain, deep and dark, familiar to me in its guttural pitch.

She spun around. She turned on the spot, the cry shifting, becoming a low wail. She clasped at her middle, and retched onto the ground. Then she collapsed, a crumpled heap with her head in her lap.

When she looked up, I recognized the face.

Elsa.

It was Elsa.

Sam

In the barn, I have Biscuit with me. Biscuit and whiskey. Neither is any use.

The fog in my head just gets darker, heavier. I feel myself unraveling, everything beneath me giving way. Can't bear to look at Merry, and yet. I need to know she'll suffer for what she's done. I don't yet know how.

From the barn, I heard tires on the gravel drive. I opened the door and watched as two cars pulled up and two sets of police officers emerged. Detective Bergstrom. I recognized her from the police station.

What now, I thought, but she did not come to our door. It was Karl's bell she rang.

Someone answered and let her and the other officer inside. The other pair walked around the property, peering into the garage and the barns. They came out holding something wrapped in plastic.

The front door opened and Elsa emerged, wild-eyed and in her tan house shoes. Detective Bergstrom put her in one of the cars and they drove away.

From the doorway, Freja stood and watched. I waved to her, but she looked away from me and shut the door.

* * *

One of the other officers walked across the field. He held up the plastic bag for me to see.

Does this belong to your son? he asked.

It was one of Conor's blankets. Blue. They had come in a set of two, the same pattern with the colors inverted.

I nodded. Yes. What is this, where did you find—

Thank you, sir, he said, and he was gone.

This is the reality. Everything around us turned to a deformed version of itself. Child dead. Wife sadistic. Neighbors . . . what? Baby killers.

They teach you that human beings perceive only a small fraction of what is around us, that our sense of sight and hearing is far inferior to that of most other species: bees with their infrared vision, dolphins and bats with their sonic navigation, horses and dogs with a sense of smell heightened enough to detect emotion. Fear, happiness, they can grasp it all.

But us, we miss more than we'll ever see, whole chunks of information lost to the ether, things happening right under our noses. Easily fooled. Willfully ignorant.

I went inside the house. It smelled of rotting waste, of all things foul. I heard the sound of the shower running. Merry, or maybe Frank. I went back out, sat down inside the studio, surveyed the equipment I'd bought. Tools of the trade. I thought of better days.

Associate professor. Acclaim for my work. Adoration, even.

That was stolen from me too. Another betrayal. Another treacherous bitch.

There was a knock on the door. Merry.

What do you want?

Sam, she said. Detective Bergstrom called. They've taken Elsa in for questioning.

I saw, I said. I watched them earlier.

She shook her head. Apparently they have reason to believe she may be unstable. There was evidence brought to their attention. This is what the detective said. That Elsa might have—I don't know—had some kind of breakdown. She was pregnant, she miscarried just a day or so before Conor was—

She stopped herself.

Jesus, I said. Elsa.

It doesn't make sense, does it?

She thinks I care now. She thinks it matters to me. But what do I feel for another man's dead son?

The thing is, she said, I saw her. In the clearing. In the place he—right in the place where it happened. She was crying. Hysterical, really... I don't know. Unhinged. Like, guilty. Shamed.

I rubbed my eyes. That woman looks like she wouldn't trample on an ant.

Merry held her arms tightly. I know. I think so too. But they found one of Conor's blankets in their barn. His blue blanket. They're testing it, trying to see if there's any trace evidence to connect her to...

Her voice trailed off. She shook her head. Anyway, I just wanted to tell you, she said. So you know what's going on.

★ ★ ★

I looked at her in the doorway of the studio. Shadow of a woman. Shadow of a wife. Nothing left but an empty shell. She looks worn out and faded, like an old shirt. Unrested, unwashed. Too thin. Bones under her clothes poking through, eyes hollowed out like the ones on the wall; look into them and there's only a void. She has a new smell, too, dank and sweet, like overripe fruit. Part woman, part something else.

I am still wearing my wedding band.

Take me there, I said suddenly. Where it happened. I want you to take me there. I want to see.

She hesitated a moment, and then nodded her consent.

Frank

I watched them from the window as they walked off toward the woods. Would they both be coming back? I wondered. Well, perhaps now that Elsa is a suspect, Sam's rage toward his wife will be a little less murderous.

Truth be told, they are both frightening. Unpredictable and wild-eyed, as though all bets are off.

I'm reminded of my father, the way he'd look after a long run of bad luck. A man with nothing is a man with nothing to lose. I caught him once in the bathroom of my grandmother's apartment, trousers down, stepping into what looked like a giant diaper. Incontinence pads. Took me years to figure it out. His determination not to leave the slot machines until he had gotten what he came for.

He took me along to the casino once, one afternoon when I was five or six years old. My mother was out of town, helping my grandmother pack up the big farmhouse in Arkansas after it was sold to developers.

My father had promised to take me to the aquarium to see the penguins. Instead, we drove to the casino, pulled into the dull gray concrete parking lot, and went in. There was a children's play area near the entrance.

You wait here, he said. It'll be fun, Frances.

There were toys, dolls with missing limbs and a big bucket of plastic building blocks; a TV screen played the cartoon channel, and there was a low plastic table full of colored crayons and large sheets of blank white paper.

I won't be very long, my father said. It'll be fun, he repeated.

There were a few other children inside the room, most of them younger than I was. A baby in a stroller, sleeping, holding in her hand one of those books made of plastic.

In the corner, a girl sat in a wheelchair. She could have been anything from eight to eighteen, her body small and awkward, her limbs all twisted in the wrong directions. Her head was turned to the side, her mouth hanging open. Her teeth looked very large. The babysitter had been trying to get her to drink from a straw, but she kept letting the juice spill out. Her blouse was spattered with red, like blood.

I picked up a crayon and drew a picture of a bird.

That's good, sweetheart, the sitter said. Later, she gave me an apple cut into slices and a bag of mini cheddar crackers.

They never remember to bring lunch, do they? she said.

It was dark outside by the time we left. I had fallen asleep on the floor. My father crouched down to wake me up. His watch and his wedding ring were missing.

Are we going? I asked.

Yes, he said.

I'm never coming back here again, I said crossly.

Neither am I, Frances, he said, but even then I knew that was a lie.

* * *

I watched from the window of the spare room this morning as they carted Elsa off.

Desperate people do desperate things.

And it isn't difficult to believe. Despair, the feeling that the world is conspiring against you, that you and you alone are suffering and wretched and punished beyond any fairness. You cannot see straight. You cannot think straight. There is only the hurt, urgent and fiery within.

Oh, I know it all too well. The longing for something you cannot have.

How my mother tried to root it out of me. We have more than most, dear. A roof over our heads, food on the table.

She had such narrow horizons, my mother. Such low expectations. I doubt it ever occurred to her that she might have hoped for more. I despised her for it. Resented her plainness, her blind acquiescence to whatever she was dealt.

How could I not want more, when it was every day flaunted in my face? Everything the other children had. Everything I had to do without.

It was Maureen who got me into the same private school as Merry. My mother wept with gratitude—as though she'd done it for her. Really, it was so Merry and I would have coordinated schedules. That way my mother could do it all. Mother to me, mother to Merry.

We've always been sisters, haven't we? Interchangeable parts. You bleed, I bleed. What you love, I love too. What you need, I must give you.

This is love. This is how it goes.

★ ★ ★

Alone in the house, I was aware of my immense boredom. Trees, walls, dull damp sky. It really could make one crazy, being quarantined here in this place.

Perhaps this is what happened to Elsa. Perhaps this is what happens to all the women around here.

Sam

There was an urgent knocking at the door. It was Karl.

Sam, Sam. They took Elsa yesterday. Why would they? What did you say to make them think she could have anything to do with Conor's death?

Jesus, Karl, I said, I don't know. I haven't got a clue. I didn't say a word.

Frank had walked into the room. He looked at her and grabbed her suddenly by the throat with one hand. The other hand he used to hold her wrists together. Bound, she was, like an animal.

You bitch, he said. It was you, wasn't it?

He spat in her face. She squirmed and protested. I did not move to get him off her. I just stood and watched.

You're a dangerous woman, aren't you? A liar, a trouble-maker.

Karl, she said, what's wrong with you?

You were the only one who knew about the miscarriage, he said. No one else.

He looked down at her terrified face and pushed her away before storming out of the house.

I watched Frank, holding her wrists, rubbing at the red marks he'd left behind.

What did you do? What's he talking about?

She shook her head. She could not speak. No wonder. Karl is a giant of a man. A minute more and he might have finished her off.

Oh, I said. Slowly it dawned on me.

You were fucking him, weren't you?

She grabbed her coat from the hook. You're awful people, she said. You know that. Awful.

She opened the door and slammed it behind her. From the corner of my eye, I glimpsed Merry hovering silently in the wings. The pair of them. Two savages.

She's a real piece of work, that friend of yours, I said.

Merry nodded. Yes, she said. Don't I know.

Frank

I walked in my rage to Sigtuna. An hour in the rain, another miserable gray Swedish day, trapped in the middle of nowhere, cut off from life, from all the action of the real world. To go from consulting millionaires about their share portfolios to this! Boiling vegetables and cleaning house.

This godforsaken place, the dull Swedes and this bland existence in the woods. Trees and sky, green and blue. Every day a repeat of the one before. It will be good to leave. It will be good to get far, far away.

In the village, I found a small café at the end of the dismal stretch of shops and restaurants, all five of them. I sat with my phone and searched for flights. I did it. Booked a one-way ticket for Sunday. I decided on Indonesia. A week at a yoga retreat in Bali, then on to Hong Kong. Nicolai it is. I sent him an email and he replied almost immediately, full of ideas for day trips and dirty weekends.

Just FYI, Frank, he wrote, *I'm still going to be seeing other women.*

Of course, I thought, but of course.

I replied with something jaunty and witty. Inside, it tightened, that part that contracts and hardens with every indignity. Cruel Karl, coward Sam, both of them so full of need, so desperate to stave off the boredom and rot. Marriage. What a hoax. And still they make it seem as though it's the prize. As though there's something wrong with you if no one's asked.

I ordered coffee and a *kannelbulle*. They might be the only things I'll miss around here.

Please leave. Please go.

Familiar words.

Thomas's words not too many months before. Simon's before that. The sting is always the same. In the gut, and something in the throat that catches and sticks. All the words you cannot say.

You don't belong here, Frank.

No, I never do, do I.

Perhaps they deserve each other. The lot of them, on this dreary island they imagine to be some kind of paradise. I despise them. I pity them.

I wondered about Elsa, alone in a prison cell. So fragile, a frail woman made of glass. Still, underneath is the thing they never see. The rage, a low-burning pit of fire that boils away, slowly, invisibly, right from the start. Maybe when they say, *Sit with your legs crossed,* or when the first boy grabs at your ponytail, or the first man slips his hand somewhere uninvited, or the first boyfriend tells you all the parts you are missing, all the ways you will never be woman enough. It's there, it's there, you try to ignore it, you try to hold it down, shhh, shhh, smile and play nice. But always it is there. And sometimes, it can take it no more. It makes itself known.

I finished up and called for the bill. The waitress was young and full in the face. I paid her and she thanked me profusely for the generous tip.

How I longed to slap the flush of youth from her.

Merry

Frank always makes sure to get what she wants. To take it. She always finds a way.

I could see it now, clear as day.

She wanted it all.

The phone rang. Detective Bergstrom.

Merry, she said. Unfortunately, there's not been much headway here with Elsa in the last twenty-four hours. She sighed. She's very fragile, very close to a breakdown, or in the midst of one. She had been trying for a child, she did miscarry, she did also— Well, she had strong feelings about what kind of a mother you were.

Yes, I said. I'm sure she did.

She is very fragile, the detective repeated. A woman on the edge. But she hasn't the stomach for murder. There were no traces of her DNA to be matched to the crime scene. Her doctor had put her on bed rest right after the miscarriage, so it's unlikely that she could have managed the trail. She'd have been too weak still.

But the clearing, I said. She was there, like I told you.

Detective Bergstrom sounded tired. No, she knows it well; she's lived here all her life.

What about the blanket? I said. In their barn.

The blanket has no trace evidence to connect it to Elsa. She also suffers from bad dust allergies—she's never in the barn. Which means it's more than likely it was planted there. Something for us to find. To distract us.

I see, I said. I suppose I couldn't imagine it would have been her.

She sighed again. I'm sorry, Merry. We really are exploring all the options here.

I know, I said.

She was quiet a moment on the other end of the line.

Merry, she said. Can you think of any reason why your friend Frank might have wanted your son dead?

I did not hesitate. Yes, I said, I can think of a few.

Merry

She came back late, shivering from the cold, red-faced and damp from the day's constant drizzle. I didn't ask where she'd been. Just poured her a glass of wine.

Here, I said, you look like you could use this.

She burst into tears. Oh, Merry, what an awful time. Everyone is so sad. So angry. Everyone is being so cruel to each other.

I watched her. I sipped my wine.

Yes, I said. We are at our worst. All of us. We have all done terrible things, haven't we. Shameful, terrible things.

She did not look at me. She took a sip of wine. She wiped at her tears.

Did you hear anything more about Elsa? she said.

No, I lied. She's still being questioned.

They really think it might be her?

Well, they found one of the baby's blankets, over in Karl's barn.

My God.

Yes. I poured more wine. Hard to believe, isn't it.

She shuddered.

Can you imagine it, I said, following me through the woods, hiding, waiting for her chance—and then taking him?

She was shaking her head. But did she mean to? I mean, kill him. Did she really want him dead?

You tell me, I said.

What?

You tell me, Frank, I said again. I was in her face, so close I could spit in her eye. I had her pinned against the counter with the force of my weight, but she was not trying to get free.

You did it, Frank, didn't you? I hissed.

Merry, please.

Say it. I grabbed a fistful of her hair; I jerked her head back. It was you. It was you.

Fire in my belly and deadly calm on the outside, I breathed in her smell and her fear.

You want to believe that. You want to blame me, she said.

She had started to struggle against me. I rammed a knee into her crotch to hold her down. Right in her cunt.

At first, I couldn't believe it, I said. That you could go that far. That you could do something so terrible.

Merry, you've always been good at making me the villain. Everything is always on me, isn't it.

I took her head and slammed it against the cupboard, heard the crack of skull on wood.

Shut up, I said.

She smiled at me. Perfect Merry and her perfect life. You're the fraud. You always have been. You're the only reason he's dead.

Again, I took her head and slammed. She turned at the last second and hit the wood side on. Her cheek split in two. Blood ran into her mouth.

So jealous. Always so jealous, so sick with envy because your own pathetic life never could measure up. Poor little Frank. So jealous you have to murder a baby.

She writhed and twisted; she was strong but I was stronger. Feral like a wild cat. Rage and hate and desperate, desperate regret. I pushed my knee in further, deeper. I wanted her to hurt. I wanted her to bleed. More, more.

You didn't even love him, she screamed. You wanted him gone. You were hurting him—you were—

She managed to push me off, to claw at my face with her nails. How we must have looked in the dead of night, scratching, biting, drawing blood. The two of us reduced to our animal selves. Primal and crazed, tearing each other apart.

This is what it comes down to. Winning is survival.

I stumbled back and fell to the ground. She was on top of me, straddling me, face up close to mine, blood dripping down in drops like tears. I tried to get away, scrambled for the living room, but she came after me, she held me against the floor.

I loved him, she cried. I loved him.

But you, she said coldly. You don't deserve to be loved. And you didn't deserve to be a mother.

She leaned closer; she opened her mouth and bit at my lip. Then she sat up. She wiped her mouth. Blood streaked across her face like some kind of tribal markings.

I know, she hissed. I know all your secrets, Merry.

The hate rose up, the adrenaline surged. I freed my right hand and yanked her shirt collar back, choking her, holding tight.

Her face was red, then purple, her eyes rolling back. I held on. I pulled. She struggled and I pulled some more. She squirmed and gagged, mouth open but no air going in. I watched.

Merry, said a voice.

I looked to see where it had come from. Sam, standing in the dark. The man in the shadows, watching the show.

I turned back to Frank, suddenly shocked by the scene. My hand opened, the release sent her staggering back against the wall. As she fell, she knocked one of the masks off of its hook. It crashed to the floor. The ancient wood cracked right down the middle, and the face split into two dark halves.

Sam poured himself another glass of whiskey, and left the room.

Frank

Detective Bergstrom is one of those overly empathetic types. She must have done her share of psychology seminars. Perhaps even a few of the more New Age varieties. Grinberg or somatic experiencing. Something bodily.

She kept watching my hands. She kept looking at my throat as I spoke, to see if I swallowed or twitched, to see if she could read my anxiety. Or my guilt. She has a tiny tattoo on her arm, in the crook of her elbow. It looks like a feather.

Tell me, Frances, she said. Where were you on the day of Conor's death?

It's Frank, I said.

Right, she said. I'm sorry. Frank.

I was at Merry's house.

All day.

All day.

You didn't go out, take a walk.

No.

You knew where she was going.

Yes.

That she usually left the baby at the clearing.

I knew she was going for a hike. I knew she went every day. With the baby.

Did you ever go with her?

No, she didn't ever want company. Now I see why, of course. It all makes sense.

Did you know the route that she took?

No.

You're certain.

Yes.

You never followed her.

Why would I do that?

Your DNA was found on the child. On the blanket used to smother him.

Of course it was, I said coolly. I was helping to look after him. You must know by now that Merry wasn't much of a mother.

You'd been with him earlier that morning. Holding him.

Yes.

How long?

I'm sorry?

How long were you with him? How long did you have him in your arms?

I shrugged. From the time he woke up. I was awake early. I played with him, fed him breakfast. Like usual.

She wrote it down. Drew an asterisk on top of the page.

Elsa, I was told, has been ruled out as a suspect. We passed one another on my way into the station. I smiled and said hello. One mustn't forget one's manners, no matter the circumstances.

Tell me about your relationship with Merry, Detective Bergstrom said. You two are old friends. Friends since you were little girls.

That's right.

Those can be difficult relationships, can't they. Lots of jealousies, lots of old upsets. Lots of secrets.

Well, I said, that doesn't sound like much of a friendship at all.

She examined my face. It's quite a gash you have there.

I touched my cheek. I hadn't even tried to cover up the dried blood and bruising with makeup before the police fetched me from the house this morning.

Looks like a fight, she said. Vicious.

I said nothing.

You want to tell me what happened? What's going on inside that house? Looks bad enough that you could lay a charge.

I don't have any intention of doing that, I said. It was my own fault.

I see, she nodded. Walked into a door or a cupboard?

I held her gaze. A door, I said.

Let's go back to this friendship. Merry and you.

We've been friends for thirty years, I said. Best friends. Like sisters.

Sisters fight.

I suppose, I said.

Do you two fight a lot?

Well, as little girls, yes.

What did you fight about?

I don't know. Silly things. Broken dolls or stolen toys. She was always at my house. My mother looked after her in the afternoons. She stayed over a lot.

You didn't mind?

Sometimes. My mother made me give up my bed. I'd sleep on the floor. I always had to be nice to her.

You didn't like that.

No.

You didn't want her there.

My mother always took her side. I was always the one who got the blame.

She wrote something down in her file. I hate that, she said.

What?

When someone tries to shift the blame onto someone else.

When you were older, what did you fight about then?

I shrugged. I don't like remembering those years. All that discontent.

Normal teenage girl things, I offered. You know, with all the hormones . . . I trailed off.

Tell me, she said.

Well, we fought about boys. Other girls. Clothes.

You were jealous of her.

Maybe.

Why is that?

Her parents were very wealthy. Big house. Fancy holidays. She had a huge allowance. She didn't have to get a job.

It wasn't like that for you.

No. My father was a gambler. We had to move in with my grandmother.

Not easy.

I shared a bed with an eighty-year-old woman every night.

You must have been very angry.

For a while.

Was Merry a good friend to you then?

I don't know. I spent a lot of time at her house. Most of the time.

A bit of a reversal from before.

Yes.

Did she mind you being there?

I don't know. We just hung out. Watched TV, listened to music. I spent a lot of time with her mother.

Doing what?

Daughterly things, I guess. Shopping, getting our nails done.

With Merry.

Just Maureen and I.

Where was Merry?

She didn't want to join us. She didn't like her mother.

You did?

I understood her.

Detective Bergstrom stretched out her legs under the table. She shook her head.

Confusing, she said.

What?

This friendship. The way you grew up.

Perhaps.

Did you resent Merry for what she had?

No.

Why not?

Because it was never enough.

How do you mean?

I mean Merry's always been . . . empty somehow. No matter what she has.

Empty, she said. Interesting.

Is it? I'd think it was more tragic, really.

The detective shot me a tight smile.

How about as you got older? As women.

I shrugged. We've always been close. Very close.

Very different paths you chose.

Yes.

And you're happy, with your life?

Oh yes, I said. It's all I've ever wanted.

A career.

It's more than a career.

Is it?

I'm very good at what I do.

She nodded. Yes, so I heard.

She smiled at me again. I wondered if she'd already have called them, if she knew the truth about my job. Or the lack thereof.

How about Merry? she said.

What about her?

Is her life a success, do you think?

Her son has just been murdered, I said.

Before that.

You can't tell, can you. What another person wants from life. What makes them happy. If they even know what that is.

But you're happy, she said. Single. Unmarried. No children.

She looked at me and said it again. No children of your own.

No, I said.

Do you want children, Frank? You think you'd like to be a mother?

I smiled. I tried to contain it. Maybe one day, I said.

And a husband.

Maybe.

Someone like Sam.

I'd hope not.

You don't like him?

He's not my favorite sort of man, I said.

What sort of man is he?

The kind who cheats on his wife.

Ah, she said. Yes.

He tried to sleep with me, I said. As though I'd do that to my friend.

Your best friend, she corrected. How extraordinary.

Funny you say that about married men, she continued. Because you were conducting an affair with Mr. Andersson.

Who?

Karl. The neighbor.

Well, I said, these things happen.

Was that why you tried to frame Elsa for Conor's murder?

She looked at me, her clear blue eyes sparkling with self-satisfaction. We're very thorough, she said. We traced the call, the tip-off that alerted us to Elsa's state of mind. Her miscarriage.

I yawned. I have not been sleeping well these past few nights.

Another strange thing, Detective Bergstrom said. Your DNA was all over the blanket the police officers found in Mr. Andersson's barn.

That's not strange at all, I said. I told you. I cared for Conor all the time. I loved him very much.

Mm, she said. Love.

We watched each other from our opposing sides of the room. No solidarity here. No sisterhood.

I wonder, Detective Bergstrom said. If it didn't make you jealous. That Merry had it all. The baby, the husband. You didn't want to . . . trade places? Or ruin things for her, somehow?

I let out a laugh.

It's a funny suggestion?

I leaned forward. Detective, to tell you the truth, I said, Merry has always been jealous of me.

Is that so?

It is.

And why would she be jealous of you, Frank?

I rolled my eyes. Come on, I said. Great school, MBA at Harvard, a fantastic career. I've lived all over the world, traveled—I have friends, a wonderful life. And I've done it all on my own.

Detective Bergstrom was looking at me. So you think that somehow Merry feels like she hasn't achieved as much as you have?

Exactly, I said. She hasn't even figured out who she is.

But you have.

Oh, yes.

And who is that, Frank?

I'm a woman who knows what she wants.

And what is it you want?

Right now, I said. I'd like to leave. Or call my lawyer.

★ ★ ★

Detective Bergstrom snapped shut her file.

Of course, she said. As you wish.

She stood up and opened the door to usher me out.

Thank you, Frank, she said. It's been illuminating.

As I brushed past her, she touched my arm lightly.

Merry's coming in tomorrow, she said. I'm sure she'll have many more insights to share on everything we've discussed today.

Merry

I watched from the window as the police car pulled up. Frank got out. She was on her phone. Laughing about something that seemed very funny indeed.

She looked like her face must hurt. Mine did. I touched the tracks her nails had left behind.

Detective Bergstrom called when she'd finished the interview.

I think we might have her, she said. I just need to clarify a few things with you tomorrow. The final pieces of the puzzle. Then we'll be in a position to lay a formal charge.

Good, I said.

I felt queasy.

The other call came from the medical examiner. They have wrapped up the autopsy and the report. They have gathered all the evidence they could hope to find.

We are ready to release your son's body, the receptionist said.

But what do we do with it? I asked.

You'll need to decide, she said gently. We usually release the body to a funeral home, for burial or cremation.

Thank you, I said.

I'd like to cremate him, I told Sam.

Whatever you want, he said.

Is that all right with you?

You were his mother, Merry, he said. It's your decision.

I wanted to say, But you were his father.

I thought better of it. I have spoken enough lies out loud. Still, he can't find out. He won't now, anyway. There is no reason for it.

I wanted to reach out and touch him. To feel the warmth of his skin. The solidness of his flesh under my fingers, the certainty of another human. The Sam who breathed life into me and made me a person.

He smelled strongly of whiskey and sweat. His beard ragged, his face unwashed. A wild man, some folkloric woodsman from deep in the forest. The kind who rescues you from danger. Or from yourself.

You really think Frank did it? he said.

I nodded.

Why? What would it solve?

She can't handle it when I have what she wants, I said.

This, he said. She'd kill for this?

I think she did.

He reached out a finger and traced the thin line of dried blood under my eye.

What kind of a friendship is that? he said.

The dangerous kind, I replied.

He took back his hand and cupped it into a fist.

But Bergstrom is close, I said. She'll get her. They'll put her away. She'll pay for what she did.

He looked at me, menace lighting his eyes. And you, Merry, he said. What about you?

How will you pay?

Frank

I was outside under the night sky, cold and starless. The houses were all in darkness, everyone inside snug beneath the covers, lost to dreams and tired bones.

My fingers cold against the glass of the bedroom window, knocking rat-tat-tat-a-tat-rat-rat-rat. Our code, like always.

I waited.

I knocked once again.

The window opened. Bleary-eyed from tears or sleep, Merry squinted at me.

Come with me, I whispered. I'll tell you everything.

She went to get her coat and boots. I helped her as she climbed out into the night. We shivered against the cold but said nothing as we walked. I had a flashlight stolen from Karl's barn to light our path, but it was hardly necessary. I think we both knew where we were headed.

The day and the night belong to different worlds. The air is strange, thicker and moister; the animals that call out to each other in the dark are the secretive kind, wilder and fiercer and tormented by the light. There was an eerie stillness, our breath heavy and dense against the night. You could see it in front of you: proof of life in frozen air.

Careful, I said, as Merry tripped on a rock. I took her arm. I smelled blood. She'd cut her hand breaking the fall.

We crossed the deserted road and headed into the forest, along the path and up toward the clearing. Merry at one point stopped and shook her head.

This is crazy, Frank, she said.

Still, we walked on, listening to the leaves and branches crack, to the burrowing of the nocturnal beasts; our coats wrapped tightly around our bodies, our hands clenched into fists within the pockets of our coats.

Everything in the night smelled sharper, stronger; life or slow decay, because everything ends up in the same state in the end. Rain caught in pools of rock or rotting leaves trodden back to mulch, clumps of thick moss and the droppings of secretive mammals.

I knew the way and so did Merry. Burned it was into the recesses of memory, the darkest and worst things; that terrible day and the ones before it.

At the clearing, I stopped.

Here, I said. I followed you here that day.

Merry was still, barely breathing.

And before. Long before, I said. I followed you, and I saw what you were doing. How you were leaving Conor by himself while you ran off.

I shined the light into the trees. The glow was enough to catch her face, the outline of eyes and nose, mouth set in a grimace. We surely looked minuscule against the trees, two beings shrunken and insignificant against a greater force. A darkness and mystery we cannot fight.

You killed him, she said, her voice a whisper.

I didn't plan to do it, I said.

But you did.

In the strange half-light, she was almost ghostly, a wisp of fragments out of the dark, dancing, shining in a sliver of white. Angelic and pure. This too, she could be, and sometimes was.

Oh, Frank, Merry moaned. She sank to her knees, her nightdress exposed under the thick green winter coat. The wailing in the trees, the echo of the empty heart.

Tell me, she said. Tell me what you did.

I was so angry, I said. At you and Sam. Asking me to leave. Treating me like a pariah. I knew what you were doing, how you were lying about being this happy wife and mother. So I followed you. I thought I'd... I don't know. Take some pictures. Have something solid to show Sam, to confront you. Oh, I don't know, really. I didn't have much of a plan.

She was listening, head in hands, the smells around us suddenly too much, too mossy, too reminiscent of bodily things. Blood and sex and death. I wanted to retch but continued.

I followed you, I said. I waited until you left him. Then I went to him. I took some pictures, to show how he'd been left alone among the trees. I picked him up. He was half-asleep, dozy and warm and soft, that delicious state of a child.

Well. I held him. I just wanted to hold him, you see.

Merry was sniffing, soft little moans of despair, a strange mewling animal.

Oh, Merry, I said, I was looking at him and seeing you in him. He had your mouth. He had that tiny, thin mouth you have. I was looking at him and thinking how you were with him. How you were so miserable. How you were so trapped.

No, she said. I loved him.

Yes, I said. I'm sure that's true too. But it was a prison, wasn't it. Motherhood.

She moaned, whimpered the air out of her lungs.

You're my best friend, Merry, I said. I've only ever wanted you to be happy. And you weren't happy. You know you weren't.

It felt liberating to tell her, to hear the words spoken aloud. Let her know how much I love her. How far I will go.

Merry, I continued. You have to understand, I did it for you.

She wailed. No, Frank, no you didn't. You didn't. Please say you didn't.

She was clutching at me, pulling on my coat. I did not push her off.

Merry, with all my heart. I didn't want to hurt you. I only wanted to help you. To set you free.

I took her face in my hands. I stroked her hair back from her forehead and looked at her, eyes bulging with tears and truth. Merry on her knees. Merry felled.

There weren't any lies, Frank, she moaned. I was happy. I was happy.

Poor Merry. Even now, she doesn't know what that means.

She moaned and rocked and shivered. I sighed.

She did not stop.

Would not stop.

★ ★ ★

Come on, I said. You can be yourself with me. Be real. Be real for five minutes.

No, no, no, Frank. She was grabbing at me again, hands clawing, shaking with violence. She pulled me down to the ground beside her.

You're a psychopath. A raging psychopath, she screamed.

I pushed her from me and she curled into a ball, hunched over her knees, shivering and sniffling. I watched her. Like this, she has always repulsed me. All these crocodile tears. Hideous. I looked away, and rose to my feet.

It's okay, Merry. You don't have to pretend anymore.

No, Frank, she moaned. Please, no.

I was above her and she was below. Begging, pleading. Roles reversed, I thought. At last.

I stood there, my hand on her head, a benediction, a pardon.

You hurt him, Merry. You wanted him gone.

She was choked now with tears, rocking on her haunches, back and forth. Pitiful.

I waited. Let her cry herself dry. She'd have to stop eventually. I let the flashlight shine out into the trees, circling us in shadows, keeping all our secrets safely within.

You were trapped, I said quietly. And I set you free.

She had stopped crying now. She was unmoving next to me, staring blankly into the ground at her feet. Letting it sink in.

I suppose she could have lunged at me, grabbed a rock from the ground and launched it at my head, bludgeoned me with her rage. It didn't matter. I didn't care.

I know all your secrets, Merry, I said. I am your best friend. And best friends can't fool each other.

She looked up at me, tears all dried. Eyes clear; glass or ice. Cold. Numb. This was Merry. Insensate. Unmoved. All roles interchangeable. She was no grieving mother.

I had gifted her with freedom. With what she'd wanted all along.

You see, I said. I did this for you.

Merry

The face you paint with a film of foundation, blend it in, cover up the cracks and pores, the thin line of blood. The eyes you make bigger, wider and more intense. Yes, these are the windows to my soul; see how they are tinged with black and blue. If you cry, they reveal themselves to be bruises, two big black eyes. Like you have been violently punished and beaten.

Perhaps this is the better look. Perhaps this is the real face you ought to be showing to the world.

For the lips, a hint of color, a shade darker to make them more defined, so your mouth doesn't appear to be just a flap of skin slashed open with a knife.

I can't go out without my face on, my mother always said. Her made-up face, the only self she wanted to know or show. Her plastic face, doing its best to keep the real one stapled and tucked underneath.

The reflection in the mirror showed me two women. Frank and me.

She smiled. You're ready, she said.

Thank you, I replied.

It has always been Frank showing me how to make up a face. We were twelve when she first took me inside the bathroom with a bag full of tricks, eye shadow and blusher and paint for the lips. This is how girls learn to play at being women.

When we're grown-ups, she said, we'll be perfect women.

In the kitchen, I tried to eat a few bites of toast, something light to line the stomach. I swallowed down a mug of coffee. The barn was still shut up. Sam would be asleep, lost to his whiskey oblivion. Unaware of everything that happened last night. Everything spoken and agreed.

I went out to the car. I switched on the heat to try and warm myself. I turned the radio to a Swedish talk show, and set off for the police station.

In my jacket pocket I had Frank's phone, stolen this morning after we hugged and I'd made an excuse to look for something in the spare room.

I did it for you, Merry, she'd said, and I had to pretend I believed it. That I was grateful, even.

You know I love you, Merry.

Yes, I see that, Frank.

In the parking lot of the police station, I looked through her phone. The photos she'd taken of the baby in the woods, captured under the date and time. He was still awake. A knife to the heart, the sight of him small and alone in his stroller, abandoned child in the middle of the trees.

He did not even have the words yet to cry out for help. Mama. Papa. We were nowhere. He was at the mercy of everyone and every cruel thing.

Frank, the cruelest of them all.

★ ★ ★

I was late for my interview but still I sat, trying to let the heat from the car take the ice out of me. Grief. Loss. Guilt. The terrible, irreversible truth.

Monster. Murderer.

But which of us is worse?

On the camera roll, one photo I'd missed. A rare one of Frank and me, two faces smiling for the camera. Sam must have taken it. Her arm is around my shoulders, holding me close, as though she is sheltering my small frame with her own.

We look happy, the way people who are happy look. A happy day, a moment outside of time. Nothing to prove, nothing to lose, nothing to take away. Just two old friends, enjoying the sunshine on a warm August afternoon.

I know all your secrets, Merry, she said.

I slipped the phone into my pocket.

Frank

It wasn't all a lie. It wasn't all the truth. What does it matter anyway? The two eventually merge into some form of reality. Some version of something half resembling the facts.

Here is the truth. The truth is, you don't always set out to do something. Sometimes, it is the buried part that takes over, the part deep and black inside you. You know it is there—it always has been—but it is kept secreted away, chained up in the basement because it is so fearful and hideous and shameful that you cannot imagine anyone ever seeing it and understanding that it belongs to you. Like your limbs and your teeth and your bloody heart, it is a part of you no matter how you try to disown it.

No, you say. You weep, you beg. Go away, leave me alone. Please, you say, I don't want you here.

It quietens; it's clever. It knows to wait. To bide its time until the moment is irresistible and you are too weak to fight it.

In these moments, it is the monster rising from the deep, the beast that gnaws off its own limb to escape the chains, the tiger at the circus who one day turns his jaws mid-performance and splits his master in two.

Enough, it bellows, shaking itself loose, snarling and spitting and howling into the night. You have kept me locked away for long enough.

Into the world it unleashes its angry chaos.

Yes. This was it. Raging me, hurt and banished, bursting with injustice. I followed Merry into the woods. I held the baby in my arms, because it was the very best feeling in the world, the weight of a small, warm human.

A baby. A baby who looks at you with wide, hopeful eyes, a baby who tells you wordlessly that you are enough, that you are loved, that you are all they need to make them feel safe and happy in the world. I rubbed his back, feeling the knobs of his vertebrae, the thin ladder of ribs, the solid thumping of his young and pure heart. He smelled of lavender baby wash and diaper cream, of something new and unspoiled.

Oh, Conor, my Conor. What a sweet, dear boy. I held him and loved him. I loved him very much. I held him and wept, for how I'd hurt him the night of the anniversary. For how I'd been so unthinkably cruel.

No. For how his mother was cruel. And for how she would never love him enough.

I held him and I looked into his little face. His mouth was open, his hand spread softly across my heart. I studied him, that impossibly smooth skin, all fat and youth, those long lashes, those shining eyes—like liquid gold.

Those eyes! I looked at him. Merry's baby. Merry's unloved baby. I watched her life in his face, a montage playing across the screen of his flesh. Merry's whole life, spent taking what she's wanted. Never a fight, never a struggle. Impervious to loss or attachment. Impervious to people and their emotions.

Thoughts you don't even know are there start to unionize. They push everything else aside and march to the front of your brain. They shake you and shout.

Merry didn't deserve the baby. Merry didn't want the baby. Merry didn't want Sam.

It was all wrong. The picture was all wrong. Unjust.

But it's not fair, my childhood self would moan to my mother.

And who told you that life is meant to be fair? she always said in reply. Pragmatic old Carol, who almost never got what she wanted.

The flash of an idea, terrible and cruel, the voice saying *yes*. Yes. Maybe I could make it right.

Take him.

Take him.

Look what you did, Merry. Look what you made me do.

I kissed Conor's mouth, a poison kiss from his fairy godmother.

Conundrum. My little Conundrum. Whatever do we do?

I kissed his sleepy mouth once more. I wrapped him in his blanket. I pulled it up gently to cover his face. The sun was streaming through the trees, breaking through the morning fog. Light dappled across the blanket. It was warm. He was still. I held him, rocked him gently, like a mother would rock a baby to sleep.

Hush, little baby, don't you cry.

Rocking, gentle, gentle, go gently, Conor, go gentle into the night.

I breathed in his smell. I hugged him close for the final breaths he would suck into those tiny lungs. I loved him. I loved him so.

After many minutes, I pulled him away. I lifted the blanket from his face. It was done. What is done cannot be undone, but I did not want it to be.

Yes. He was gone. I had taken him. I had taken what she did not deserve. What she did not want. She would thank me, somehow. It would be what she wanted. What she needed.

I have always been so good at knowing what she needs.

I set Conor gently back into his stroller. I pulled the strap over his limp body to hold it in place. I laid the blanket over his legs, as it had been before.

There, there, Conor, I cooed. Mama will be back soon.

I had done it. For you, Merry, for you. Because I know you far better than you know yourself.

All right, all right. Here is another truth.

The operating table, the smell of sterility. The anesthetist saying, Count backwards from ten. Ten, nine, eight, seven . . . When you wake up, we will have taken out all the malformed parts of you.

It's for the best, the doctor had reassured me.

I don't see a future with you, was what Thomas had said, and he wasn't the first man to say it either. . . .

And why? Because you are broken, because you are not enough. Now I was broken worse than before. Irreparably, in fact.

★ ★ ★

They cut you open and scrape it all out, scoop it from you like the innards of a melon. The knots of flesh and malevolent cells. Scoop, scratch, snip. It's all gone. Everything that sat there waiting inside you, biding its time from girlhood to womanhood, knowing all the secrets, promising all the gifts.

One day, your body whispers in your ear, one day you will perform miracles with your flesh.

Ovaries, womb, gone, eradicated. You weep for what is lost but the tears wash nothing away, they just empty you out even further. The parts of you that make life are broken. The parts that do the opposite are strong.

Menopause, the doctor said, outlining the symptoms that would soon set in. Old woman symptoms, the kind that make them rant and sweat and dry all over. It can't be me, it can't be me but it is.

Oh, here's a fun little fact: It's only in the Western world that women experiencing menopause suffer from hot flashes. The heat is shame, red and urgent despair at the loss of one's place in society. Everywhere else, menopause is but a gateway to another glorious stage of life.

I almost told Sam that one night. I thought the anthropologist in him would get a kick out of my snippet of wisdom.

My mother, dying slowly and alone in the hospice while I spent two weeks in Ibiza with a tech entrepreneur who'd brought three women along just in case he got bored.

She'd been too late for any lifesaving operation. All those years living with a gynecologist, she'd decided she didn't need to consult one outside the home.

It was stage three cancer when they found it, a thick ball of malicious cells, their roots twisted deep into the wall of her womb. Genetic, a little gift she'd pass on to me later.

I was by her side when she died, my father lied. I was holding her hand when she went.

Later, when I spoke to the hospice nurse, she told me that my father hadn't visited in days. Fortunately, your friend was here, she said. Merry. She came every day to visit.

She was with her at the very end.

Unfair. Unjust. You ache for all the lost things, but it doesn't bring them back.

Count yourself lucky. This is what my gynecologist had said. Oh, yes, lucky old Frank. Always showered with such an abundance of good fortune.

I was given two weeks to recover from the surgery. My boss sent flowers and my personal assistant, Jill, visited me in the hospital. She bought a pile of magazines for me to read, and a folder full of documents for me to sign.

Shall I pick you up when you're ready to leave? she asked.

I'll take a taxi, I replied.

Back at home I shuffled around the apartment clutching my lower half, pressing at the hollows, waiting for the symptoms to kick in. Thirty-five! I was thirty-five.

I'd told none of my friends. I received no visitors or phone calls. It was just me, alone in that beautiful London apartment, walls and ceiling, windows that looked out on a park full of strollers and children chasing puppies and brightly colored plastic balls. I shut myself inside the bathroom and screamed till my ears screamed back. You have nothing, all this you have built and still you have nothing.

In the mirror the woman is flawless, long and lean and tan and tight, everything she's supposed to be in order to be considered beautiful. No unwanted hair, no fat, no lumps of cellulite. Breasts high and round, belly flat and smooth.

Exhausting, it is, the constant upkeep.

Skin still youthful, face not yet marked with lines of time or hardship. Hair long and thick. In good shape, well put together, that's what they say. Often it's enough to turn heads, to warrant a line rehearsed and smooth. You feel the eyes track you, top down or in reverse, depending on what their thing is, ass man or tits. Then the approval, an inward grunt you can almost hear. You'll do.

And still, it's not enough. You're an eight or a nine, real quality, they say, but when you open your mouth, their faces cloud over. They tell you that you plummet.

You're too intense.

You're too needy.

You're too ambitious.

You're too everything.

And now this.

Now this.

I curled up on the bathroom floor and stayed there.

It was Jill who found me. She'd come for another signature; she had a spare set of keys. The doctor was called, the wound ruled septic, the patient ruled broken down, though not yet beyond repair. They drained the yellow pus and pumped antidepressants into my veins. The psychologist asked me useless questions and made notes in a file.

Jill called to say that the boss recommended I take a leave of absence.

Six months, she said. To give you all the time you need.

Of course we both knew what it meant.

I looked around the apartment. I knew I could not stay.

It was then that I called Merry. Merry, stranded on her island in the frosty Baltic, sent into exile by the shameful husband, trapped with a child. I wanted to see it, Merry and Sam in Sweden, a pantomime not to be missed. I wanted to see her misery. I wanted to use it to soothe my own. I waited until I was cleared to fly and booked my flight.

Ah, the best-laid plans. Well. I can't say I didn't try. For a moment I thought we could all get what we wanted. For a moment I thought we could both win.

Me, happy. Merry, free. It seemed possible. It seemed to make sense.

And then not. It was just a confusion. A great and awful confusion.

I told her last night I did it for her.

I didn't.

I did it for me. For all the rejection and cruelty, for all the things stolen, for all the ways I have been left robbed and bereft. Tit for tat, this for that.

She's with the police now. The detective will be making her notes, searching Merry's face as she speaks. Why did I do it?

Why did I tell her everything, or at least a version of everything?

Because I wanted to give it to her, my cards revealed. I thought, let her decide which truth she wants to tell. I'll accept the outcome, whatever it is. I am ready. I welcome it. I am too tired of fighting against it.

We hugged last night. We held each other tightly. This morning she gave me a weak smile. She is making as if she understands. As if it is all settled between us, truths balanced out on a set of scales. But who can ever tell?

Fate, that other coldhearted bitch, the most ruthless mistress of them all. I want her to have her way with me. I want her to decide this for once and for all.

See, Daddy, turns out I'm a gambler too.

Merry

Detective Bergstrom wanted to slap me. I could tell by her face, by the way she held her hands under the table, out of the way.

I said it again. I just don't think she could have done it.

But just yesterday you said—

I realize that I was only projecting my anger onto her. It wasn't fair. It wasn't her. She's my friend, Detective Bergstrom. Why would she ever want to hurt my child?

You're taking back everything you said about her.

I sighed. I made a horrible mistake. It was a terrible thing to even suggest. I realized that last night.

So suddenly she wasn't jealous. She wasn't trying to steal your husband. She wasn't manipulative and malicious.

She's my best friend.

So she didn't know where you were going.

No.

She was at home all morning. She never left.

She'd been baking. She couldn't have left the house with the oven on.

Baking, she said. And I suppose she'd had contact with Conor in the morning? Enough to explain DNA transfer. On him. On his blanket. On the blanket used to smother your child.

That is correct, I said. I can confirm it all.

Merry, you understand what you're saying here?

I do.

You're absolving her of all blame. You're making it impossible for us to prosecute Frank.

Why would you prosecute her? I said. She didn't do it.

Detective Bergstrom pressed at her temples. Exasperated, and who could blame her?

Merry, do you understand that the investigation will probably turn back to you?

I shook my head. Well, actually, no, I said. It won't.

Someone did this, Merry. And I sure as hell won't rest until I know who.

Detective Bergstrom, I said. I think we both know that the investigation will need to be wrapped up soon enough.

She folded her arms across her chest.

I did some research of my own, I said. These cases are almost impossible to prove, aren't they? Babies who die from asphyxiation. What is the saying? "The only difference between a SIDS death and a suffocation is a confession."

That's it, isn't it. There's no real way to tell.

Unbelievable, she said. Merry, you are quite something.

You have no confession, Detective Bergstrom. It wasn't me. And it wasn't Frank.

I've been very open with you, I said. I've given you all the information I could. I've told you everything that happened.

I took a sip of water. I tried to remember all the things I had wanted to say.

★ ★ ★

I'm grateful, my husband and I are truly grateful, for all your efforts. For everything you've done to get to the bottom of our son's death. But what if you've been wrong this whole time? What if it's just an awful, tragic case of sudden infant death. Inexplicable. No one's fault.

Detective Bergstrom slammed a hand on the table. But it is someone's fault, Merry, she hissed. And you and I both know it.

I shook my head. No, I said. I really don't think that's the truth at all.

She sat and stared at me from across the table.

Truth, she said at last. Let me tell you what I've learned about truth, Merry. It always comes out eventually. It always finds you out in the end.

I stood up. I'd like to go home now.

Of course, she said. But before I forget—the strangest thing.

She smiled at me, a smile far from friendly or kind.

Sam, on the day Conor died. Well, you should ask him where he was, she said.

And why.

She opened the door and ushered me out.

I drove home, stomach lurching as I pulled into the drive. I looked over at Karl and Elsa's house. It has been deathly quiet for days, no movement in or out. I wonder where Freja is. I wonder if we will ever again have a barbecue with the lovely Swedish neighbors.

At the paddock, I could see Mr. Nilssen busy with his horses. You are welcome to bring your son over to feed them, he told me, the first and only conversation we ever had. He looked up and gave me a somber wave.

I went inside the house. There was a half-eaten sandwich on the kitchen counter. I picked it up and took a bite. Then I went into the bathroom and washed the makeup from my face. The water was icy. It would not turn warm.

Frank was in the spare room. Her suitcase open on the floor. She was packing the last of her things inside.

I leave tomorrow, she said. First thing.

Good, I said.

I took her phone from my pocket and placed it on the bed. She glanced at it and then back at me.

The case is over, I said.

She nodded. She didn't look surprised, or particularly relieved.

You didn't tell her.

No.

Our secret, Merry. Just for us. She gave me a little smile. Everybody wins, she said.

I held myself up against the doorframe.

Frank, I said.

What is it?

I never want to see you again.

How curious the words felt in my mouth. How untrue.

She continued to ball socks and wedge them into the suitcase, seemingly unperturbed by all the events of the last few weeks, by the possibility of prosecution, by the certainty of banishment from my life. Inside me, the knot twisted.

Do you hear me, Frank? I said. Never, ever again.

She looked up and gave me a smile. Of course, Merry, she said offhandedly. Whatever you say.

I left the room and walked over to the barn. Sam was awake, hunched over a box, putting together the pieces of what looked like an old train set. He barely noticed when I opened the door.

Sam, I said. I just came to tell you. It wasn't her. I wanted it to be, I wanted to blame someone. To have an answer. But it wasn't Frank who did it.

He looked at me. There's evidence, that's what you said.

I know. I wanted to explain it. But we can't change the truth. The truth is, it wasn't her.

That's what you believe? he said.

It is.

And the detective?

I don't know. These cases, it's hard to find answers. It was more than likely sudden infant death. Just cold, cruel fate. God-awful bad luck.

Bad luck, he repeated. Huh.

I looked at him. Why was he not angrier? Why was he taking my word for all of this? Sam, I said. Where were you the day he died?

His hands were on me in an instant, pinning me to the wall, holding me in place.

He put his face up close to mine. He smelled rancid, sour and stale. His beard scratched at my chin. He turned and spat at my ear, the glob of spit landing on my shoulder.

You don't get to ask me questions, he said. Understand?

You're hurting me, I whispered.

Hurting, he said. You don't even know what that means.

He turned from me and went back to the trains.

I ran inside to the bathroom, to throw up, to wipe his smell from my skin. The bruises on my neck were thick and blue, welts of disgrace and shame.

Bad luck, I'd said.

I pictured Val in Connecticut, dropping her daily button on the rug.

Perhaps *fate* is more accurate.

Sam bursting through the bathroom door to catch me with the pregnancy test in my hands, a pregnancy test I had planned to discard under a pile of vegetable peelings and crumpled tissues. A pregnancy I'd already decided to have terminated. Only there was Sam, home early because he'd just been fired.

Fate. An intervention from above.

I did it for you, Merry, Frank had said; the ever-loyal friend. I did it so you would be free.

In the mirror, my face twitched. Ever so slightly, around the mouth. Just that one word. One little word.

Free.

You are free.

As the bruises darkened with blood under the skin, I stood and watched.

I could not help but smile.

Frank

It is over at last. My final night.

Outside, the wind rattles against the door like an angry houseguest locked out. Me, perhaps, in elemental form. The air is bitter, biting. It snaps at the flesh and turns everything blue.

It will be a long winter. A harsh one. There will be no escape from its icy grip.

I look around the room that has been my bedroom, already just the spare room once again. I thought I might feel a twinge of something, sadness or regret, but looking at the bed and drawers and wardrobe, the cheap brass lamp and the throw that itches against my skin, it all seems suddenly the stuff of another life. I check the shelves and under the bed, I open and close the wardrobe doors one last time. I put the last of my toiletries into my suitcase. I curl a hand to the bottom to feel for Bear.

A small something to take with me. A reminder.

Of me, there is nothing left, not a single trace of the months I spent in this room, within these four white walls. I will leave tomorrow; the taxi will come before the sun is even up. The first flight out. I would have gone sooner, but it might have raised suspicions. Fleeing the scene, and all.

I wonder if Merry will see me off at the door in the morning, to make sure I leave. To make sure she is rid of me.

Packing up my mother's belongings after she died, I came across a small pile of photographs and letters in an old cookie tin. My parents on their wedding day, cutting a rented silver knife through a cheap supermarket cake. My mother in a bathing suit on the Santa Monica Pier. My father holding up newborn me, my face twisted in an unhappy cry. And then there was a photograph of two little girls, eight or nine years old, hair braided into matching pigtails, smiles wide, arms around each other's shoulders, holding on tight. On the back, my mother had written *My girls, 1988.*

You'll be friends for life, she always told us. Your first friend is the only one you'll ever need by your side. You'll look after each other.

Had she said it to me or Merry? I cannot recall.

I kept the photograph beside my bed, cased in a thin oak frame. In the faded colors of the sun-bleached photo, we could easily be mistaken for the same child. Same height, same hair, same wide smiles, both with a tooth missing from the top and from the bottom.

From time to time, I would get asked about the two little girls in the photograph. Is that your sister? Or sometimes, Is that your twin?

Yes, I'd always say, in reply to both.

I imagine I will look back at this time in Sweden like you remember a peculiar dream, a hazy blur of images and actions that make no real sense in the light of day.

It was a terrible tragedy, I'll say, if anyone brings up my old friend Merry and her dead baby son. A most dreadful time for all of us.

I want to be gone from this place. From all its reminders of lost things. Onward and upward, a new chapter ready to unfold, the pages blank and waiting.

Yes, I think. This is exactly how it should be. I have no regrets.

Merry, I can't imagine what lies ahead for her. Or Sam. Perhaps they will stay right where they are, prisoners of their wretched and gloomy cabin in the woods, bound by contracts meaninglessly declared before God. Perhaps they will simply cease to exist, the trees and vines growing around them, covering the house, blanketing the husks of their bodies inside these walls for an eternity—or more.

Merry, Merry, Strawberry. She thinks we will be out of each other's lives. But you cannot cut off a part of yourself and believe that the memory of it will disappear. You adapt, of course. But the absence is never gone, the nerve endings and synapses never stop expecting the missing piece to return.

She will come back to me. She always does. I know it. It might be nothing more than a postcard, a year from now, a decade. The photograph will be something generically beautiful, a dramatic fjord, a snowed-over lake surrounded by ancient pines, the blues and greens of the Northern Lights in full splendor. Maybe somewhere else entirely—an exotic beach, a city teeming with life. There won't be any message, any trace of her name. But the postcard will be message enough. I'll know what it's meant to say. I'll get it right away.

★ ★ ★

You're forgiven.

You're missed.

It will say, *Thank you, Frank. You've always been the very truest friend*.

Merry

The case is officially closed. Files sealed, evidence boxed and put away. Detective Bergstrom called us in one last time. Sam and I in the familiar windowless room.

If there's nothing more you can add, no more information. We just don't have enough for a prosecution.

What about Frank? Sam said.

The detective looked at me. Your wife seems certain it wasn't her. She corroborated everything Frank told us. Anything that might have been used against her, Merry has dismissed.

She gets away with murder, Sam said.

Detective Bergstrom eyed me.

I don't know, Mr. Hurley. I sincerely hope someday the truth comes out. For now, it will be ruled a case of sudden infant death, with suspicious circumstances. There are many unanswered questions. For you and for us.

Sam and I, alone in the car. It was a strange feeling. Too intimate. Too close. We had driven most of the way in silence.

You should come back inside the house, I said, standing in the kitchen. I'll leave. I'll go away. I tried to keep the panic from my voice.

He shook his head. No, he said, not yet.

He has something in store for me. This I know. I won't run. I won't do him the injustice of missing his chance.

We drove to the funeral home.

We're here, we said to the woman behind the desk. To collect our son.

The office was bright and airy, like a chiropractor's reception room. Everything white and gleaming, fresh flowers in a vase, a framed Monet print on the wall: *Woman with a Parasol.* We'd seen the original at the National Gallery of Art on a trip to Washington some years ago, sent a postcard of it to Sam's mother.

The receptionist gave an apologetic smile. I'm very sorry about your loss, she said. She must say it all day long.

The ashes they give you in a simple cardboard box, the name of the cremated person printed neatly on the side. Inside, another container holds the remains, scooped up after cooling into a sturdy plastic bag.

I carried the box in both hands, walking slowly and carefully back to the car. Sam opened the door and I climbed inside. I held the box on my lap and traced my finger over the name printed on the label. Conor Hurley.

We drove out of the parking garage, exited left to make our way back home and out of the city. It felt so foreign to be around people. To be moving about a city like we had any place in it.

I think it's going to be a long winter, I said, for something to say.

But also because it struck me. Time, stopped at the moment of Conor's death, and at the same time stretched out in front of us, elastic and seemingly endless. A long winter, then another, then another.

I had an idea for Conor, Sam said. For the ashes.

That day, he said. In Finnhamn. Remember?

I do, I said. It had been a good day.

It was this past spring. Conor must have been five or six months old. Mid-May, the first truly warm weekend. We'd driven into Stockholm and taken the public ferry across to the island. The boat was called *Cinderella,* and we'd smiled about that and made a joke about turning into pumpkins.

We took a long hike around the full stretch of the island, following the grassy path, Conor on Sam's back, the sun warm, the sky the bluest we'd seen it in months. We found a secluded bay and in the heat decided to strip down, to take a dip in our underwear. Conor was asleep and Sam laid him out gently on a blanket in the shade, our clothes bundled to cushion him in place.

We'd shivered in the water, which was nowhere near thawed after the long winter. But I remember that feeling, the sheer pleasure of the elements after months indoors, the relentless dark and cold. It was like being held in captivity. All of it, really.

The weather can drive you mad, someone had said when they heard of our move. No more than five hours of daylight.

We'd shrugged it off. It's only weather, isn't it. But the first winter had been punishing.

We'd bought the lamp, the high-dose vitamin D from the pharmacy to stave off the worst of it.

You'll get used to it, Karl told us, but it seemed like another reminder of our strangeness in this place.

In any case, that May day was the first of the best, a spring and then a summer that seemed to open a portal into another world, the lightness a sudden and welcome respite from its seemingly endless opposite.

Sam in the water put his arms around me.

We're making a good life here, he said, and for the first time it felt almost true.

There are almost one hundred thousand lakes in Sweden, I said. How many do you think we'll manage to swim in?

There was a future in that question, he and I, old and gray, hearty and hale. Holding on to each other and taking tentative steps deeper into the icy depths of the water.

I don't know, maybe it was all just another attempt to will it.

In wet clothes, we ate *köttbullar* and potatoes in Finnhamns Krog, overlooking the lake and touching hands across the salt and pepper. Conor was smiling or sleeping; the fresh air and the walk had tired him out. We missed the last ferry back and found a cabin for the night, rustic and charming among the trees. We made Conor a nest out of pillows and laid him at the foot of the bed.

In the morning we picked up fresh bread rolls from the farm store and waited at the harbor for the ferry to take us back to Stockholm. It looked like a postcard, the three of us a blur in the corner of the bucolic scene.

I think I can be happy here, Sam, I said.

It had been a good day.

★ ★ ★

I looked down at the brown box held tightly in my hands. All that remains.

My idea, Sam said. I want to go back to Finnhamn, scatter Conor's ashes in the lake where we swam that day. It's a good spot.

I swallowed and he turned to look at me, menace in his eyes. A man with revenge in mind. He has said nothing more about Frank. About me letting her go. Perhaps words are useless. Perhaps it will all come down to actions in the end.

Good idea, I said.

Sam

In Stockholm, we parked the car and walked toward the harbor, where the archipelago ferries line up in the bay. The sea was rough, the water thick gray below us, unfathomably deep. We were the last people to board. At Finnhamn, we disembarked. The sky had cleared a little, the rain on hold, but the clouds hung low and ready.

We walked along the water awhile and then followed the footpath along the edge of the island toward the bay. There was a lone pair of hikers, wrapped up warm in their all-weather gear. They passed us on the path and smiled hello.

Hej, we said in reply, like it was an ordinary day.

The cold was bracing, the island more brown than green, with many of the trees already empty of leaves, the winter setting in fast. Soon it would be all ice and snow, a barren land and its myriad frozen lakes.

I watched Merry walk ahead, brittle and small, her movements slow but determined, like an animal being ushered into the abattoir. We didn't speak.

When we reached the small bay, we perched on the rocks. Merry's fingers around the box were blue. How do we do this? she said.

We just scatter them here, in the water.

She nodded.

You know, I said. I was seeing someone. This past year.

I heard her suck in a breath.

Her name is Malin.

Merry said nothing.

She's a therapist, I said. I went to her for therapy.

Therapy, she repeated.

I was trying, you see. I was trying to do better. To be a better man. To get out of old habits, destructive patterns. The things standing in the way of real happiness.

I sounded like a brochure. Oh, Malin. She had such high hopes for me. She made me enact scenarios. Gestalt therapy. She made me talk to pillows as though they were my wife and mother; she made me say the unsayable things.

I hate you. You scare me. I want to destroy you all.

She thought I was making progress. Slow but steady. Baby steps, she always said.

I looked at Merry, staring out at the water. I'm going to do it, she said.

She opened the box carefully, pulled out the container and then the plastic bag from inside of it. A pile of gray sand, the weight of a baby. She handed it over to me.

We walked carefully down the rocks and toward the water. I opened the bag and took a handful of the ashes into my fingers, feeling the rough remains of pounded bone. I drew back my arm, and sent it all into the sea.

I passed the bag to Merry.

She took a handful, cupped her hand, and threw it into the water, shielding her eyes from the ashes as the wind blew them back into her face.

We took turns passing the bag back and forth, scattering handfuls of ashes into the bay, watching as they were swept up by the wind and then the water, as soft and weightless as kisses.

When the bag was emptied, we stood and stared out into the abyss of the sea below. Conor was floating away in the current, particles carried off to join the infinity of the tides, back and forth, from the Baltic to the Atlantic, light and mutable, in and out; timeless and weightless and eternal. It was a fitting resting place, I thought.

Come, I said to Merry. Quickly.

There was no justice, but I would have it all the same.

I pulled off my boots and jeans, my socks and my underwear. She looked at me and understood. She shrugged off her clothes and together we went in, water freezing against the skin, burning the flesh red.

I went under, and Merry followed. Heads submerged, air suspended, all life on pause. I opened my eyes. Merry was watching me. We came up gasping for air, the sea salty on our lips, the gray dust nowhere and everywhere. I licked, tasted it, sucked it in.

Merry, water and tears, frozen and shivering. She looked at me standing opposite her; two broken halves.

You ruined everything, Merry.

She was looking at me, blank slate, numb. I was starting to shiver, the icy water too much. Only a while more. It would be enough.

Everything I did for you. Everything I built. And you betrayed me, you betrayed me in the worst way.

Her eyes were streaming, her gaze unblinking. Looking at me, knowing what she had to do.

Forgiveness. It does not come cheap. Nor should it.

I'm sorry, Sam. I'm so sorry for it all.

She searched my eyes, maybe for signs of mercy. I gave her nothing. Merry nodded. I'm sorry, Sam, she said again.

Her head went under. This time turning away from me, swimming farther out, into the frozen nothingness; oblivion and certain death. Obedient wife. I knew she'd do it.

The water was a blade, stinging, cutting right to the bone. My lungs were straining, the chest constricting with the effort of breathing in such cold. I stood, unmoving, watching her shape blur under water, retreating farther and farther away.

Go, I thought, die in pain, tortured by knives of ice.

She deserves nothing less.

You fear women, Malin told me. You are afraid they will take things from you. Take your power. The way your mother did to you as a child and a young man.

I hadn't even told her the half of it.

I have tried. I have done whatever I could. And what good did it do? What did I get in return? This. Only this.

I shuddered. I needed to get out of the water. I wiped my eyes. I looked for Merry but she was a vanished speck in the deep. Going, going, gone.

I was alone, and she was gone. Conor gone. Frank. All of it, gone.

I looked at the water, a sea of nothingness, an indifferent mass. The cold cut the flesh; outside the water, the wind was howling, the sleet ready to fall.

I let out a howl of rage.

No sound came.

Alone. I screamed again.

How I moved I don't know, but I propelled my frozen limbs forward into the water, heart pounding, head in flames. I swam, fast as I could, slicing into the cold with the weight of all my fury, swimming, swimming, harder and harder, head under, eyes open, searching, frantically searching, for Merry in the depths. A shadow, an almost imperceptible shadow, then a halo of dark hair.

I swam toward it and there she was, heavy like lead in my arms, the weight of a thousand men, the weight of a wife. The cold no longer felt cold—the worst sign, the surest way to die. I heaved her under my arm and dragged, kicking, pushing, straining against the current and screaming into the void. I could see the rocks, the place where land met sea, our clothes still scattered where we'd left them; the remains of a shipwreck.

Merry in my arms, pulling us under, down and deep—*Come, come, sings the mermaid, I know just the spot*—because an end is too tempting, too easy; a final surrender to the gods. *Yes, yes, we are on our knees.*

The water begs you to let go, the limbs ache to succumb. Float, sink, let the water take you. Let it all be over.

I shouted, *No,* and on we swam, pulling, dragging. Waist height in the water, I stood up and walked, primordial man arising from the sea. *Look, legs and lungs, now you are human, now you are born anew.* The cold air stung against the cold wet, singeing the skin.

Pulling her along with me, I walked and dragged, until onto the rocks we collapsed, Merry beside me, her body seemingly empty of its blood. Cold as death, colder still, but even so I knew dry land was not enough. Man possessed, I rolled her on top of me, naked flesh upon naked flesh, willing the heat, willing the life.

Breathing, blowing. I wrapped her in my arms, enveloped her in her entirety. Her eyes were open, she was not drowned, just frozen stiff, the ice maiden.

Rub, I said, forcing hands, breath, skin upon her, pounding the life back into the body. Slowly she put her icy hands on me, she breathed into my neck, again and again, hot and warm, faint and then forceful. Her bones were pressing into me, the rocks under us cold and rough and unforgiving. With my hands I rubbed heat into her back, her thighs, I kept her frail body tightly in my arms, that body, always so frail, fragile like spun sugar, breathing my mouth onto her small blue face, against her cheek, into her stiff lips, feeling her against me, her pounding heart beating life into mine.

Merry, I said, Merry, you're okay. I've got you.

Truth. Bare and cold. Nothing left to hide.

No, always more.

We held on to each other on the rocks until we could feel our blood warm, two strange and wretched creatures washed ashore.

Merry. Wife.

Mother of my child.

Merry

We lay a long time in each other's arms. Saying nothing, just feeling the warmth of soft breath against blue skin.

After we dried off, we made our way back to the ferry. It was too long to wait for the next one; we were too cold, chilled to the bone.

Come, Sam said, shivering.

We rented one of the cabins, like last time. We pulled the extra blankets from the cupboard and slipped naked into the bed, the only way to recover heat.

I closed my eyes. Moved my toes to try and circulate the blood. I felt the familiar solidity of Sam's shape against my back, his smell and the pattern of his breathing. Shallow, and a little bit urgent.

He could have left me. Should have, perhaps.

What did I feel in that water, apart from the ice? Not regret. Not even sadness.

Just absence.

Sam, looking at me with all that disgust, all his great, aching disappointment at the lost things.

Under the water, I drifted with the current—how you live is how you die, perhaps. Floating, floating, no anchor, no compass. Just the pull of some unknown direction, calling me toward it.

You are free. You are free.

Frank's gift to her friend. I could see how she would think of it this way. How she would believe in the mercy of what she did.

But a gift is sometimes a curse. Freedom, freedom. What are you supposed to do with something so precious as this?

Poor Frank. Crushed. Banished once again, when she wanted only my heart. This could have been my gift to her. All she has ever needed.

But I could never give it.

Conor's face I saw, down in the depths of the water. Not crying, not smiling, just that blank stare he saved for me. Watching, waiting to see what I would do next.

My son, my child. I wanted to feel sorrier. Sadder. I wanted to feel more of anything. I looked at his face, the child wronged. The lie in the lie in the lie. I floated and drifted, weightless and frozen all the way through. I'm sorry, I'm sorry; I have always been a sorry woman. It is the end, I thought, and what of it? I surrendered. I would make no fuss. I would resist no fate. I never have. I expect I never will.

I think that was when I felt Sam's arms. Coming for me. Cutting through the water and the silence. Pulling me out. Claiming me for his own.

I was alive.

Perhaps I was forgiven.

Or born anew.

Here we go again, Merry.

Now we are here. Sam and Merry, Merry and Sam. This must be what fate has settled on. I stretched my limbs, felt the blood now hot under my skin.

I am here. I am here.

In the bed, which smelled of mothballs and lemon soap, Sam moved his body so that he was facing me. He smiled, a different face from earlier. Something new in his eyes. He wrapped me close and bent his head low against mine. Then into my ear, he whispered softly the words.

Let's make a baby.

Acknowledgments

I am eternally grateful to the dream team at Writers House: the unrivaled Amy Berkower and Genevieve Gagne-Hawes, whose masterful insight, support, and guidance are absolutely everything a writer could wish for. Immense thanks also to Alice Martin for her incisive edits on later drafts, and to Maja Nikolic and team for their deft handling of foreign rights.

I am indebted to Reagan Arthur, Emily Giglierano, and the team at Little, Brown and Company in the United States, and Kate Mills and the team at HQ in the United Kingdom, for their endless enthusiasm, expertise, and care in the handling of both book and writer. I could not have been in better hands.

I will forever be grateful beyond measure to my parents, Norman and Avril Sacks, and my sister, Lara Wiese, for their unconditional love, support, and wisdom, and for being my first storytellers, best readers, and eternal cheerleaders.

For my dearest friendships, I am hugely grateful to Lisa King, Carla Kreuser, and Frankie Morgan.

And finally, my deepest gratitude to Maroje, for his wholehearted love and support, for his input, patience, and transcendental hugs through each draft, for making my life infinitely more wonderful—and for booking us that cabin in the Swedish woods.

About the Author

Michelle Sacks grew up in South Africa. Her first short story collection, *Stone Baby,* was published by Northwestern University Press in 2017. Her earlier writing has been published in *African Pens* and *New Contrast,* and by Akashic Books, and she was shortlisted for the Commonwealth Short Story Prize in 2014. *You Were Made for This* is her first novel.